# POISON
## and
# PREJUDICE

# POISON
## and
# PREJUDICE

## A Rare Books Cozy Mystery

# DAPHNE SILVER

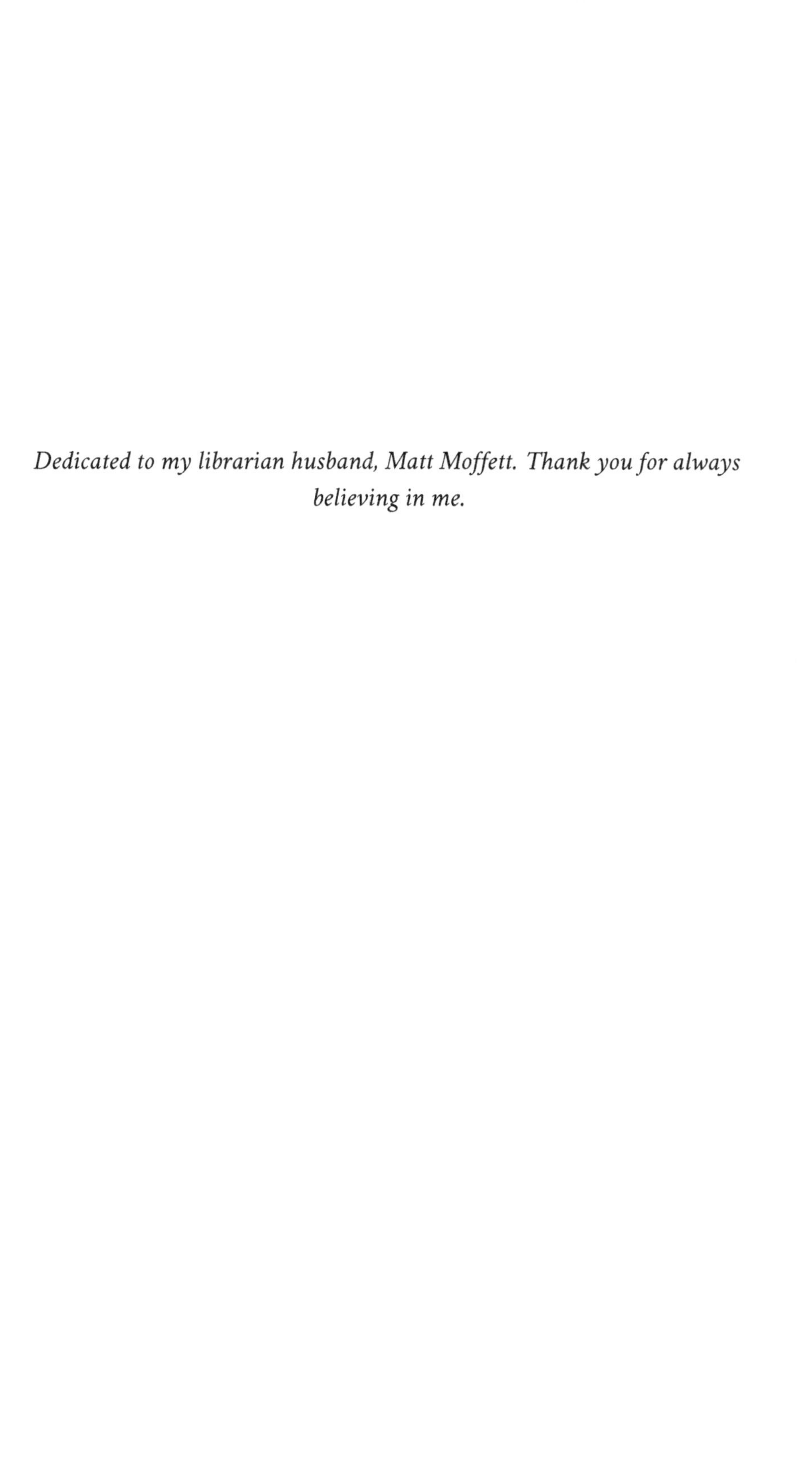

# Chapter One

Librarians are used to carrying boxes. We're tenacious. Powerful. At least, that's what I told myself. I piled up another of my sister's overflowing storage boxes into my arms to cart to her new storage unit. My biceps strained under their weight, but I assured myself I could manage. How many cartons of books had I carried before? This was nothing. Right?

"You can do this, Juniper," I reassured myself. "Librarians are strong. You are strong." With the small tower of boxes in my arms teetering, I wobbled slowly down the hallway.

Not that it helped with my pep talk that the Chessie U-Store facility was so dark and unwelcoming. Cavernous, really. Only one out of every three lights above me appeared to work. A strange odor emanated from somewhere down the corridor, while something dark ran in a long river across the concrete floor. I didn't think it was water. I might be naturally curious——overly so, my sister would say——but that weird liquid was one mystery I was fine not solving.

"Where is everyone?" I asked aloud, seeking out my sister Azalea and her husband Rory. I paused, wondering if I should still include the adjective "estranged," even if it was simply in my mind's narrative. The two had been carefully mending their marriage. I figured that's why he was here helping us clear out the Carriage House—to continue building good graces with Azalea. I was glad to see them reconnecting, especially since they shared a daughter, my four-year-old niece Violet. Fortunately, their issues had been more about their situations in life, and they seemed ready to resolve those together.

How much further was her unit? At least it was on this floor. Right? It was, wasn't it? I had considered getting a storage unit of my own here, but that was before I had visited this dreary place. Still, just like Azalea needed one before our parents visited for Rosh Hashanah later this week, I needed one to finally clear out my Washington, D.C. townhouse. I couldn't continue making the trek between D.C. and all the way down here to Rose Mallow, Maryland, so frequently. It was time to really consider moving here permanently.

Did that mean I'd have to find a place of my own? I shuddered at the thought. But I couldn't keep taking up one of Azalea's guest rooms. She was trying to run a business, having turned our late grandmother's century-old mansion into the Wildflower Inn. At least I paid for the space, but it wasn't helping the business's reputation grow, having me living there.

On the wall to my right was a flyer for an auction happening later this morning. I had heard of storage unit auctions but never seen one in person. Were they similar to the reality TV shows? Would there be an auctioneer and people bidding over abandoned and unseen units? I had participated in a few rare book auctions during my career, so attending this one might be interesting to check out if we finished in time.

I concentrated on carrying my stack of boxes and working to maintain my footing. Seeing anything beyond the unwieldy tower was proving difficult. I didn't hear anyone, so I kept trudging along until I ran into someone.

Boxes—and flowers—flew everywhere. I crashed to the floor.

Flowers?

"Oh no, I'm so sorry." I'd fallen smack on my bottom, surrounded by the contents of the boxes and dozens of red rose petals.

Standing in front of me was a young man with a sheepish expression. I figured he was a little older than my twenty-eight years. Maybe thirty-five? I wasn't sure, but I doubted he was older than that. Even in the dim hallway, I could make out sandy brown locks and piercing dark brown eyes. He could have been a magazine model.

"Are you alright, miss?" He offered me a hand.

"Mostly fine." I accepted his assistance to stand up. "Although I may die of embarrassment." Reviewing the scattered bouquet of roses, I knelt and began picking them up.

"It's okay. They'll survive." He picked up one rose and thrust it towards me to demonstrate the flower's hardiness. It drooped pathetically. "Well, they'll be good enough."

"I couldn't see with all my boxes." I cradled the sad-looking rose. A thorn pricked my finger. I waved my hand in pain.

"Let me take a look," he offered.

"Are you a doctor?"

"No," he said with a laugh. "Just a realtor. But I was an Eagle Scout. And I've kept up on my CPR and First Aid training." He examined my finger. "I think you'll be okay."

"Thank you…sorry, I didn't catch your name."

"Noah. Noah Danvers," he replied with a toothy smile. Being a realtor, I half expected him to pull out a business card and was pleasantly surprised when he didn't. "And you?"

"Juniper Blume. A pleasure to meet you, Noah," I said. "So, where were you going with your roses? I don't mean to sound rude, but a storage facility doesn't exactly scream romantic date."

Noah laughed. "No, I suppose not, but my girlfriend's working a job here, so I thought I'd surprise her." He started picking up my boxes and working to get the various papers and scattered supplies back inside. Meanwhile, I collected his roses—but with a little more care this time.

"That's sweet. What does she do here?"

"Her family runs a cleaning company. The U-Store is one of their clients."

"That's good."

"I'm glad they hired her," he said. "This place really needs some attention. I hope they'll let her do some handyman jobs too. You can see how much they need it." He waved towards the burned-out lightbulbs overhead. Thank goodness it wasn't simply me who thought this facility was an old dump.

"If she cleans here regularly, is she able to give you the inside scoop on these storage unit auctions I see advertised?" I nodded my head towards the nearest flyer.

"Unfortunately, no," he said with a laugh. "I've attended a couple, and they're rarely worth the time spent, let alone the twenty bucks or whatever the opening bid is."

"I've seen a couple of TV shows, but I've never actually gone to one. What happens?"

"The Chessie U-Store will put up for auction any units that have gone unpaid. I do know from my girl that this place's administration is vicious. They basically put up any unit as soon as rent is past due."

"No grace period?"

He shrugged. "I don't think so."

"So they announce the auction, and people show up to bid?"

Noah nodded. "Lots of places have moved their auctions online these days, but Chessie U-Store isn't exactly super tech-savvy. They're pretty stuck in the last millennium."

Looking around, it felt like I had stepped back in time, and not in a good way.

"They'll put up flyers and ads in the newspaper and on the radio station. People come, peek at the opened-up unit, but no one can go inside."

"Is there an inventory of what's in the unit?"

Noah laughed. "Nope. If you can't see it, there's no way to really know what's in there."

"Have you ever won anything?"

His smile grew mischievous. "If I tell you, I'll have to kill you. Seriously, I tried a couple times. Thought I could get some items cheaply for staging houses for sale."

"No dice?" I asked.

He shook his head. "Most of the furniture was either broken, out of style, or missing components. The decor was even worse. One time, I got these green and black patterned curtains..."

He paused and shuddered.

"They weren't originally green. Or black. Or patterned."

It was my turn to shudder, considering the implications of his words.

"Gross."

"Are you taking things in or out of storage?" Noah asked.

"In. My sister runs the Wildflower Inn, and she's cleaning out the Carriage House."

Noah's face lit up. "I've seen that place during my morning runs along the boardwalk. Historic area, right? Bright old yellow house with a sweeping verandah and a gorgeous garden?"

"That's the one. Yes, it backs to that boardwalk and the Chesapeake Bay, so you wouldn't miss it," I replied with pride. My sister Azalea had worked diligently to transform our late grandmother's historic Queen Anne-style mansion into a boutique hotel. She and my four-year-old niece, Violet, had finally moved into the Carriage House out back, so we needed to get the remaining boxes out of there. Especially with our parents coming in a few days for Rosh Hashanah.

"You must love working there," Noah replied.

"Me? Work at the Wildflower Inn?" I laughed so strongly I wheezed.

"I'm sorry. Did I say something wrong?"

I waved my hands. "No, no, it's just…if you thought I was a klutz with these boxes, try imagining how horrible I'd be at taking care of that beautiful house. I'm actually a librarian."

"At the Rose Mallow Public Library?"

"Private librarian, actually."

His eyebrows arched. "People have private librarians?"

"I specialize in working with rare and historic books and ephemera. I'm currently working on a family's personal collection," I replied, keeping the details purposefully vague. I worked for the rich and powerful Calverton family, and not everyone in Rose Mallow was such a fan. Besides, I took the trust Dorothea "Dor" Calverton bestowed upon me to work with her family's artifacts seriously. Well, that, and the non-disclosure agreement I had signed. It didn't say I couldn't tell people I worked for Dor Calverton, but it made clear the strictness of procedure around the contents of their collection. I figured it was easier just not to mention her by name.

"Wait, so you work with fragile and irreplaceable papers and artifacts, but you don't trust yourself to work with a house?"

"Well…yeah, when you put it that way. I don't know. For some reason, my general klutziness disappears when it comes to books." I shrugged. It was my superpower. When it came to books, I became magically equipped with the patience, expertise, and curiosity to properly handle them, catalog their contents, review their condition, and make minor conservation efforts to ensure their long-term stability. Perhaps not the most exciting of superpowers, but I was grateful for it. I loved my job.

"We all have our quirks," he said with a smile.

We finished collecting my boxes and his bouquet. While his flowers looked worse for wear, at least the roses were still red. Okay, the stems that still had flowers on them, anyway.

"Can I pay for a new dozen?" I asked.

Noah shook his head. "If I have even one, it'll be fine. She'll understand."

"That's really nice."

"Do you need a hand getting these to your sister's unit? There's probably a cart around here somewhere."

I shook my head. "I'll pay more attention this time." I made a mental note to search out the cart on my way back to Azalea's minivan. "Go enjoy surprising your girlfriend."

"Thanks, Juniper. Nice to meet you." Noah waved as he disappeared around a corner.

# Chapter Two

I gathered up my boxes, leaving some of them on the ground for another trip—but away from that mysterious wet trail—and continued on my trek. As I rounded a corner, I found an employee in a Chessie U-Store branded shirt with a matching baseball hat, pulled down low. Thick blonde curls poked out from underneath the cap. Oddly, she wore sunglasses, even in the semi-darkness. Maybe it wasn't a stylish look, but reflected a medical need?

"Do you know if there are any carts around here…uh, Lizzy?" I asked, noting her name badge.

"You passed them on the other end of the hall." She pointed back down the long corridor I had walked. Naturally.

"Ah. Thanks."

She nodded once and walked off.

"Oh, wait, one other question."

She paused but didn't turn back towards me. Instead, she stood incredibly still, like a statue. It was impressive.

"Do you know where the auction will be?"

I noticed her shoulders relax.

"First floor. Third hallway on the left. Look for 12A," she replied without turning back to me. Then she continued away. Not exactly super friendly. But then again, maybe that's why she was working at a storage unit. She might just not be the most social of people. I shrugged and headed off.

Eventually, I found my sister and Rory. It took a few more trips, but we eventually finished loading everything into her unit.

"I'm wiped," said Rory as we locked up the space.

"Me too," agreed Azalea. "I can't wait to go home and put my feet up."

"I can massage them," he added, a little too eagerly. I appreciated that the two of them were working things out, but I could do without any massage banter. My face scrunched up tight. I'd been the third wheel between the two of them going back over a decade, as Azalea and I used to spend our summers here. She and Rory were high school sweethearts. I had hoped they'd grow out of acting this way, but renewing their relationship must have brought back their public discussions of affection.

"Sorry, Juniper," Azalea said, but her voice was punctuated with little teenager-like giggles. She definitely wasn't sorry. Oh well. At least I was happy that she was happy.

"Before we go, though…" I pointed to an auction conveniently posted on the opposite wall.

"Right, right, the auction," Rory said. "I'd forgotten you'd mentioned it."

"Several times," Azalea added, not bothering to conceal her eye roll.

"I'm curious. Aren't the two of you?"

Azalea's head bobbled. "Maybe a little. What do you think might be inside?"

"I don't know. That's what makes it interesting," I replied.

She looked at Rory. He shrugged. "I'm game to find out more. We got done early anyway, so Aunt Harmony isn't expecting us back yet. She can keep watching Violet."

"And Clover," added Azalea with a wink at me. My rescue pup was best buddies with my niece, and I was grateful to Rory's aunt for babysitting the two of them this morning. I hope she hadn't spoiled them too rotten. Harmony ran the Purple Oyster Coffee Shop, which made amazing cookies for kids and dogs.

"Let's go!" I said, leading the way. As if I knew the way. Lizzy, the Chessie U-Store employee, had given me directions, but in this labyrinth, they were somewhat nebulous to follow. I knew it was at least on the first floor.

* * *

When we got down there, I listened for the sounds of people. Fortunately, the voices echoed through the facility, so it didn't take long to find a large crowd. They hovered around a large storage unit with a drop-down metal door. I didn't recognize most of the people there, but to my surprise, my good friend Nuri Cho was among them. I weaved through the group until I joined up alongside her.

"Looking for books for Boardwalk Books?" I asked, nodding to the enormous backpack on Nuri's back. My friend ran the used bookstore on Rose Mallow's public boardwalk. She'd recently acquired the space next door, so I figured she was looking to expand her inventory.

Instead, Nuri flinched when she realized I was there. "Oh, hey, Juniper. Didn't expect to see you." She gave a half-smile and a sad wave. "Oops, I need to…" She didn't even finish her sentence before disappearing into the crowd.

That was strange.

Nuri had been friends since being in graduate school together to become librarians. We lost touch after she dropped out in the last semester, but had quickly resumed our friendship about a month ago. That's when I discovered she was working with Boardwalk Books. Now, we texted almost daily. Mostly, we shared silly memes we'd found online about books, libraries, and bookstores. Most of them were ridiculous, but every time it made me smile.

Plus, I'd been spending time helping her with the store expansion. Since she lived in an apartment across town, she spent a lot of time using the Wildflower Inn as a convening spot. We'd go through books together or toss around ideas before walking up the public boardwalk behind the house to her store. Azalea had started referring to Nuri as our third sister.

I was tempted to go after her, but Azalea and Rory had sidled up to me. "Did you see inside that unit?" my sister asked.

"Such a mess," said Rory.

"How much can you see?" I asked, struggling to see over the throng of people. It didn't help that I barely crested above five feet tall.

"Go take a look," Azalea said. "They're not starting for a few more minutes."

I weaved through the people until reaching the front. I couldn't go into the unit, but even if I had been allowed, there wouldn't have been room for someone to sift through. The unit was overflowing with jumbled heaps of torn trash bags and old, stained cardboard boxes. I couldn't really tell what was inside any of them, but give the water damage and trash, I doubted they were in good shape. Then I noticed the flies. Ugh. No, thank you.

Who had abandoned this place? Why did they leave all these items behind? There had to be a story here. I felt awkward that any of us could take everything home for only twenty bucks.

"Watch out!" someone called. "Back up."

I realized the person was shouting at me. I had gotten too close to the unit. Putting my arms up in surrender, I shimmied to the side to get out of the way.

A heavyset man in a Chessie U-Store polo waltzed through the crowd, which opened as if he were parting the Red Sea. His forehead was beaded with sweat, and large, graying stains crept out from under his arms. Seeing as how it was early October on a mild day, I knew this wasn't from the temperature.

He wiped at his nose a few times, scratched his unshaved chin, and then coughed loudly to get everyone's attention. "Alright, folks, welcome to the first unit of the day. We'll start the bid at twenty dollars. Do I hear twenty dollars?"

"Not worth it, Gary," said someone in the crowd. A few people laughed.

Gary shrugged. "Fine. Ten dollars? How about ten dollars?"

People looked amongst each other.

"I'll do five," came a voice.

"Ah, come on, folks. You can do better than that," Gary replied with a head shake.

"Fine. I'll go seven."

"Make it ten, and it's yours. You never know how much treasure is buried inside." Gary wiggled his bushy eyebrows.

The man considering the unit shrugged. Then he waved his hand. "Ten. For you, Gary. Only reason why."

"There we go! Congratulations. Let us know when you find a million-dollar treasure inside. And make sure to tell your friends."

"Sure, sure, Gary. Honestly, you should be paying me ten bucks for taking this heap off your hands."

The crowd laughed again.

I had expected a storage unit auction to be exciting to watch. Not like this. The ones on television had made me expect high stakes, trash-talking amongst the bidders, and unbelievable discoveries. Guess it was a reminder not to believe everything I watched, even if it was labelled as reality TV. Perhaps especially if it was labelled as reality TV.

* * *

I flashed back to my first experience with an auction. Funnily enough, Nuri had been there too—although that was the only similarity with what was happening now.

We'd been back in graduate school for library science. Our professor offered us a chance to attend a live auction for rare and historic books. He told us that it would be a good professional development experience and how he was friends with the auctioneer, Barbara Jacobs, who he described as the "consummate professional."

Like always, my curiosity won me over. I couldn't wait to attend. I was surprised when Nuri and I were the only two from the class to go. We felt severely underdressed when we arrived. At least I had worn a dress, but it was a polyester one from the late '60s that I'd had scored for three bucks at a thrift store. The bright orange and yellow geometric patterns clashed with the other attendees' more traditional business formal attire. Nuri's attire choice was worse, wearing one of her favorite punk band t-shirts with ripped black jeans.

"He should have warned us about what to wear. Everyone's staring at us," she said. "We should go."

"We're already here. We'll just sit in the back and watch," I suggested.

"But we don't belong here. Everyone is staring."

"Nuri, it's fine. No one will care. I promise," I said. She made a face but

11

stayed with me as we found two seats in the back of the small room, filled with about thirty other people. Everyone was much older than us, except for the staff, which consisted of twenty-somethings scurrying around for last-minute preparations. There was also a bank of people on phones against one wall.

The auctioneer appeared at the lectern in the front of the room. Without saying a single word, she immediately commanded everyone's attention. With a quick nod, the lights dimmed, and a dramatic spotlight appeared on a column in the middle of the stage.

"That must be Barbara Jacobs," I said quietly.

"She's like the maestro of an orchestra," Nuri replied.

Before the first item, Nuri attempted to go up and introduce herself to the auctioneer, but other staff asked her to take her seat again.

"She didn't even bother to say hello," she grumbled with her arms crossed.

"She's busy, Nuri. We're not here for a social visit."

She bobbed her head. "True. I guess I'm just nervous. I'm not used to things like this."

I put a reassuring hand on her arm. "Neither am I. But isn't it exciting? At least a little?"

A small smile crested across her face. "Yeah, I guess so."

"Let's just enjoy ourselves, okay?"

"Okay. Thanks for being here with me, Juniper."

"Anytime."

An assistant brought out the first book. It was carefully placed on the column, while Barbara described the details of its contents. She then kicked off the auction. Things moved swiftly, and I could barely keep up with the flow of bids. People lifted paddles with numbers, and sometimes there were proxies making bids from phones. More paddles raised, people nodded, and it was a strangely quiet experience of small shuffling, except for the auctioneer's powerful voice, acknowledging each bid and amount and then moving on to the next.

The auctioneer shared the story behind each book, including its full provenance or ownership history. I loved listening to the book's histories. I wondered where the books sold would go and hoped that many would find their way to museums and public archives. Nuri and I didn't have the money to bid on anything, but it was still exciting. The auction was an elegant affair, although I couldn't afford anything.

Then Barbara called out the next book. "A *siddur* or Jewish prayer book from Kalynivske, Ukraine, from the late 1800s."

"Oh my goodness," I whispered.

"What?" Nuri asked.

"That's where my family is from. My great-grandfather immigrated from Kalynivske at the turn of the twentieth century. It was a Jewish *shtetl*," I said in shock.

"A what?" she asked.

"Yiddish for a small village of primarily Jewish people."

"Do you think that was your family's book?" she asked.

"Well, it may have been small, but there have been thousands of people who lived there over the years. Until World War Two."

"I'm afraid to ask," she said.

I nodded. "The Nazis came through. Not many survived. I remain thankful my ancestors left long before then."

"So this could have belonged to someone your family at least knew?" Nuri asked.

"Maybe. Not likely." I didn't want to believe the chances were strong. But from what I recalled, the town rarely had over a thousand people at any time.

"But not zero."

"True, but still. Even if it wasn't theirs, it was from their city," I said. "Can you imagine the people who have touched that book? Turned to it in times of trouble?" I wasn't particularly religious, but my Jewish heritage was important to me, especially anything connected to my Ukrainian history. Here was a piece of that history right in front of me. I could almost touch it.

The bidding began, and to my shock, Nuri shot up her placard.

"Number twenty-three. In the back. At one hundred dollars," acknowledged Barbara.

"Nuri, what are you doing?" I whispered again.

"Getting you that…what did he call it?"

"A *siddur*. But no, you don't have to do that. We don't have the money."

"Don't worry about it," she replied. When someone else outbid her, her placard went back up immediately. This happened several times. The prayer book reached over three hundred dollars.

"Nuri, please. You don't need to keep going." Where had my friend gotten this kind of money that she could bid in an auction? We shopped at thrift stores not only because they were fun but because we didn't have much money. Not that long ago, I had overheard her trying to work out a deal with the financial aid office on the phone. Had something changed?

"I'm in it to win it," she said with a wink.

"Do I hear three twenty-five?" the auctioneer asked. No one else responded. He looked around again and then nodded. "Sold to number twenty-three."

Everyone clapped politely. A few turned and appeared surprised to see two young twenty-somethings participating. I noticed a few popped eyebrows, but no one said anything.

"Thank you, Nuri. I'll treasure this," I said.

"I know you will."

"How did you afford this?" I asked.

"Don't worry about it. I'm good." She winked again.

After the auction, Barbara Jacobs, the auctioneer, came over to congratulate us. Unlike the nervous Nuri at the beginning of the event, she now appeared confident and secure, gripping her hand in a tight shake that seemed to startle her.

"What are you going to do with your prayer book?" she asked us.

"Take it home to my family," I said truthfully. "My family is from that area of the world, and there are so few pieces left. This will be a connection to our history."

Her bright smile increased, and she nodded in appreciation. "That sounds wonderful."

I left that auction feeling on cloud nine.

* * *

This so-called auction, on the other hand, left me feeling vacant inside. Not only did I not know what was in the unit, I knew nothing about the history or the people who owned it. Had these been treasured items for them? It made me nauseous how people were underbidding each other to get someone's life at as low a cost as possible. The items might not be valuable, but perhaps they had been to their owner.

I turned away, unsure if I wanted to attend any more. Looking anywhere except at the action, I noticed an odd door at the end of the hallway. As a librarian, I'm endlessly curious, so I walked up to examine the strange metal structure. It was grated, but I could see lights beyond the grates, going down some stairs. It seemed older than the rest of the facility, and I wondered about its history. Where did it go? When was it added? I walked down the hall to examine the oddity.

# Chapter Three

"Employees only," said a female voice.

"Oh, sorry." I turned to face a tall woman. It was Lizzy, the employee I'd met earlier. She had her arms crossed. I couldn't see her eyes through her dark sunglasses, but that didn't stop the feeling of her death stare boring into me. I wasn't sure why she projected such hostility. It wasn't like I was going through the grated door. Even if I was curious. Besides, it was obviously locked.

"Auction's that way." Lizzy pointed back the way I came.

"Yes, I know. I just thought the architecture was fascinating."

"The architecture?" Lizzy sounded dubious.

I nodded and pointed to the door. "It's so different from the rest of the place. It looks almost medieval."

"You really should head back." Her voice was tight.

I looked over my shoulder towards the auction and sighed. I turned back to Lizzy and asked, "Are the auctions always like that?"

"Like what?"

"Depressing."

Lizzy didn't respond for a moment. I couldn't read her expression with her hat and sunglasses covering so much of her face. I again wondered how she navigated this dark building. She didn't have a cane or other walking tool, and she didn't seem to have issues seeing me. So why the get-up? The blonde hair protruding from the hat appeared obviously fake, so I wondered if she had a self-esteem issue. I hoped everything was okay.

Then she shook her head. "No, not always. You're giving new life to those items in the auction. New homes for them. Someone let them go, and you're picking them back up."

"I hadn't considered that," I said. "I like that thought."

"Why do you care anyway?" Her demeanor shifted slightly. She seemed less angry and more interested.

"I'm a librarian. Specialize in rare books. Each one has more than one story. It sounds like it might be the same with the items in the storage units."

"What do you mean?" she asked.

"Well, there's the story that the book tells. *Peter Pan, Huckleberry Finn, The House on Mango Street*. The stories we read that someone wrote," I said, getting on a roll. You couldn't say I wasn't passionate about reading. "But then there's the story of its reader. Of us. We each take something different from these books. And we add something to their history. I think that's likely true of most things in a storage unit. Or at least, I hope so."

To my surprise, Lizzy smiled. "You get it, don't you? How special an object can be. I wish more people did." Her smile soured. "Most people do not. Most people don't understand that anything can be special."

"I'll think about what you said. About how we can give things a new home. Thank you," I replied, earnestly.

She nodded with a thin and tight smile. At least I thought it was a smile. It wasn't as hostile as she'd been previously, at least.

As I wandered away, I looked back over my shoulder. Lizzy stared at me. I still couldn't see her eyes through her glasses, but her face was definitely studying me. A sudden, cold shiver sent up my spine, but I ignored it, waving and smiling instead.

* * *

I found Azalea and Rory by another unit. Nuri hopped from foot to foot, as if she needed the restroom. Even after talking to Lizzy, I didn't feel excited about continuing with the auction and planned to see if they wanted to head home. All the work of moving things into the storage unit had made for a long morning, and I wouldn't mind some brunch. Maybe Nuri could be convinced to come as well? It would be nice to catch up with my old friend. We could discuss what was selling in her store, the latest books coming out, and if she might be available to join us for Rosh Hashanah dinner. I had been a bad friend, forgetting to ask her sooner. I was sure Azalea wouldn't mind one more at the table.

However, before I could say anything, the auctioneer opened the next unit. Like the others, it was filled to the gills, but this one was organized and orderly. I spotted boxes stacked high, each with handwritten labels. Being a librarian, I was drawn to the labels. They were obviously codes: letter, letter—number. It wasn't a system I recognized.

Definitely not Dewey Decimal nor Library of Congress. Instead, the codes consisted of a bi-partite system, using two letters and one number, as opposed to the tri-partite system many museums used. I thought back to my library school days. How many different coding systems had we studied? Yet, this didn't remind me of any of them. What did it mean?

The boxes also caught my attention. They weren't the re-used, worn-out, and taped-up boxes I'd seen in the other units. No trash bags here. Instead, I recognized that these as high-end, museum-quality containers, like the kind of containers an archive used to protect its documents and artifacts. The boxes were made from a thicker material that looked identical to ones I had used in previous repositories. Acid and lignin-free to provide high-quality protection. Definitely a hundred steps better than that first unit with the trash bags! Best of all, there wasn't a single fly.

Why were these in a storage unit? I mean, I understood that the unit was indoors and supposedly temperature and humidity-controlled, although I doubted this place withstood Maryland's extreme temperature shifts well. But it wasn't an appropriate place for collections storage. And who had abandoned such a well-maintained unit?

Curious, I snapped a few photos with my phone. But Nuri stuck her hand in front of my lens.

"What are you doing?" I asked.

"That's not appropriate," she replied.

"Why? I saw other people doing it earlier."

"Just…" She struggled for words. "Just don't. Please."

I didn't understand my friend's erratic behavior, but she was my friend. I nodded and put the phone away.

* * *

The auctioneer Gary started up. I could feel a difference in people's interest. I guessed that everyone had noticed this one was unusual. No one underbid this time. When he started at twenty dollars, multiple hands went up.

"$400," called out a voice. Everyone turned, and several people gasped. It was Noah Danvers, the realtor I'd met earlier. Where had he come from? I thought he wasn't interested in things like this.

Nuri waved her hand. "$500."

The realtor glared at her. "$1000."

What was happening? I looked over at Nuri. She looked like she had been punched in the stomach.

"A thousand dollars? Are you sure?" I whispered. It felt like the prayer book auction all over again, but it was also different. There was a desperation here that hadn't existed before.

"I have to beat his bid," she replied. "Somehow."

I inched closer to her. "Why is this unit so important?"

Nuri shook her head. "I can't explain. Just that it is."

"Can you go higher?"

"No, that was my best amount. I didn't think I'd need that." Tears welled in her eyes.

I put a hand on my friend's arm. I didn't understand all the details, but I knew there was more to this story. Like Lizzy and I had discussed, there is always a story behind the story—the one the reader brings. I didn't know what Nuri brought to this, but it was evident this unit was critical to her. She had once done something incredibly generous for me. Perhaps I could do the same for her?

I ran some mental math. Not exactly my forte, but I could manage some basic figures. I had been planning to sell my D.C. townhouse, and my employer paid me well while I lived with my sister. I had some extra funds. Then, I raised my hand and called out, "Two thousand dollars."

Everyone turned. Noah Danvers' face melted.

"Three thousand," he replied.

My sister Azalea sidled up to me. "What are you doing?"

"Helping a friend in need."

She must have seen the determination in my face, because she backed off. I was relieved that our sisterly telepathy worked today, because if she asked me to explain better, I wasn't sure that I could. I simply knew that Nuri needed this. This time, I could be the one to help out. That was enough.

"Five thousand dollars," I said, hoping I wasn't being an idiot.

Behind me, Rory asked my sister where I was getting the money. She replied that it probably was from my boyfriend. I gritted my teeth. I didn't need his money. Just because Leo was incredibly rich didn't mean I thought of him as a piggy bank. Besides, I had my own assets. Not many. Most of it was tied up in my D.C. townhouse. And sure, I had a decent job and paid my sister a small rent, but it's not like I had several thousand dollars lying about. But it also didn't mean that I needed Leo to save the financial day.

"Are you sure?" Nuri asked me. I nodded. "I'll pay you back."

"Don't worry about it. I'm just returning the favor," I said.

She looked confused. "What favor?" Had she forgotten the prayer book auction? I didn't have time to remind her then. We could discuss it later.

I noticed a woman had slid up behind the realtor. She whispered something in his ear. Was this his girlfriend? The one he surprised with the roses? Noah's face whitened, draining of all color. He looked like a vampire. What had she told him?

He slipped away with her. I looked for them through the crowd, but the crowd began swarming around me. Many hands patted my back, some more boisterously than others.

"Wow, that was something."

"Incredible work, miss."

"Hope you got some good treasures."

The auctioneer, Gary, has pushed his way through the mix with his hand outstretched. I took it, instantly regretting the choice, given how clammy his thick palm felt.

"Congratulations, little lady," he said to me. "That has to be a record for the Chessie U-Store!"

I mumbled a thank you, awkwardly accepting the people still patting my shoulders and shaking my hand. I had become a mini-celebrity here, which I could have happily done without.

I looked again for Noah and the woman, but I didn't see them anywhere. Why had he put up such big numbers and then darted out? Something she told him had appeared to scare him, but what? Was it related to the auction? Was it why Nuri had such big emotions for this one?

Speaking of which, I pried myself away from the crowd to find my friend. However, Gary caught up with me first, explaining that we'd have to handle paperwork and payment before I left. I nodded and thrust a credit card at him. He didn't take it, but said we'd work it all out in the office.

"There are still some units I need to auction this morning," Gary said. "But if you want to peruse your winnings, you're welcome to explore."

"Really?" I asked, surprised.

He shrugged. "Anything for our big winner."

"Thank you."

* * *

I found Nuri not long after Gary left with the horde of people. They had moved on to where the next auction was being held, somewhere in this strange labyrinthine building. Nuri slumped alongside Azalea and Rory, appearing to shrink with every passing moment.

"What just happened?" Rory asked me.

"I won a unit," I said, trying to sound like this had been perfectly normal.

Rory didn't appear amused.

"It'll be fine," I promised him.

"Are you going to need help paying for this?" His voice sounded a mix of fear and compassion.

"No, I've got it." Sure, it meant I'd be in some debt until the house sold, but I could manage that. Right? Nana Z would be shaking her head at me if she knew what I'd done. While she was born after the Great Depression, she had learned from her parents—my great-grandparents—the importance of remaining debt-free. Then again, she had the biggest heart of anyone I'd ever known, and if I had explained that this was all for a friend, she would have been first in line to help out.

Rory shook his head, appearing not to comprehend what had transpired. I didn't blame him, not being certain myself. All I knew was that I saw a friend in need, and I could help her.

"Thank you," Nuri said softly.

"Can you tell me more about what's going on?" I asked.

She shook her head. "I wish I could. Please don't ask me again. I'll pay you back."

"I know it will work out," I said, although I had no intention of holding her to that promise. I wouldn't have spent so much money if I had felt like it required someone else's help.

"Shall we see what you purchased?" Azalea asked.

"I can't wait to see," Rory said, charging ahead.

We walked up to the outer wall of stacked boxes. While my sister, Rory, and I gazed up at the towers of boxes in front of us, determining where to start, Nuri took a different approach. I noticed her reaching out, touching the codes, shaking her head, and checking the next one. Apparently unsatisfied, she disappeared into the maze.

Did she know what the codes meant? Was she looking for one in particular? I wanted to ask her, but I knew Nuri wouldn't tell me. Not yet, anyway. I might have felt angry if I didn't feel more confused and concerned for her.

"Oh my goodness," Rory called out. I turned to see him opening one of the boxes.

"What's inside?" I asked.

He didn't answer. Instead, he pulled out some sort of action figure, still in its plastic case. I looked closer. It was from *Star Wars*. Rory held the box in one hand and covered his mouth with the other.

"What is that?" I asked.

"Original Chewbacca figurine. Pristine condition. 1977. In its original case." He handed it to Azalea and pulled out another from the box. "Han Solo! And Luke. Leia." Then he gasped even louder. "Darth...Vader." He could barely get the words out.

"From the original movies?"

"Do you realize how much this is worth?" Rory asked me.

"No, but I'm guessing it's a lot." I knew a lot more about books than toys, but I knew how rabid a fan base the movies had. Original toys in excellent condition were likely akin to first edition books in well-cared for binding. And the more well-loved the author, the more expensive the books were valued.

He nodded. "Azalea knows how much I love *Star Wars.*"

Under other situations, I would have expected my sister to roll her eyes, but today, she shivered in apparent anticipation. If anything, she struck me as barely keeping it together. Did she also love the movies more than I realized?

"We're looking at thousands of dollars here," he said. "You may have just made back your money with this single box."

"Wow" was all I could muster.

"Look at you," Azalea said with a laugh. "You're normally the one telling us how much everything is worth and giving us all the tidbits."

"Turnabout is fair play," I replied, giving her a playful push. "Happy to learn."

"This reminds me of how much I used to love antiquing with Nana Z. Well, thrifting really," Azalea said. "She'd give us what, five dollars each, and send us around the store..."

"Telling us whoever found the most unusual item would win," I finished the memory. It was a favorite activity of ours when we spent summers here.

"Get anything good?" Rory asked.

"You tried convincing us that a cow-shaped creamer was actually a magic lantern for cow-shaped genies," Azalea said. We burst out laughing. I'd forgotten about that one. Nana Z had been amused by my creativity but deducted points for lack of credibility.  Especially when she turned the creamer over and pointed out that my not-so-vintage cow had been made in China recently.

"Okay, but what about when you offered up a half-used candle because you claimed it smelled like her garden after the rain?"

"She loved that one. I won that round."

"Well, yeah, that candle really did smell like her garden," I admitted.

"See?"

"What happened to your candle and creamer?" Rory asked.

"Probably in one of the boxes we moved in this morning," Azalea replied. "Although I think I used up the candle back home. I used to light it whenever I missed Rose Mallow."

"Oh yeah," I added. "You used to light that candle every time you and Rory got off the phone." Although we summered in Rose Mallow, we lived the rest of the year with our parents in Baltimore. Not that far, but far enough for two teenagers, especially when Azalea didn't get to see Rory all that often.

"That's sweet," he said, giving her a quick kiss. It was nice to see them reconnecting. After having nearly divorced, I was glad to see them falling back in love. Even if my teenage self would have been gagging at the moment.

"Now I'm excited. What else is in here?" Azalea asked. She opened another box, thinner and longer than the *Star Wars* one. "Oh, look at these…" She pulled out a series of prints. Each was a gorgeous photographic study of the Chesapeake Bay in black and white. They could have easily hung in a museum. "Aren't they gorgeous?"

"They look familiar," I said, but uncertain of the details.

Azalea studied them more closely. "I know this artist. Can't make out the signature, but I know I know them. I think they were in Nana Z's artist group."

"The Rose Mallow Artist's Guild?" I asked. Our late grandmother had been a talented watercolor artist and active with nearly every civic group in town. She was undoubtedly president at some point.

She nodded. "That's the one." Then she snapped her fingers. "Oh, I know. We have one framed in one of the guest rooms."

"That's what it seemed familiar," I replied.

"But I don't remember who took the photo."

"We'll check later."

Azalea put the prints back in the box and went to look for another. She disappeared into the labyrinth.

Meanwhile, I looked for Nuri, who was still somewhere inside the maze. Although not a big unit, I couldn't find her quickly. I wandered in deeper. When I peeked around a corner, I spotted her stuffing something into her backpack.

Before I could ask what she was up to, my sister screamed from the other end of the unit.

I raced over to find her burying her face in Rory's chest. He grabbed her hard. I looked where she had turned from. On the ground, nearly hidden by the box towers, lay a man.

I kneeled next to him and checked for signs of breathing or a pulse.

Nothing. He was cold to the touch. Worse, there was a puddle of dried blood beneath him.

"Is he?" Rory asked.

"He's dead," I replied quietly. Since moving to Rose Mallow this summer, I'd unfortunately become accustomed to finding bodies. I still felt upset, but I no longer wanted to throw up, as I had the first time. It wasn't a habit I'd wish on my worst enemy.

"Could he have died here naturally?" Azalea asked. She was hoping I'd say yes. I looked around at the towers of boxes. They appeared unscathed. If he'd had an accident in here, that wouldn't have been the case.

"I'm not the police, but it doesn't look good," I replied.

"Oh no," Azalea covered her mouth. Rory grabbed her tight. "Another murder."

Nuri came over to us, saw the body, and fainted away, collapsing into a series of boxes. Fortunately, they didn't topple. However, she ended up in a strange position, half held by boxes and half on the floor. I left the man's side and sat beside her, making sure she didn't hurt herself as she slowly came back.

Rory kept one hand around Azalea's waist while pulling out his cell phone with the other. I was thankful he would be the one to call 911 this time. I had done so too frequently in recent months.

"Do any of you know who he is?" I asked.

Everyone shook their heads.

# Chapter Four

The police cordoned off the storage unit. As I watched them put up tape, I couldn't help noticing one of the boxes appeared askew. Nowhere near the body. It also wasn't one of the ones Rory or Azalea had rifled through. I had never made it into any. The memory of Nuri hiding something in her backpack flashed through my mind. What had she taken? Why?

"Juniper," said Detective Lakshmi Gupta. Like always, the detective wore a well-tailored suit, complemented by a lime green blouse and a gold necklace. Her long, dark hair was pulled back into a crisp bun, not a single strand out of place. "Want to catch me up on what happened?"

"I'd say good to see you, but…" My voice trailed off. I explained about purchasing the unit. I debated leaving out the unusual bidding war, but I knew the detective would find out soon enough. Besides, what if that realtor guy—Noah Danvers—was somehow involved? Had he known about what was inside the unit? Had he been involved with the death?

"Juniper, earth to Juniper," said the detective.

"Oh, sorry. My mind's hopping."

"I'm sure. It's obviously been a trying morning. You were telling me about this other guy jacking up the price? But why did you meet that?" she asked.

My mouth opened, but nothing came out. How could I explain that Nuri needed the unit but wouldn't say why? Would I have to reveal that she appeared to have known the strange code and taken something from one of the boxes? Was that relevant? I wanted to believe it wasn't, but I knew that this wasn't my decision to make. I needed to tell the detective everything.

"I got caught up in the heat of the moment," I said. "I mean…"

"Whoa, Detective, look at this!"

We both turned around to see Deputy John Torres pouring through another box. Like Detective Gupta, Deputy Torres was normally a stoic man, so I was surprised to hear the excitement pouring through his voice. We'd had our differences—well, as had the detective and I—but I had hoped we'd come to a place of understanding. I wandered over to see what he had found. Besides, it gave me some more time before I needed to explain more details about the auction to Detective Gupta. I would tell her everything. Soon enough.

"What did you find?" the detective asked.

"*The Amazing Fantasy #15*. First edition," he said.

"Okay?" Detective Gupta didn't sound impressed.

Torres' eyes nearly bugged out. "First time we meet…" He paused. "Spider-Man."

"Are you sure it's not a facsimile?" I asked.

"If it is, it's a really, really good one." The deputy held the open box towards us. I peered in at the comic book. While I wasn't anymore a Marvel expert than I was on *Star Wars* toys, I did know about preserving comic books. This had been carefully kept in a mylar bag, surrounded by acid-free paper. Someone understood the value of maintaining this book.

"How much is it worth?" the detective asked me.

I shrugged and looked at Deputy Torres. He smiled like a boy on his birthday, ready to open presents.

"One of these sold a few years ago for $3.6 million." He practically giggled telling us. It was hard to believe this excited young man was the same frosty individual I had dealt with.

Now it was the detective's turn for her eyes to bug out. "That's a lot of money."

More than enough to kill over. But no one needed to say that part out loud.

"Okay, but that was a 9.6," the deputy added.

"A what now?" she asked.

"The grade given by the Certified Guaranty Company—or CGC. A 9.6 is nearly impossible to get. Means the comic book is near mint," he explained.

It felt like I was in an upside-down universe where the deputy was giving out the sort of details on books I usually had. But I wasn't upset. If anything, it always thrilled me to hear someone so excited about books. And that very much included comic books, in my opinion.

"Does this one have a CGC grade?" I asked.

He pointed to the large number in the upper corner of the mylar bag. "It's a 9.2. Still worth hundreds of thousands. Maybe a solid million."

"Wow. Combine that with the *Star Wars* toys..."

"*Star Wars* toys?" Deputy Torres repeated. He practically drooled.

The detective's brow crinkled, and she coughed once into her fist. That was enough to pull the deputy out of his reverie. This was, after all, the scene of a mysterious death. Even if it was also fast becoming a room full of strange and unexpected treasures. Who had owned this unit before? Was it the man inside? Where had all these things come from? And why was the unit abandoned?

"Hello, Detective Gupta," said my sister Azalea. She then turned to Deputy Torres and nodded at him. His face immediately reddened. When Rory came up behind her, both men's eyes hardened, steeling their gaze on each other. I tried not to roll my eyes. When Rory and Azalea had separated, she and the deputy had flirted with each other like middle schoolers. While the deputy claimed to understand why she went back to Rory, he obviously didn't like it.

It felt like someone had turned down the temperature by at least ten degrees. I instinctively rubbed my arm.

"Azalea. Rory," said Detective Gupta. "And where is your other friend?"

I looked around. I didn't see Nuri anywhere. "I'm sure she's here somewhere."

"Well, none of you go far. I want to talk with all of you."

"I need to go to the office and settle up everything," I replied.

"I'll join you."

* * *

As we walked over to the office, I asked the detective, "So, what do you think? It's definitely a murder, isn't it?" I knew full well it was unlikely she would respond with much.

To my surprise, she said, "Not sure. I'm not going to rule anything out, but it's certainly suspicious."

"So you agree it's murder then," I said.

"Juniper, you almost sound like you want it to be murder?"

My mouth gaped. "No, it's not that. I'm sorry. I don't mean to be so callous. It's just that…" For once, I struggled to find the words. "It's just becoming a pattern for me, I guess."

The detective patted me on the shoulder. It was one of the friendliest moves she'd made. "This isn't your fault, Juniper. I just can't rule on the cause of death until the medical examiner makes an analysis." She sighed. "But between you and me, you're likely right."

"He looked like he had been hit on the back of the head. I don't think you can do that yourself," I said.

"Agreed."

"Do you know if the man owned the unit?"

She shook her head. "I don't know yet. Part of why I'm walking with you to meet the manager."

"It's so surreal," I replied. "The unit was locked before the auction started. No windows. No other way in. He was in the back. A traditional locked room mystery. Like Agatha Christie, Arthur Conan Doyle, or Seishi Yokomizo."

"Seishi Yoko…?"

"Seishi Yokomizo. He was a Japanese author who wrote detective mysteries."

"Never heard of him," she replied.

"Well, although his first mystery, *The Honjin Murders*, was originally published in 1946, it was only recently translated into English. I definitely recommend reading it."

Detective Gupta laughed. "There's the Juniper I expected. Encyclopedia

Blume."

I blushed. "But not on comic books or action figures, unfortunately."

She put a hand on my shoulder and gave it a quick squeeze. "Not yet anyway."

"Detective!" another deputy called out. She turned to him. Then she turned back to me. "Go ahead to the office. I'll catch up soon."

# Chapter Five

As I walked up to the ajar office door, I heard a voice inside. Gary, the manager, was on the phone with someone, saying, "No, I haven't any idea who he was. No, it was a woman…you know, what's her name…" I could hear him shuffling through papers. "Esme Vienna. She owned it."

I tapped on the open door. Startled, Gary looked at me, grunted, and told the person on the phone he'd call him back.

"Our big winner." His voice wasn't so cheerful this time.

"I came to pay up," I said.

"I'd hope so."

I didn't care for his biting, sarcastic tone, but seeing as I just wanted to get this day over with, I let it go. For now.

As we worked through the paperwork, another employee popped in. Her name badge read "Gladys." Gary and Gladys. A female version of him with a lot more hair, which she sported in a classic Farrah Fawcett style, although it was more silver than blonde. She must have been his sister.

"Have you seen Lizzy?" Gladys asked. She nodded at me.

"Not now. I'm busy." He didn't bother looking up at her.

"I haven't been able to reach her since the…uh…auction."

He shrugged. "She'll turn up. Probably hasn't even heard the chaos about 12A yet."

"That's what I wanted to tell her. Make sure she knew what was going on."

"You call her?" he asked, still futzing with various papers on his desk.

"Left a voicemail and text message telling her to call me back."

Gary stayed focused on his paperwork. "She's likely doing her job. Probably on an upper floor. I'm guessing she has her phone on do not disturb—like you're supposed to during work hours." He wagged an accusing index finger in her direction.

Gladys rolled her eyes. "This isn't about me."

He finally lifted his head and grunted. "Oh, really? You don't want to be the first one to gossip about 12A?"

She pursed her lips and put her hands on her generous hips. "Mama didn't raise us to be gossips, Gary."

He bellowed at that. "That's rich, given how much Mama spilled the tea." He turned and winked at me. "That's what you young ones say these days, right? 'Spilling the tea' for gossiping."

I remained blank and didn't respond, but he didn't seem to notice.

"Are we all set?" I asked.

He nodded. "Thank you for your business." At least he sounded more sincere than when I first came in. He put out a hand to shake mine. I tried taking it quickly, but he grabbed my hand hard, so I was forced to match his vigorous shake. His grip was strong and unpleasant.

Eventually pulling my hand free, I turned to go, but before doing so, I asked, "I meant to ask, what's with the old grate door?"

Gary and Gladys looked at me like I'd spoken in Yiddish.

"Which grate door?"

"The one at the end of the first-floor hallway," I said.

They traded glances, appearing to speak telepathically. My sister Azalea and I could do that, but only sometimes. Other times, we definitely sent each other mixed signals.

Gladys spoke, "That's where our sub-basement is. You know where the boiler and electrical systems are. That sort of thing."

"It looks medieval," I said.

She shrugged. "Guess it's simply old-fashioned."

"I hate going down there," Gary added. "All the spiders. And makes me claustrophobic."

Gladys smiled, looking triumphant. "I'm the one who handles all the facility issues."

* * *

As I walked out the door, I nearly collided with Detective Lakshmi Gupta. She nodded at me before continuing into Gary's office.

Maybe it's my curious nature—I am a librarian after all—but I stepped just outside of the sight of the office door frame and listened in.

"I'm going to need to see the security footage," the detective told Gary and Gladys.

"You have a warrant?" Gary asked.

"I'll have it soon."

He grunted again. "You know it's bad enough what happened. Now to have your hordes of people here."

"My hordes?" the detective repeated.

"All these police. Your flashing lights. A gazillion cars in the parking lot. People are going to ask questions. Feel like this place is unsafe. You have no right to make my customers want to leave."

"Gary..." Gladys sounded as if she was trying to comfort him, but he was not having it.

"If I find out people are moving out because of all of you police folks..."

"Sir, there was a death in one of your units."

"I know that! But can't you investigate...you know, more quietly? Subtly?"

I couldn't see her through the door, but I could picture the detective shutting her eyes tight and attempting to keep her face straight. I knew from experience that she would be boiling underneath. She hated when people interfered with her investigations. Guess how I had discovered that? First-hand knowledge indeed.

"If you give me the footage, things will go easier."

"Hah. It's bad enough now. If people hear that I handed over their privacy without a warrant. No, ma'am. That is not happening."

"Gary," his sister's voice was more trill.

"Gladys, not now. We have a business to run."

"And how is business running?" the detective asked.

"Fine," said Gary.

"It's been better," said Gladys.

"Gladys!"

"Well, that's the truth.  Isn't that why you're so worried about our customers?"

"I'm worried *for* our customers," he replied.

"Sheesh, Gary." She paused before saying, "Listen, detective, my brother is right to be concerned about perception. Business could be better."

"Could be worse," he murmured.

"Shush. If it was worse, we'd be shuttered."

I heard feet stomping like an unhappy child.  I assumed it was Gary throwing a tiny tantrum at his sister, revealing their truths.

"Did you know what was in the unit?" the detective asked.

"That there was someone dead inside? Heavens, no," Gladys replied.

"No, no. I mean, did you know what was stored in there?"

Gary laughed. "Most of these units are full of rubbish.  Things people forget are even here. Those TV shows people have watched with the units full of treasure are fairy tales."

He obviously had no idea what was in 12A. I knew the detective well enough to know she wasn't about to illuminate him on the findings. I had found a fairy tale. Or was it a nightmare?

* * *

I rejoined Azalea, Rory, and Nuri by the front of the storage facility. With the police reviewing our unit, we wouldn't be able to go back into it yet. Once it was deemed a murder site, I wondered when we would be able to return.

"Did you learn anything?" Nuri asked.

"Nothing definitive," I replied with a sad shrug.

"We need to get Violet," Azalea said, checking her watch.

"Yeah, Aunt Harmony said she needed to get back to work this afternoon,"

Rory replied. His aunt had been watching their four-year-old this morning, but she also ran the Purple Oyster coffee shop, so she couldn't take the entire day off.

"Then I've got to prep for everyone leaving the Wildflower Inn tomorrow before our parents come in later this week," she said, turning to me.

"I'll help," I said with a cheery smile, but my sister rolled her eyes at me.

"For someone who is great with fragile books, cleaning is really not your strong suit." She gave me a playful nudge on the arm. She wasn't wrong. I couldn't cook or clean well.

"Your parents are coming to town?" Nuri asked. The first she'd spoken since we'd discovered the body. I wondered if she had been in shock. I worried for her.

I nodded. "Rosh Hashanah—the Jewish New Year—is coming up soon, so we're getting all together for a big family meal. You'd be welcome to join us."

Azalea gulped but quickly recovered and nodded voraciously. "I'm making all sorts of goodies—lekach, which is apple honey cake, a couple kugels, and rugelach. Plus, I want to try this recipe for a challah bread pudding that I found in our Nana Z's materials. Oh, and I also saw one for a flourless orange-saffron cake that I'm curious to test out." She counted on her fingers as she listed the various goodies. It was going to be carb-tastic, and I couldn't wait.

"And I'll get them from the airport," I said. "Although I'll need your minivan. My little Karmann-Ghia roadster only fits two people." I loved my vintage convertible—which I called "KG"—but it wasn't exactly the most practical of vehicles.

"Sure, we'll work it out," Azalea replied.

Rory looked confused. "Airport? Don't they just live in Baltimore? They teach at Johns Hopkins University, right?"

I nodded, explaining, "Yes, but they're also in a klezmer band."

"Klezmer?" Nuri asked.

"It's a traditional type of music for Jews from Eastern and Central Europe. They're taking a sabbatical this semester to do a tour with their band across Europe, so they're flying here just for the holiday," I said.

"Oh wow."

"It's pretty cool. More reason for you to join us. It'll be a fantastic party. A great way to welcome the new year."

Nuri looked at me and shrugged. "I'll think about it."

"Please do," I said, putting a gentle hand on her shoulder. She shivered under my touch. I hated to impose on her, but I knew what it was like to find your first body. I needed to make sure she was okay.

"Nuri, could we ride together back? Since Azalea and Rory need to get Violet?"

She toed the dirt on the sidewalk but nodded.

# Chapter Six

In her car, Nuri remained uncharacteristically silent.

"Okay, spill the beans. What is going on? It's just the two of us now," I said in a voice that I hoped was firm but compassionate.

"I can't talk about it," she replied.

"You took something from one of the boxes. I could tell."

Nuri pulled over to the side of the road. She slumped in her seat, sighing, before unlocking her seatbelt and reaching into the back. She pulled her backpack onto her lap. Inside was an archival file folder. She handed it to me without explanation.

Curious, I carefully opened the folder. Inside were several old letters, interspersed with sheets of acid-free paper.

Normally, I would handle old papers with my bare hands, but since I hadn't washed them, I carefully dug out a pair of purple nitrile gloves that I always carried in my bag. It was strange how frequently they had come in handy since I moved to Rose Mallow.

I studied the letters. They appeared very old. The paper was thicker and yellowed, and the handwriting was a dark sepia brown in beautifully slanted cursive.

"My dear Cassandra," I read the greeting. I also examined the upper right-hand corner where the writer had dated it to early March at Chawton Cottage. "Chawton? Why does that sound familiar?" I turned to Nuri. "Can you tell me more about these?"

"They're from…" She paused, twisting her mouth. My brain also twisted, trying to remember where I knew the word "Chawton" from.

Then it dawned on me.

"Jane Austen," we said at the same time.

"You knew?" she asked.

"It took me a moment. But Chawton was Jane Austen's home," I said.

"Yes, where she wrote all six of her novels."

"Well, she had already drafted several, including *Northanger Abbey, Sense and Sensibility,* and *Pride and Prejudice.* She finished them there," I replied.

Nuri shook her head. "Of course, you know that off the top of your head."

"It's on my literary bucket list trip to England. I want to see Chawton Cottage, Greenway Home where Agatha Christie lived, Stratford-upon-Avon for Shakespeare, and even 221B Baker Street. There's a museum dedicated to Sherlock Holmes there, I think." I counted on my fingers. Truth was there were several more places I wanted to tour one day, but these were some of the highlights.

"That would be nice," Nuri said in a faraway voice.

"How did you get these letters?" I asked, hoping to bring her back to reality. Maybe me too. As much as I wanted to continue planning my ideal itinerary, there was a more pressing matter at hand. "Did you know they were in one of the boxes?"

She looked out the driver's side window, away from me. "Do you remember how I left school abruptly?"

"Of course. It wasn't long before graduation."

She tapped on the steering wheel. "Well…" She paused and sucked in her breath, as if summoning all the courage in the world. "These letters are why."

I didn't understand. "What do you mean?"

"They're mine. I needed them back."

"They're yours? What were they doing in the unit?"

Nuri looked as if she was holding back tears. She waved her hands, as if attempting to wipe away my questions.

"I wish I could tell you, Juniper."

"How did you know they were there?"

She cracked her knuckles. "I've said too much already."

Why was she continuing to only give me half answers—ones that caused more questions? "Do you know Esme Vienna?"

Her eyes and nostrils flared.

"How do you know that name?"

"She owned the unit. I heard them mention it in the front office."

I could almost see the arguments in her head playing out across her face. She wanted to tell me what was going on, but I didn't know why she felt she couldn't.

"Who is she?" I asked.

She swished her lips around before saying, "Esme comes to Boardwalk Books often." That made sense. Half the town came to Nuri's used bookshop on the boardwalk. It was one of my favorite places, and I had been thrilled when she took it over.

"Okay. Anything else?"

She shook her head.

"Give me something here. I put a lot of money out for you."

She turned to face me fully. "I know, I know, and I'm grateful. I want to tell you. Everything. But I shouldn't have shown you these. I shouldn't have said anything at all." Her voice rose with anxiety.

"You haven't told me anything, though. I don't know what's going on," I replied, hearing my voice rise to meet hers.

"Please stop asking me all these questions, Juniper."

"I deserve to know what's going on. I bought the unit because I could tell it was important to you, and I don't know why. Do you know who that man was in the unit? Was he connected to Esme somehow? And why were your letters in her unit? Letters you removed from a possible crime scene." I didn't care how upset I was getting. Why was she stonewalling me?

Nuri shut her eyes tight. Tears welled in the corners. Normally, I'd feel sympathy. She'd been through a lot. We all had. But this was getting under my skin.

"I…" Nuri said, but then stopped. "I can't answer this."

"Why not?"

Her face hardened. "I need you to stop interrogating me."

"There is a man dead, and you stole something from the site."

Her face flushed. "Stole? Stole! I didn't..." She gripped the steering wheel hard. "Look, Juniper. I know I'm supposed to be thankful. You did something to help me. And yes, no, I am grateful for that. But it doesn't entitle you to know anything more." She released the steering wheel and grabbed the folder from my hands.

"It doesn't entitle me to know anything more?" I couldn't believe what I was hearing. "I spent five thousand dollars. And there is a body inside. And *Star Wars* toys and expensive comic books and...these letters." I gestured to the folder. "Why would you show me the folder if you aren't willing to explain?"

She shook her head. "I never should have. It was trying to say thank you. Trying to explain what I could. You don't understand."

"No, I don't. I need you to help me out here."

Her voice oscillated between anger and pain. "I wish I could. But I can't. I just can't."

"Why not?"

She hit the wheel with a free fist, honking the horn loudly. "Can't you trust me?"

"Trust you? I think I've demonstrated that. I stepped up for you."

"I need you to do it again. One more time. Please."

"I can't let this go, Nuri."

Tears streamed from her eyes, and I felt them hot and wet in my own.

"Juniper, if you don't stop prying..." She paused again. "You'll need to find another way home."

"Are you serious?"

She nodded. "I can't do this. Not now. Maybe not ever."

My mouth gaped.

"Can you tell me *anything*?" I asked.

She shook her head without looking at me.

"Fine. Then I'll get out." I released my seatbelt and put my hand on the door.

Nuri mumbled something.

"What?"

She put up a hand. "Be safe."

"You're leaving me on the side of the street, Nuri."

"You can stay if you end the barrage of questions, Juniper."

"I apparently can't do that any more than you can tell me anything."

"It's safe around here. You have your phone, right?"

"Sure," I replied.

"Juniper, I'm sorry."

"So am I, Nuri. So am I."

I got out of the car. Nuri sped off, leaving me in the dust on the side of a small and quiet street, backing to woods and a few random homes. At least it wasn't a busy road. Nowhere in Rose Mallow proper is far from one another, but the Chessie U-Store is beyond the town limits, so I had a few miles ahead of me to walk. At least with it being the start of fall, the weather was decent.

Or it was until the thought crossed my mind. Then the wind picked up and the rain started. Naturally.

# Chapter Seven

Fortunately, my boyfriend Leo Calverton was available when I called, so he swung by, picking me up in a used Subaru. Some kind of electric-powered one. I didn't know much about modern cars, but he told me he'd changed cars because he wanted something better suited for going off-road. While most of the archaeological digs he oversaw were in Europe, he still had the occasional local project. Even better, he'd purchased the used car from the dealership where Rory worked. He didn't need to buy used, given his hefty trust fund, but he said it was a good value and he was happy to support a local business.

Thank goodness the rain had been light. He handed me an old hoodie from the back seat and turned on my seat heater. So fancy! I curled up in his hoodie. It smelled like him—an earthy but luxurious scent, befitting my globe-trotting archaeologist.

Leo had a classic movie star quality to him. He had dark hair with a natural white streak, like lightning. His piercing eyes matched the deep color of his hair. I could stare at him all day.

"What happened, Juniper?"

I explained everything to him. Well, almost everything. I knew everyone assumed that Leo would cover the five thousand dollar cost, since his family were billionaires, but I hated being dependent on him. Nor did I want him to think I was invested in our burgeoning relationship for money. I could manage my own decisions.

"You said the storage unit was owned by Esme Vienna?" he asked.

"Yeah, why? Do you know her?"

"That name is familiar." His eyes lit up, and he pulled out his cell phone, scrolling through his contacts. "Oh, yes, of course. I know her well. She owns Victory Cleaners. They clean my condo. You might have seen her van. It has a Rosie the Riveter logo plastered on the side."

I briefly remembered Noah Danvers saying his girlfriend cleaned at the Chessie U-Store. Was that a coincidence? I'd need to check if they used Victory Cleaners. Either way, I was surprised that he contracted an outside company.

"But doesn't the Calverton family have its own army of maintenance and custodial staff?" I remembered seeing many employees there during my brief tenure with their library.

"Yes, but I don't want people who my parents oversee cleaning my condo."

"What do you mean?" I asked.

"They may not be around much, but that doesn't mean they don't keep tabs on us Calverton siblings," he replied with a shrug.

"You think your parents spy on you?"

He laughed. "I don't need to think it. They've made it clear that they like to know what each of their kids is up to. So this was one small step I could take to keep them out of the minutiae of my life."

It was strange to think about any of this, especially since I hadn't even met his parents yet. I now worked for his grandmother, managing the family's personal library at her own historic home. But Leo had made it clear that although she was the matriarch of the Calverton clan, she was very different from his parents, who ran multi-national companies in banking and real estate development.

"Besides," he added, "it's an easy way to support a local business." He paused and then added. "You know, I don't think she lives far from here."

"Are you suggesting we pay a visit?" I asked.

"I'm certainly curious. What was Esme doing with all of those things? And who was the man in her unit?"

I reached over and squeezed his arm. "This is why we're a good pair. I'm curious about this too."

"You're a bad influence on me, Juniper Blume," he said with a laugh.

"You didn't suggest anything bad. Just that we stop by. Maybe find out why she lost such a valuable storage unit?"

"Nothing more," he said.

"Nothing more," I repeated, knowing full well that I had pushed the boundaries one too many times in previous investigations. I couldn't help being curious. And everything with Nuri made that feeling ten times stronger.

* * *

We pulled into a residential neighborhood of adorable but modest Cape Cod Revival-style cottage homes from before World War II. Esme's house was quaint but unremarkable. What had I expected? Had I thought there'd be big signs of a Rosie the Riveter? Or maybe something connected to the eclectic collection of expensive materials in her unit? Or perhaps I expected it to be severely run down since the unit had been abandoned? Instead, the house and landscaping appeared managed and modest. There was nothing to indicate anything strange.

We walked up to the door and rang the bell. No one answered. I looked through a small vertical window on the side of the door, but the glass was diffused and impossible to see through. All I could tell was it appeared dark inside. The larger windows surrounding the house had the blinds and curtains drawn. Because I couldn't help myself, I attempted knocking loudly, but it wasn't a surprise that didn't have a different response.

A neighbor walking his dog yelled out to us. "Don't bother. She's not home."

We wandered over to him on the sidewalk. Leo stooped to pet his sweet lab mix.

"You looking for Esme?" he asked. "Guessing your clients, too?"

I nodded. "She takes care of his condo, and I'm looking to have her company take care of my home." It was a white lie, but honestly, not much of one. I wondered how much it'd take off Azalea's back if we hired someone to clean. Or if I did get my own place, I might need to bring them in. I was

45

no domestic goddess, unfortunately.

"Well, you won't have much luck."

"Oh? What happened?" I asked. Leo stood up, also emanating concern. The lab went back to his person.

"She won a cruise all around Europe," the neighbor explained, breaking into a big smile. "It's so exciting." The lab barked once in apparent agreement. I took my turn kneeling down to give him some generous pets. What a sweet dog.

"A cruise to Europe? Wow." I hadn't expected that. Every time I turned around, there was something else strange about it all. "How long will she be gone?" Could that be why the unit was abandoned? Maybe she had gone to Europe and accidentally forgotten to pay the bill?

"She left…" He paused to think. "Maybe a week or so ago. But she had to leave immediately. I remember hearing that."

"From Esme?" Leo asked.

He shrugged. "No, I think another neighbor. So I'm not sure when she gets back." He smiled. "You know how hard she works with Victory Cleaners, since you're clients. I do remember her mentioning not having had a vacation in a long time. So I was glad to hear that she was getting some time to herself. Although, I miss having her clean. She was always more friendly to chat with than that other girl."

"What other girl?" I asked.

"Oh, you know. Her niece. What's her face. Definitely didn't have the passion Esme brought to the work. Never quite as friendly. Esme and I could have chatted for hours."

I could tell, given how much he happily shared with us. He and his dog headed off, waving brightly. We smiled and waved back.

As we walked back to Leo's car, I asked him, "Did all seem weird to you, too? That Esme won some exciting trip and left immediately? And no one knows when she'll return?"

He nodded. "Very odd. What are you thinking, Juniper?"

I made a face. "Not sure yet. But we need to find out more."

My stomach grumbled. Loudly. I could have collapsed in shame.

Fortunately, Leo was a gentleman and didn't mention anything. So instead I added, "Do you have time for lunch?"

"A great idea."

# Chapter Eight

We headed over to the Purple Oyster Coffee Shop, as it offered more than simply coffee. Rory's Aunt Harmony wasn't there since she'd been taking care of Violet all day. My sister and Rory said she planned to return, but obviously that hadn't happened quite yet. I was sorry to miss her.

I loved the Purple Oyster, which stood on the northernmost end of the boardwalk. Each wall was painted a different color: yellow, orange, or, of course, its namesake purple. Harmony regularly changed out the paintings and prints on the walls from local artists. I looked around for any matching our black and white Chesapeake Bay photographs from the storage unit, but nothing looked the same.

The other thing I loved about the Purple Oyster was the food. As a vegetarian, I normally found something to eat, but it was often the same things: salad or pasta. Here, Harmony whipped up everything from wraps with roasted squash, sauteed spinach, and goat cheese to quiches with tangy feta, caramelized onions, and crunchy asparagus. Best of all, she offered vegan options for Leo, too, even managing to meet his gluten-free needs as well.

I felt for Leo. It's hard enough being a vegetarian, but a gluten-free vegan must be tortuous to manage in public. He ordered some turmeric-roasted cauliflower with a side of rosemary garlic fries. I hoped he wouldn't mind if I stole some. Or maybe half.

As we sat down waiting for our lunch, a young woman stomped over in deep eggplant Doc Marten boots. She came up behind Leo, throwing her hands over his eyes. Her long fingernails practically matched the boots, although they clashed with her neon pink hair. She sported a black lace babydoll dress and tattered fishnets. I felt like I'd time-traveled back to 1995. A little more recent than my mid-century vintage vibe. But more importantly, who was this woman?

"Must be Annie!" Leo jumped up from his seat. Annie squealed and clapped her hands. They hugged tightly. He turned to me, but before he spoke, Annie shushed him.

"Wait, don't tell me…" She cocked her head to the side and leaned across the table to stare at me. I shrank back, unsure of what she was planning to do. "Wow, your aura keeps changing color on me. I've never seen that before. You must be in a state of transition."

"My aura? State of transition?" I asked.

She nodded solemnly. "Keep yourself open creatively to inspiration and new possibilities."

"Okay. Sure." I wasn't positive how to respond to her abrupt reading.

"Annie, this is my girlfriend Juniper," said Leo. "Juniper, this is my younger sister Annie."

His sister? I hadn't expected her to be a Calverton. But underneath the cat's eye eyeliner and dark lipstick, I saw the resemblance. I'd only met Leo's younger brother Cecil. He had been smarmy, having brought a date to the family's collections storage for some alone time when we interrupted them. Annie appeared older than Cecil, although also younger than Leo, who was the eldest sibling. I tried remembering how many brothers and sisters he had overall. Was it five of them in total?

I put out a hand, but she waved it away and pulled me into a surprisingly strong bear hug. "Leo has told me so much about you, Junie bug! And so has Grandma. They speak the world of you."

"Junie bug?" I mouthed silently to Leo from over her shoulder. He shrugged and quietly laughed.

As she released me, I replied, "It's so nice to meet you."

Annie must have noticed my staring at her hair, because she said, "Don't you just adore today's wig? I was trying to decide between this and electric blue. But looking at my chart, it's definitely the season for shocking pink. Don't you agree?"

"Always," I said. "What chart?"

"My natal chart. I'm big on astrology. When were you born?"

I didn't answer the question, because I realized I had used one of her wigs earlier in the summer. Nothing so exciting as electric blue or shocking pink, but a brown wig that made my *Amelie*-style bob longer. Leo had given it to me for an earlier case. However, it hadn't survived well. "I wanted to tell you how sorry I was for messing up your wig in June…"

Annie laughed. "That old thing? Leo told me." She winked at him. "No worries. As long as you continue working for the family, I won't bother suing."

"Suing?" My body shook in alarm.

"She's kidding. You're kidding. Right, Annie?" Leo asked.

Annie leaned back and crossed her arms. "Maybe I am. Maybe I'm not." Then she smiled like a child who had successfully stolen a cookie.

"Don't scare Juniper, please."

She dropped her arms and stuck out her tongue at her brother. "Such a spoilsport. Okay, fine, Juniper. I promise I'm only joshing you a little. I have like five hundred wigs. And that one was at least three years old."

"Five hundred wigs?"

"Something like that. It's mainly to mess with the judges' heads anyway."

I was about to ask what she meant when our orders were called out as being ready.

"Will you join us for lunch?" Leo asked.

She pulled out a pocket watch on a chain. "I have enough time for some coffee before my client meeting. I could use the caffeine."

Something clicked in my head: suing, judges, and clients. She was a lawyer. Granted, she wasn't like any lawyer I'd seen before. When I lived in D.C., the lawyers there all wore black too, but they were finely tailored, nearly matching suits—not retro goth baby doll dresses with bright wigs and steampunk style accessories. Did she dress like this in court? She must be a sight to behold.

As we sat back down with our food and drinks, I asked, "You have a client meeting on Saturday?"

Annie made a face like a teenager asked to do chores. "So boring. Now that the Port Chesapeake project is over, I'm handling the bureaucratic fallout. There are deals with developers, land owners, businesses, all sorts of people. It's such a mess."

I knew what she was talking about. The Calverton family had planned to essentially bulldoze Rose Mallow and replace the historic charm and character with an ultra luxury, cookie-cutter development, renaming the place Port Chesapeake. Fortunately, Leo and I had convinced them to change course.

"I'm glad you all decided to invest in the town itself instead. My sister runs the Wildflower Inn. She's excited to apply for one of the new grant opportunities."

"Yes, yes, yes. It's exciting." Her voice suggested otherwise. "It's just so much paperwork. So utterly boring. I'd much rather do my normal work." She stole a french fry from his plate. He batted at her hand, but she simply laughed and lunged for another one.

"What do you normally focus on?" I asked.

"Oh, you know, taking down drug cartels. Destroying human trafficking rings." She waved her hands as if she had described a normal, everyday activity.

"That is seriously impressive," I replied.

Annie shrugged and sipped at her coffee. "It's not easy. But honestly, I think it's less of a bureaucratic nightmare than undoing Port Chesapeake. What were you thinking, Leo?"

Leo smiled, looking relaxed but confident. "You found your way of fixing the world, Annie. This is a small way we can help." The way he looked at me made me melt in my seat.

"Always the idealist, but I respect that. I'm glad you stood up for your ideals, big bro. It may be annoying for me to work through, but it should make a difference to Rose Mallow," Annie replied, patting his shoulder. "Well, I have to go. The law waits for no woman. A pleasure to meet you, Junie-bug."

With that, Annie waltzed out.

"Your sister is…" I struggled for the right word. I wasn't sure what I thought of Annie yet, but she definitely left an impression. I wanted to know more about her.

"Larger than life? Yeah, most of my family members are."

"She seems to have a good heart."

"She does," he agreed. "Ignore her teasing. She likes to keep people on edge. I think she gets strength from people underestimating her. Like someone else I know."

"Who?" I asked.

Leo laughed. "Look in a mirror. You both change lives. Don't worry. Annie will make sure that Rose Mallow is treated well. This is her home, too."

"I'm glad your family is keeping its commitment to investing in our community."

"Me too. But that's mainly because of you, Juniper."

"You mean Junie-bug?" I said with a laugh.

"I promise not to call you that without your permission."

"Thank you." I put a hand across the table, and he grabbed it tightly.

# Chapter Nine

Back at the Wildflower Inn, I helped Azalea with cleaning. Well, helped might have been an overstatement. But with our parents coming into town later in the week for Rosh Hashanah, it was all a hands-on deck project getting the Wildflower Inn ready. Not that my sister didn't keep the place immaculate already for her guests, but she was excited to show off the place to our parents. I was proud of how beautifully she had transformed our Nana Z's home into the boutique inn. Our parents had missed the grand opening of the Wildflower Inn as they had been on tour, but they had promised not to miss Rosh Hashanah.

"Their plane's delayed," Azalea announced from the top of the stairs. I climbed up to join her. "Bad weather in Frankfurt."

"Oh no. Will they make their connection in London?" I asked.

"Not sure. They're seeing if they can make it to Paris."

"There's still plenty of time. We have several days before they're supposed to get here."

Azalea nodded, but I could see the anxiety creeping across her face. With this being her first big holiday event, I knew she wanted everything to be picture-perfect. While I had faith that would happen, it was evident from the way Azalea pulled absentmindedly at her hair that she was less certain.

"Let's focus on cleaning," I said, although they were words I despised. Who enjoyed cleaning? Well, if it was conservation work on an old book, I got pretty excited, but dusting corners, removing cobwebs, and sloshing through a sink of dirty dishes? Not my idea of a good time. "Maybe we should hire a cleaning company?" I thought about Noah Danvers' girlfriend. He said that she had a contract with the Chessie U-Store. Maybe we could bring someone in, too. But maybe not them, given how strangely he acted at the auction.

"Hah. That's a good one. Unless you have more money hanging out that I don't know about?" My sister arched an eyebrow.

"Nope. Today was my one-time generous blitz," I said.

"Then cleaning is on us," she said. "Although I meant to tell you that I also got a message from Great-Aunt Lilac."

"Let me guess…not coming?" I said.

She nodded.

"Not a surprise. When was the last time we saw her?"

"Nana Z's funeral, I think," Azalea replied.

"That sounds right. But it must not be easy when you're in Hollywood." Nana Z was Aunt Lilac's older sister, but they couldn't have been more different. While our parents were professors by day and Klezmer musicians by night, Aunt Lilac was a serious Hollywood star. Although it had been some time since her last movie, so I wasn't sure why she didn't have the time for us.

"Yeah. And the cousins are doing their own thing." Azalea's voice dropped.

I put an arm around my sister's shoulders. "It's going to be a great holiday. Mom and Dad will make it. And we'll have Violet, Rory, Aunt Harmony, Keisha, and her sister, plus Leo and each other. That's ten people right there."

"Sure," she said, sounding still disappointed. I knew Azalea had been looking forward to hosting a large bash to have as much family together. At our grandmother's holiday gatherings, we sometimes had twenty to thirty people squeezed into the house. I figured that's the barometer Azalea had in her head for a successful event. I hoped she'd find a way to make her own version of success.

"Plus, I can feel Nana Z here, too. She's always with us. She'd be so proud of you."

"You think so?"

"I know so." I hugged her tight, feeling her relax into my embrace. "You're going to do a great job."

"Thanks, Juniper."

"You know, when Esme Vienna comes back to town, we should talk to her about cleaning. Take some of this off your plate. I'll shift the money around somehow." I wasn't sure exactly how that would happen, but I wanted to help my sister ease up a bit.

My sister stiffened. "Who did you say?"

"Esme Vienna."

"How do you know her?"

"She owned the storage unit."

Azalea's mouth gaped. She blinked several times before finally saying, "*She* owned the unit?"

"Yes. Apparently, she's out of the country, having won some sort of vacation."

Azalea waved her hands. "Wait, wait. How did you figure out she owned the unit?"

I recounted overhearing the name from the general manager. And about how her cleaning company took care of Leo's condo. He was very complimentary. I left out about my strange and unsettling conversation with Nuri, or how she left me on the side of the street. It didn't seem relevant.

Azalea sucked in her lips. "She's on vacation?"

"That's what I heard."

"And Leo works with her company?"

"Well, I don't know that I'd say 'works with.' He hired them for his condo. It sounds like Victory Cleaners is pretty successful." The name of the company had finally popped back into my head.

Azalea shook her head. "Don't you think it's weird that someone with a successful company and on vacation lost her storage unit? With everything we found there? And of course..." She made a gesture that I figured referenced the dead body. I understood why she wouldn't want to say it out loud.

I agreed that it was unusual. "Maybe there was a mistake."

"Yeah, maybe."

"I'll reach out to her once she gets back."

"Where did you say she went?" Azalea asked.

"Some cruise through Europe. A neighbor said she won it."

"Huh. How did she win this cruise?"

I shrugged. "When she returns, I'll find out. And we'll get you an extra set of hands."

"No, thank you," Azalea said with surprising firmness.

"Is it the money? I can help." I kept talking like I was Miss Moneybags. I think I just had this tendency to want to save everyone. And money could make a difference.

"Like you paid five thousand dollars for that storage unit?"

I didn't care for the tone of my sister's voice. "I already explained that I was helping a friend. And I'm good for it." As soon as I sell my townhouse in D.C. I left that part out.

Azalea tsked. "It's bad enough that you're paying me to stay here. I'm not going to have my little sister paying for a cleaning service, too. And certainly not from *Esme Vienna*." The emphasis on her name threw me.

"Why not? What's wrong with her?"

Her lip curled briefly, like a wolf ready to growl. But she quickly composed herself again. "Just that's enough. I put my foot down." She disappeared into a room, not allowing me to respond.

I stood for a few more seconds at the top of the stairs. What had just transpired? It was apparent that Azalea knew Esme but wouldn't share the source of her anger. Of course, maybe it was simply pride.

# Chapter Ten

I tried to relax that evening, but it was hard to unwind after everything that had happened earlier in the day. I probably opened and shut ten different mysteries. I attempted a bubble bath but got bored five minutes in. Fortunately, Clover was happy to take the bath instead. Some dogs hate being washed, but Clover won't turn down a warm pool of water, especially if bubbles are involved. I flashed back to attempting to give him and Violet a bath a few weeks ago—one that ended with me in the tub instead. At least now I was laughing at the memory.

Afterwards, we went downstairs, where I gave him some dinner in the kitchen at the back of the house. He gobbled it up quickly so he could get back to playing with Violet. The two of them headed up front to the library. Far enough away that they could play, but not too far that we couldn't hear them.

My sister was in menu planning mode, having several different cookbooks spread out across the tables. Some looked older than we were. Others seemed to have been purchased that same week.

"Thinking about Rosh Hashanah dinner?" I asked.

"Uhm hmm. We're going to have a house full of people, and I want it to be perfect," she replied. I was relieved she no longer seemed annoyed by our conversation earlier. As curious as I was about what set her off, I didn't feel a need to revisit.

"Anything you do will be perfect," I reassured her.

"Thanks, Juniper." She closed the book in front of her and turned her attention to me. I poured water into the teapot and started up the stovetop.

"You know something silly?"

"What? I'd be overjoyed for silly right now."

"Well, okay then. You know how everyone makes New Year's resolutions in January?"

"Sure, although I have pretty much given up on them. I can never seem to maintain any of them," I said.

"Same here. It's a lot of pressure we put on ourselves. But I was thinking that I might like to make one for the Jewish New Year," she said.

My teapot began to gurgle as the water heated up. I pulled out a mug and waved it at her. She shook her head, so I only kept the single mug and got some of my favorite Darjeeling black tea ready. I also found an old jar of honey. Fortunately, honey was the one food never to go bad.

"You're going to need more honey for the holiday," I said.

"Good thinking. I'll add it to the shopping list."

"Anyway, what were you saying about making a resolution for the new year?"

She sighed. Her face seemed to shrink, and she appeared oddly childlike. It was a surreal experience watching her morph, especially since she was my older sister. "You won't laugh?"

Was Azalea embarrassed? My sister? I couldn't remember the last time I had seen her embarrassed by something.

"Of course I won't. What is it?" I asked.

She clasped her hands in front of her face. "I'm thinking about…"

"Tell me."

"I'm thinking about taking a painting class."

Right then, my teapot whistled. I turned off the stove and moved it to a cooler burner. Then I turned back to her. "That sounds like a fantastic idea."

"You really think so? You don't think it's silly?"

"Why on earth would I think that?" I poured the water into my mug with the tea leaves and honey. Then I dug into a drawer for a small spoon to stir it together. "What kind of painting?"

"Watercolor," she said.

"Like Nana Z."

Azalea nodded. "Exactly. I mean, I don't have her talent, but…"

"Don't sell yourself short. I'm glad you're going to take the class. I hope you have fun with it. I think it's a lovely idea. Truly." I brought my steaming mug of tea over and joined her at the kitchen table.

"Have you ever thought about doing something like that?" she asked.

"A watercolor class? Maybe. Did you want me to join you?"

"Oh, no. I mean, you can, but I meant, is there anything you'd like to do for the new year?"

I hadn't considered it. My life had been such a whirlwind lately. Moving to Rose Mallow and leaving my old job was enough on its own, but in the couple short months I'd been here, I'd switched jobs *again* and inadvertently solved multiple murder cases. I hoped that this morning wasn't going to mean another case for me to take on. Maybe I should get my private investigator license? But I didn't think Azalea would appreciate the joke.

Instead, I sipped on my tea. The water had been too hot. I nearly burned my tongue. I blew across the mug. It was a simple blue and white one with a logo for the town of Rose Mallow.

"I'm going to have to think about it. I honestly don't know."

"You don't have to answer right now," Azalea reassured.

"But before our parents arrive?" I asked.

She smiled. "Not even then. And if you do decide on something, you don't even need to tell me. But I'm glad I shared with you. Thanks for being there for me."

I put a hand on top of hers. "Of course. I hope you have a great time."

# Chapter Eleven

Late that night, something woke me up. I wasn't sure what it was. I didn't hear anything. I looked out my window. While I enjoyed a spectacular view of the Chesapeake Bay, I couldn't see anything below the roof of the wraparound verandah. My dog Clover slept soundly on the bed next to me. Nothing seemed out of the ordinary, but I couldn't shake the feeling that something felt wrong.

I put on a robe and went for the door. Hearing the pitter-patter of my feet, Clover bounded next to me. He followed me downstairs.

The front door was open. I went to close it, but as I did, I spotted something out of the corner of my eye. Not something. Someone. They were in the library. I turned and saw them rummaging through my Nana Z's book collection. Dressed all in black and alone in the dark, I knew that it wasn't one of our guests in the hotel.

"Hey, I've got an attack dog here," I called out.

However, instead of growling, Clover trotted over happily to the invader. I recognized the stance. My dog wanted to play with them.

The mysterious person shrieked, apparently believing my bluff. They mowed me down while running out the open door, escaping the playful terror of my twenty-pound lovebug, Clover.

As I sat up in the doorframe, I watched headlights turn on and a car speed off down the street. Clover joined me, licking my face. "Well, you scared them off. Good boy." He put his fluffy white head to the side, as if attempting to understand me. I pet him generously.

After getting up from the floor, I closed the front door. Huh. It wasn't locked. When and why had it been unlocked? We never kept it unlocked unless there was someone stationed at the receptionist desk. At least there was our newly installed security camera. Maybe that would give some information.

I turned on the lights in the library to scope out the damage. A flutter of books had fallen to the floor, although none seemed worse for wear. I picked them up and returned them to their rightful places on the shelves. Looking through the collection, it didn't strike me that any were missing.

Besides, why would our would-be thief want these books? Nana Z had a nice collection of books, but none were valuable. Mainly mysteries from the past few decades, histories on Rose Mallow and Maryland, several coffee table books on the Chesapeake Bay, and a host of popular fiction, new and old—although the old ones were recent reprints, not first editions.

It didn't seem that the intruder had even attempted to grab anything else—none of the artwork or antiques on display in the library. All of those were exactly where they were supposed to be, and nothing even appeared askance.Those had to be more valuable. Had I simply interrupted the person early in their search?

I glanced at the grandfather's clock. It was nearly two in the morning. Should I call the police? I hated waking Azalea or worse, our guests, but was this really up for debate? No, of course not. We had someone break into our house. I couldn't solve this by myself.

"Let's go get Aunty Azalea," I said to Clover. He raced ahead of me down the hallway, as he knew that along with Azalea came his bestie Violet, her four-year-old daughter. We went outside to the Carriage House to wake them up.

* * *

Before long, Azalea and I hovered over the main laptop in the receptionist area to check the security footage. Clover had lain down with Violet, and the two quickly went back to sleep.

I watched over her shoulder as Azalea reviewed the film from the front and back doors, as well as peering out into the yard. Not long before I came downstairs, the thief appeared like a shadow crossing the front lawn.

"I can barely see him," Azalea said.

"Yeah, it doesn't help that Rosh Hashanah is about to start."

She looked up at me with the same face Clover made when he didn't understand what I had said. "What does that have to do with anything?"

"Rosh Hashanah is also Rosh Chodesh," I said.

Azalea shook her head. "It's been a long time since my Bat Mitzvah. I don't get what you're saying. Baking traditional Jewish goodies, I've got down, but I don't remember all the minor holidays."

"Oh, sorry. You remember that Rosh Hashanah is the Jewish New Year, also known as the 'Head of the Year.' Well, Rosh Chodesh is known as the 'Head of the Month,' beginning with the new moon of each month. Rosh Hashanah always falls on Rosh Chodesh."

My sister's eyes blinked rapidly. Then she nodded. "I see. So you're saying that it's nearly time for the new moon. But what does that have to do with our break-in?"

"Just that it's even darker than usual because there is barely a visible moon."

"Ah. I follow you now," she replied. "Looks like we should add more exterior lighting, especially for when there is little moonlight."

I nodded in agreement while Azalea went back to reviewing the footage. Neither of us could see the person well, but it was clear that they didn't struggle opening the door.

"How did they get inside?" I asked.

Azalea appeared stumped. "The door is always locked. I check it twice before turning off the lights."

"You did add a security code to the door," I pointed out.

"But that's for guests to go in and out after hours. I don't think this was one of the guests."

"I don't think so either," I said. "Do you think one of them might have given the code to someone else?"

"Why? If they're staying here, they could have let the person in themselves."

Azalea had a point. She snapped her fingers.

"I can at least confirm that's what happened."

"What do you mean?" I asked.

She pulled up a different screen on the laptop. "Every time the code is keyed in, the time is logged in our security system." She scrolled through the page. "Look, there it is. The intruder keyed in the code at the same time as the camera caught them coming inside. So they definitely used the code."

"I wish I could have seen them better. I'm sorry I don't have a better description," I said. Azalea patted my arm.

"You didn't do anything wrong. This person did." She smiled at me.

"Thanks."

"In the meantime, I'll change the code. I should do it more frequently. Fortunately, all of the remaining guests are leaving in the morning," she said.

"That's good. I'd hate to alarm them."

"Agreed. I don't want to make people think the house is unsafe or start putting up reviews about break-ins." Azalea shuddered. "We'll let the police know about the intruder after breakfast."

"Are you sure you don't want to call now?" I asked.

"It's not like they actually stole anything. You must have scared him away."

"I hope so," I replied.

"Not sure that a few hours will make much difference. Scaring off intruders is good, but I don't want to upset our guests. What if they talk about the break-in during reviews? Or tell their friends that it's not safe to stay here?" she argued. It was strange to hear my sister rationalize holding off on reaching out to them, but I understood her hesitation. The Wildflower Inn was beginning to pick up traction. It was a fragile time for her business, and we couldn't risk jeopardizing that. Besides, she wasn't arguing to never call the police, just to wait until after our guests checked out in a bit. I could respect that.

Besides, neither of us could sleep after what happened. A body and a break in all in a single day. My body shivered. After going over the footage several more times and wandering through the library a dozen more, Azalea headed to the kitchen to prep for breakfast.

I was in the library when the newspaper was delivered. Picking it up off the porch, I took it back to read, but when I saw the front page, I quickly ran down to the kitchen.

"What?" Azalea whipped batter in a metal bowl.

"The storage unit death made the front page," I said. *"Comic Books, Collectibles...and a Corpse: Shocking Discovery in Storage Unit.* Quite the headline."

Azalea breathed in deeply, but said, "That's not surprising. Did Luna Moray write the article?"

"You know she did." I met Luna during a previous case. She was Rose Mallow's mini media mogul, running the *Chesapeake Chronicle* newspaper as well as the local radio station. I believed she had a blog too? And she was in charge of our local cat rescue. When did the woman sleep? Luna and I had not gotten along well at the beginning, but by the end of the case, we had become friendly. She even did a piece featuring the Wildflower Inn recently, which was incredibly positive.

"What does she say?" Azalea asked.

I skimmed the article. "Looks like they've identified the body now. Marcus Howard. He's a local artist. Could he have created the photographs?"

Azalea shrugged as she poured the batter into a pan. Smelled like banana bread. I hoped she needed a taste tester.

"I know that name, but I didn't know what he looked like. Or if I did, it was a long time ago. If I remember correctly, Nana Z was in the Rose Mallow Artist's Guild with him. Trying to remember what medium he specialized in. I looked at the print we have, but I couldn't make out the signature." She snapped her fingers. "You know, Esme was in the group too, if I recall."

"That might explain why she had her artwork. And the photographs, if it's from her, Marcus, or another guild member."

"Yes, that would make sense. I'm sure they've all been friends for decades."

I kept reading. "The authorities are asking the public for any help regarding how he ended up in Esme Vienna's abandoned storage unit. Luna mentions that Esme couldn't be reached for comment."

"Does she talk about the bidding war over the unit?"

"Unfortunately, yes, my name comes up. She has a quote from someone who watched the auction. He claimed it was the most fun he'd had in years at the Chessie U-Store, and how it reminded him of how intense the auctions used to be when it was run by the previous family. Thank goodness she doesn't describe what else was found in the unit," I replied, relieved that she was apparently unaware of the expensive items I had now purchased. "She also doesn't mention the Wildflower Inn…"

"Oh, that's good. I don't want this place associated with heavy things ever again." Azalea put the pan into the oven.

"I don't blame you. No one wants that."

After closing the oven door, Azalea wandered out of the kitchen and down the hall. She came back holding a brochure, which she handed to me.

"What is this?" I asked.

"About the Rose Mallow Artist's Guild. They have a small gallery on the boardwalk, so I added their brochure to my little nook for the guests, featuring local businesses. Did you know several are offering them discounts?"

"That's lovely." I perused the brochure. The gallery opened later today, so I decided to stop by.

Azalea went back to working on breakfast. I wanted to do something helpful, so I started some tea. I could use my favorite Darjeeling black tea to keep pepped for the rest of the day. I left a mug for Azalea and took one back to the library.

As I wandered the room, I reflected on how bizarre it was that I'd felt more surprised than scared during the break-in. Why hadn't I been terrified? Had I become immune to criminal activity? That didn't feel right, though. Clover hadn't been scared either. He hadn't even growled once. I sat in the coziest chair and stared at the library walls, as if the great mystery authors there could somehow answer my questions.

Was it because all the thief would have gotten away with were some well-loved copies of Agatha Christie and Dorothy Sayers? Sure, there were also some Jane Austens, Jules Verne, and Mary Shelley, but again, they were all modern editions—nothing old or rare. They didn't touch my grandmother's art books. Not even the one on Rose Mallow's local artists. I should probably look through that. That must have been printed years ago.

If I recalled, Nana Z was featured inside, a photograph of her painting in her garden during the summertime. I likely had the dress she sported still. I missed her greatly.

# Chapter Twelve

The next thing I knew, a crush of feet stomped down the stairs. I squinted, bright sunlight streaming into the library. My mug sat on an end table, completely cooled off. Azalea must have added a plate beside it with a slice of delectable-looking banana bread. I stood up and stretched, only to realize I was still in my robe and pajamas.

I sank back into the chair and looked over the side. I felt like I was five years old, playing hide-and-go-seek. The guests chatted loudly with each other, heading across the lobby into the dining room. I crossed my fingers no one would come in here.

When it seemed that most of them had gone across, I ran across the lobby and down the back hallway to the kitchen, hoping no one would notice me.

"Hey there, sleepy head." Azalea plated pastries and quiches for the guests. She had another pan of banana bread ready, too.

"What time is it?"

"Nearly nine."

"No. You're kidding me." I rubbed my face, catching a wayward strand of hair. "Oh no, no, no." I searched out a metal surface and tried to make out my reflection. I could only imagine the bedhead I sported. My perfect French bob had likely exploded.

Azalea giggled. "You looked so peaceful. And you needed the sleep."

"Really? You couldn't have gotten me before the guests awoke?"

She shrugged, but her face beamed with mischief. The joys of living again with your sister. I'd have to figure out some way to return the favor.

"Wait, what about Violet and Clover?" I asked.

"Both are up and playing in the room under the stairs together. I'm sure we'll see them soon enough. They're fine. Head upstairs. We've got this."

Maybe I wouldn't return the favor after all. My sister knew I needed sleep, and she had taken care of everything else. Also, the joy of living again with your sister.

"Thank you, sis."

She winked at me. "Now go while I distract everyone with food."

"Good idea."

* * *

Upstairs, I quickly showered and changed. My phone remained plugged in on my nightstand. At least it was fully charged. However, it was flooded with text messages and voicemails.

Some were from our parents. Their flight was delayed again, but they were working on an alternate route. They thought they'd still make it for Rosh Hashanah.

Several were from Leo checking on me.

A few were from Luna Moray, trying to get my side of the storage unit story. She also invited me to join her on her daily radio program. No wonder I wasn't in the article.

One was from Nuri. It was a brief voicemail, simply apologizing for everything. She must have been up as late as we were, as it came in the early morning hours.

* * *

After a quick breakfast, I took Clover for a walk up the boardwalk behind the house. I loved how the boardwalk connected us to Redbud Park at the southern end and a row of local businesses on the northern end. In between were a row of historic houses like ours, all backing to the beauty of the Chesapeake Bay. Watching the water roll across was therapeutic after all the stress of the past twenty-four hours. Seagulls cawed and dove, and a few boats breezed along.

We wandered north towards the businesses. I popped by Boardwalk Books to check in on Nuri personally, but the place was dark. She had placed a hand-written sign on the door, saying the store was closed for a "family emergency."

Concerned, I tried calling her, but the phone went straight to voicemail. I didn't leave a message but sent a short text, saying I got her message and wanted to connect soon.

Unlike the bookstore, the Rose Mallow Artist's Guild gallery was open. Curious, I poked my head in. The small place was crowded with people.

"Are dogs allowed?" I asked a person near the door.

"Well-behaved?" the woman responded.

"And leashed," I said.

"Come on in." Her smile was bright. We came inside, and fortunately, Clover showed off his good manners for once. I silently thanked my pup. "Are you here because of Marcus?"

"I wanted to pay my respects," I said truthfully.

"We're discussing a vigil for tonight. Right here on the boardwalk," she said.

"Do you have some of his work on display?"

"Always. He was such a master craftsman."

I had expected her to show me black and white photographs of the Chesapeake Bay, but instead, she led me over to a display in the middle of the gallery. Marcus had been a woodworker. He sculpted abstract pieces from local felled trees, according to a small artist's statement.

On another shallow pedestal was a piece he created with local driftwood, setting up moss and branches. It reminded me of the sculptural nature of bonsai, although he hadn't trained any tiny trees.

Clover went closer, and I had to hold him back. "Not something you want to mark." He slumped back, appearing defeated.

Other groups of people chatted around us. Some discussed the impromptu vigil. It sounded like it'd start around seven that evening, although a few people pushed back, wanting to begin earlier. I heard someone else discussing bringing food and if the gallery had any extra tables.

To the other side of Clover and me was another small cluster, but my ears perked up when I realized they weren't talking about Marcus but about Esme.

I turned to them and said, "I heard she won a cruise."

"No, no," said a man. "She's on a silent retreat. At one of those places where you're not allowed cell phones."

"Or electricity," added another.

"Oh," I said, thinking that might explain why no one could reach her. After the conversation dwindled, I resumed wandering the gallery, weaving in and out of people. Several seemed happy to see Clover, and he enjoyed many pets. I hoped he wouldn't jump back and have people rub his belly, but the one time it happened, the woman cried with laughter and gladly obliged.

On the far wall stood a photograph matching the style I spotted in the storage unit. Sort of. It was the same size. And the same tones of black and white. But the photograph wasn't of the Chesapeake Bay; it was of a smiling couple. Maybe an engagement shot? Still, there was something about the composition that struck me as by the same artist as in the storage unit.

"Getting married soon?" A woman nearby thrust out her hand.

I took her offered hand to be polite, but was shocked by how strong her grip was. "No wedding bells at this time. Simply paying my respects."

"At this time, you say?" She released my hand, and I had to shake it slightly for the feeling to return. Then she stuffed a business card in my poor palm. "Olivia Carroll. Rose Mallow's resident and premier wedding photographer."

She spotted Clover. "Also do family and pet photography too!"

My dog, recognizing another eager customer, again lay back and happily accepted more belly rubs. Fortunately, Olivia quickly obliged.

"Your style is distinctive," I said. "Have you ever taken photos of the Bay?"

Olivia gazed up with a smile and a faraway look in her eyes. "My favorite subject. I love getting out there whenever I can. But my business keeps me busy. Most of my work is with people—and the occasional puppy, yes, dear, I mean like you, such a cutie pie." She spoke to Clover, who ate up the attention.

"Did you ever work with Esme Vienna?"

Olivia's expression suddenly soured. "Hah. She wishes she was even half the artist I am."

"She's a photographer too?"

"Photographer?" She waved in another direction. "No, she created whatever that is. Little sculptures out of things she found at the places she cleaned. Isn't that strange?"

"Things? Like she stole things?" I asked.

"No, no. Like from the garbage. Pieces of lint. Scraps of paper. Used paper towels. Stuff like that."

"How…" I searched for the appropriate word: "Creative."

Olivia shrugged. "More like weird. But sure. See, look at that pedestal."

I followed where she pointed and saw a solitary pedestal with a beam of light on it. I would have assumed it was empty except for some dust, but when we walked closer, I saw that it was a tiny living room. I peered closer at the miniature room. Everything was made from different colored pieces of dryer lint. The room was surprisingly intricate. There were different colors for the walls and floor, as well as a sofa and rug. She'd even hung a small "painting" on one of the walls, set up a mini coffee table, and a planter.

"Is that a dog?" I pointed to a small whitish-gray creature. It looked like a teeny-tiny Clover.

"Maybe," said Olivia. "Or maybe it's dust?"

I found the creation fascinating. How had she discovered this art form? How did she attach things together? Was it just lint, or did she use some sort of special glue? Microscopic nails and hammers? Staring at the piece was oddly transfixing, even meditative.

"I heard she's at a silent retreat." I stood back up.

Olivia stood up and belly laughed. "A silent retreat? That busybody? No way."

"Someone else said it was a cruise."

She wiped her eyes. "That's a good one, too. No, I know where she actually is."

"Where?"

She leaned in closer to me and then made a "drinky drinky" sign with her hand.

"You think she's at a rehab?" I whispered.

"I don't think. I know." Olivia tapped the side of her forehead.

"How?"

"Her niece, Susannah. She mentioned something suspicious to me when I last saw Esme. Artist's Guild stuff. Susannah said something vague about her aunt being away for a while."

"And that meant rehab?" It sounded too vague to mean much of anything.

"Well, if you'd seen Esme at other Guild meetings and parties, you'd know that she might be older, but she could put away her share of chardonnay. There was something in Susannah's tone that made it clear her aunt was going to try fixing it. Say what you will, but good luck to her."

"When was all that?" I asked.

Olivia thought. "A few weeks ago. Maybe more recently. I'd have to look at my calendar."

"You said it was at an Artist's Guild meeting. Is Susannah also an artist?"

"Not sure what that girl does. Except mooch off everyone. Especially her aunt. I call things like I see them, and while I know Esme had her issues, Susannah wasn't helping them as far as I could tell," she said. I knew I shouldn't feed into a person who loved to gossip, but it was hard to turn away. My inquisitive nature might have been my superpower at times, but it was also my weakness.

"Really?"

Olivia nodded. "She's capable of so much more. Smart girl. But lazy. She doesn't even try to make her own artwork. I think she just tells the computer to make something and out it pops." She waved towards some prints hanging on a back corner of the wall. They were abstract with bright neon colors and thick black shapes, reminding me of early digital artwork made in the 1990s.

"They're interesting."

"Sure, I'll give you that." Olivia's voice dripped with sarcasm.

"Did Esme and Susannah get along with Marcus?"

Olivia sighed. "I hate to speak ill of the dead…"

"Was Marcus not a nice person?"

"Heavens no. He was the loveliest. Just that…how shall I put this?" Olivia paused. "Esme was always in love with that man."

"Did he love her back?"

"He was polite about it. But he hadn't dated anyone since his wife…well, you know."

"Since his wife? What?" I asked.

She sighed again, like a bellows releasing. "Since she's been gone."

"Gone?"

But before Olivia responded, her eyes lit up. "Oh! My next client!" She pulled out another business card and darted off without even a goodbye.

Having lost his new friend, Clover pulled towards the door. I nodded at him, and we left the gallery. I decided I'd stop by the vigil later that night.

# Chapter Thirteen

Back at the Wildflower Inn, Detective Lakshmi Gupta was talking with Azalea in the library. They stood in the middle of the room. Clover took off, seeking out Violet.

"Juniper, there you are! I thought you were just taking Clover out for a walk."

"The walk took longer than I'd planned." I shrugged. "Detective, good to see you."

"Juniper," she replied with a short nod.

"Is anyone else still here?" I asked Azalea.

"No, everyone's checked out. Just us. I was catching the detective up on the break-in."

"You should have called overnight," Detective Gupta replied. "And you…" She turned to me. "You know better than to tidy up a crime scene."

"I know, but we're running a business. My reputation is on the line," Azalea jumped in. "Besides, nothing was taken."

"That's interesting because something was taken…from Esme Vienna— well, now Juniper's storage unit."

I held my breath. Had she discovered the missing Jane Austen letters in Nuri's bag? I kicked myself mentally. Why hadn't I told her about that? Nuri had kicked me out of her car. I owed nothing to her, right? And yet, I couldn't shake my loyalty to my old friend. There was no way she had hurt Marcus. I knew that deep in my core.

"There was a box open in the unit." She pulled out a photo of an open book-sized box. It was another archival-ready one, but it wasn't the right size for the letters. It was different from what Nuri had taken. "Can you tell me anything about this?"

"It looks like the other boxes in the unit. Really nice. Museum-grade, acid-free, made to last a while. And custom sizes for the objects inside. I don't know what was inside, but those boxes weren't cheap."

"Do you recognize these numbers?" she asked, pointing to the black numbers on the side, like the other boxes had.

"No. I saw there were codes on the boxes, but they're not a system I'm familiar with. I know several used by libraries and museums, but this is different."

A flash of disappointment crossed her face. I hated disappointing her, especially when she sought my advice. "I don't recognize the box, but I should tell you about something…"

I felt a swift kick at my right ankle. What was that? Out of the side of my eye, Azalea was sucking on her lips with her eyes wide. She looked like a balloon ready to burst. I didn't know the details, but our sisterly telepathic link kicked in. Not that it required much mind-reading to recognize that she didn't want me saying anything.

"What?" the detective asked.

"Oh, uh…I heard that the person was Marcus Howard. Have you learned anything more about how he passed away?"

The detective's face softened. "It was definitively ruled a homicide."

"How was he killed?" Azalea asked.

"He was hit by some sort of blunt instrument. But it wasn't left at the scene," the detective replied.

"Oh my goodness. Do you know who did it?" Azalea asked.

She shook her head. "It's just the beginning of the investigation." Then the detective turned to me. "You were telling me yesterday about how you ended up purchasing the unit."

"Oh, that."

"That."

I sighed heavily. "Well, the boxes actually were part of what caught my attention."

"Why?" asked the detective.

"All of the other units were absolute messes. Things in garbage bags, stuff sticking out every which way. What I could make out didn't look like it was in good shape or quality."

"But this unit was different?" We both knew she had seen the place, but I knew the drill. I had to answer anyway.

"Completely.  Appeared lined up and organized in high-quality boxes. Even that strange, unknown code was curious to me, but it was apparent that there was a logic to it."

"Okay, so I understand that. But five thousand dollars? That's a good bit of money for someone in their twenties," the detective asked.

"I read something that most Americans can't afford to spend an unexpected four hundred dollars. Even in emergencies," Azalea mentioned. I looked at her, trying to send a telepathic message, "Not helping." She put her hand to her mouth and smiled in seeming embarrassment. She'd gotten the message.

"I got caught up in the spirit of things.  When that realtor guy started digging in, my adrenaline spiked. I couldn't resist getting into the action." Since Azalea didn't want me explaining about the missing items, I assumed she wanted me to stay quiet about Nuri. How had she learned about Nuri's involvement?  Or was that her expressing that the unit was important to me? I hated to leave these details out to the detective, but I wanted to talk to Azalea first. I could always go back to the detective afterwards.

"Probably doesn't hurt that you're dating a billionaire." Detective Gupta threw it in casually.

My cheeks flamed. I gazed over at my sister, who simply shrugged. Did she think that, too? Even after I had explained otherwise? How rude.

"*That* has nothing to do with anything. Leo doesn't even know how much I spent."

"Okay, then where did you get the money?" Detective Gupta asked.

That was intrusive. Why did everyone assume I didn't have any money? But I wasn't going to do anyone any good holding back. Even if I wasn't sure how I was going to pay for it quite yet.

"I'm doing well. I have a good job. And I'm going to sell my D.C. townhouse soon. That will more than cover the cost. In the meantime, I'll manage. I'm not hurting." I hoped I sounded more confident than arrogant. I looked over at Azalea, but her expression suggested she remained doubtful. If I couldn't convince her, would I be able to convince the detective?

"Did you know Esme?"

I shook my head. "Never heard of her before."

"You had no idea it was her unit then?"

"Not a clue."

Something clicked in my head.

"Wait a second, Detective. Did you want my help, or am I a person of interest in this case?"

Her face went full poker mode. "There are just some curiosities that I'm trying to get straight. But I am serious in saying that you have been helpful before. I think you'll be helpful again."

"I'll do my best."

"And don't you think it's strange that a book-sized box is missing, and then last night, someone broke into your house trying to steal one of your grandmother's books?" she asked.

"Yes, definitely strange."

# Chapter Fourteen

That evening, I caught up with Leo, who agreed to meet me for the Rose Mallow Artist Guild's vigil in Marcus Howard's memory. I wandered up the boardwalk from the Wildflower Inn north until I reached the art gallery. Leo looked out over the water, chatting with his sister Annie. Again, she sported the '90s goth babydoll dress aesthetic, although today she sported a bright purple wig.

After greeting me, Leo said, "Annie's agreed to work with me on overseeing the Calverton grants to local businesses."

She gave a half-hearted shrug. "I'll delegate most of the work to my team. And if not, to Leo." She winked and smiled in a way that assured me she was teasing. Or at least I hoped that was what she meant.

"Thank you, Annie. That'll mean a lot to so many people around here."

"Your sister applied for the Wildflower Inn?" she asked.

"Yes. It's a great place, well worth supporting…"

"Whoo, hold up, tiger. I'm not on the grants committee. Neither is Leo," she said.

"So you won't be deciding who gets the money?"

Annie shook her head. "No, but I'll make sure her application gets the attention it deserves. And if she has any questions—or wants our honest feedback on it—we can help her there, too."

"Any Rose Mallow business," Leo added.

"Thank you. I appreciate that."

"You know…" Annie tapped her matching purple lips. "We could use someone like you on the grants review committee."

"Wouldn't that be a conflict of interest if my sister is applying?" I asked.

Annie smiled. "You would simply need to abstain from voting on her application. Easy peasy." She wiped her hands together.

"I'm not sure." Which was true. I'd moved to working with Dor Calverton as a private librarian to be less entrenched with the bureaucratic controls of the Calverton family. The idea of joining a committee screamed everything I had tried moving away from. Besides, when would I fit in another commitment?

She shrugged. "Think about it. We have a meeting coming up on Tuesday night. We'd be happy to have you attend."

"Even after everything that happened with the museum?" I was surprised she wanted to include me after I had lasted such a short time with my previous project. Not to mention how that one had also turned into a murder case.

Her smile softened. It looked more real, even with her bright purple lipstick. "Juniper, I'll be honest with you. I want you on that committee because of what happened. Not just because Leo has sung your good graces, but because I looked into it. You stood up to some powerful people and spoke the truth. That's something I admire. And something we need."

"You're stronger than I think you give yourself credit," Leo added.

"I'll think about it," I said.

"Great. Leo, can you text Juniper the meeting details?"

"Sure thing, sis." He pulled out his phone. Within moments, my own pinged with the details for the Tuesday evening meeting. I hope I hadn't overextended myself.

Something screamed from Annie's pocket. Sounded like someone dying. I stiffened with concern. But Annie simply pulled out her phone. Was that her ringtone? "It's Zurich." She stuck out her tongue. "That's why I gave them the death metal song. As much as I'd prefer talking to the both of you, I need to take this. Ciao."

"Ciao," I repeated reflexively.

As she walked away, I turned to Leo. "She remains quite the character."

"Yeah, she's something. I always think she'll end up the youngest member ever of the Supreme Court."

"Can you imagine? With the purple hair?"

Leo laughed. "Actually, I think it's good she's getting involved with the grants. She does so much international work that I'm happy to see she's finding some time to help out locally. And I'm glad you're going to get involved."

"Thinking about it."

He put an arm around my waist. "And I'm really glad to see your idea taking off."

"It wasn't just my idea," I said, but I couldn't hide the blush forming on my cheeks. "I only helped push along the thought that your family should invest in the community, not tear it down and rebuild with something…" I struggled to find the polite word.

"Boring? Cookie-cutter? Waste of money?" Leo supplied. This was why we dated. He and I were on the same wavelength, even with something as deeply personal as his family's community priorities. That didn't mean much with most people, but when your family runs multi-national corporations, it had a lot more impact.

"Something lacking the history and charm of Rose Mallow," I added.

He grabbed me tighter. I was half-tempted to give him a deep kiss, but then seeing the people behind us jolted me back to reality.

The memorial.

"Later, *tiger*," I said, repeating his sister's phrase.

"At least she didn't call you Junie-Bug today."

"True." I laughed, but then quieted down. More people were strolling up to the gallery. A considerable crowd began to swell around us on the boardwalk.

"Did you know Marcus?" I asked Leo.

Leo nodded. "Marcus used to make artwork for my family's annual charity ball each winter."

"You have an annual charity ball?" Why was I surprised by this?

"It's a big social event. One of my other sisters works on it with my parents. Essentially, her full-time job. You'll see. Quite the party."

"I can only imagine," I said with curiosity.

"Mark your calendar for this winter."

I made a face. "Oh, I have to go to it?"

Leo laughed. "I normally try to find an excuse to be out of the country, but this year, my parents have made it clear that I'm expected to be involved. It'll be a lot nicer if I have the best date there."

My cheeks warmed. "If I can make it easier for you, I will definitely be there." Plus, was he suggesting we'd still be dating this winter? My stomach fluttered. Was this what it felt like to have a serious relationship? None of mine in the past had ever been more than casual dates. I don't think I'd ever simply assumed I'd be with someone months from the moment. It made me feel...how would I describe it? A mixture of nervous and excited.

"Are you okay, Juniper?"

"Oh yeah. Sorry. Marcus made artwork for the big event?"

"He was a true Renaissance man. Could do anything: woodworking, paintings, a fancy scroll one year celebrating my parents' anniversary."

"I'm so sorry," I said.

Leo sighed and shrugged sadly. "Hearing he was killed...it's a real loss to the community."

"So it seems."

"And in your storage unit. Such strange circumstances. Takes me back to when his wife disappeared."

"She disappeared? I thought she passed away," I said.

Leo nodded. "We all think she did, but no one knows for sure what happened."

"What happened?"

Leo started to respond, but someone came by, handing out candles. Another person shared flyers featuring Marcus's photography and obituary. We each took one. I looked over the biography. It mentioned how he was hopefully reunited with his long-lost and beloved wife, Betsy. They didn't appear to have any kids.

"Oh," I said.

"What?" Leo asked.

"He used to teach at my graduate school." I spoke softly, expecting the ceremony to begin shortly.

"Did you take any classes from him?"

I shook my head. "No, he was in the arts department. Never took any classes there. Although I think Nuri took a few. I wonder if she ever had him as a teacher."

I looked towards her store. Through the crowd, it was difficult to tell if it had reopened. I'd need to check after the vigil.

On the outskirts of the group, I spotted Olivia—the photographer I spoke with at the gallery. She appeared to be arguing with someone. A person in the crowd moved, and to my amazement, the person she argued with was Noah Danvers—the realtor who dipped out of the auction after running up the amount. How did the two of them know each other?

"I'll be back," I whispered to Leo. He nodded.

I wove through the group towards Olivia and Noah. Locked in their heated exchange and with everyone else around, they didn't appear to notice me.

"I'm free now," Olivia said, waving a camera at him like a baton. "You can't do this."

"It doesn't work that way," Noah replied.

"No. You don't get to do this to me."

"You signed the contract, didn't you?"

"There's no way..."

Olivia noticed me and closed her mouth. Her hand with the camera dropped to her side. Noah turned, following her gaze.

"You," he said. But he didn't say anything else. Instead of coming towards me, he sprinted away.

"Wait, Noah!" I tried to go after him, but too many people had appeared for me to easily navigate. How many people could this boardwalk hold? At least the weather was holding out for us. Not that helped at the moment.

As I traversed towards Olivia, I ended up knocking into her. "I'm so sorry."

The camera fell from her hands in the process. I dove to get it, but Olivia cried out. The lens cap, apparently loose, rolled off as it hit the ground, and to my surprise, a liquid spilled out. Olivia fell to her knees. She quickly grabbed the cap and swiveled it back on.

"Are you okay?" I offered her a hand to stand up, but she refused, clutching her bizarre camera instead. "Is your camera okay?"

"Fine, fine," she replied brusquely.

Even looking at it this close, it appeared like a real camera, but it was clearly not. Was it a flask? Had she been drinking? Maybe she was distraught over Marcus's passing? A million thoughts clouded my mind.

"Was that Noah Danvers?" I asked.

Olivia smoothed down her clothes. As she did, she seemed to morph into a completely different person. A smile grew across her face, and she replied with a cheery voice, "Yes, it was. We're discussing a booking. Yet another engagement photo shoot! Always busy with business when you're Rose Mallow's premiere wedding photographer."

"Okay," I said, unsure of how to respond to her sudden change of demeanor. "But you looked like you were arguing."

"Arguing?" Olivia laughed loudly. Too loudly. A few people looked over their shoulders. "No, my dear, we were just haggling. I may offer great rates, but it doesn't mean they aren't worthy of my professional expertise." She blinked several times.

Could that be the contract he had alluded to? One for the photography shoot? I wondered if he was planning to marry the girlfriend he was giving the roses to. And if she was the same person at the auction who pulled him out?

Leo waded through the group to us. "I think they're getting started shortly."

"Oh, ho, ho, look at this handsome devil," says Olivia. "Aren't you two a stylish pair?" She thrusts a business card at Leo. "Olivia Grover, Rose Mallow's premiere wedding photographer. I was just telling your…what was your name again, honey?"

"Juniper."

"Right. I was just telling Juniper about booking an engagement shoot, if you two are interested." She wiggled her eyebrows.

Leo's face flushed the brightest shade of red I'd seen. He looked like he had summited a volcano. I couldn't help giggling, although I tried keeping it under my breath.

"No, we only recently started dating," I said to Olivia.

"Never too early to think about. Besides, I book up quickly. You should come by my studio. We can chat."

Before I could respond, someone tapped on a microphone and asked the obligatory "Can you hear me?" sound check. The three of us turned towards the art gallery. Standing on top of a chair was another artist from the guild. Her eyes were red and swollen, and even now, she had a hard time not crying. She started to say something, but instead, she cried. The microphone was quickly handed over to someone else.

A man I thought may have been in the gallery that morning took her place on the chair. It wasn't the best impromptu stage, but at least it got him over the heads in the crowd.

"Marcus meant the world to us. He died way too soon." He continued on, welcoming everyone for attending and how much it would have meant to Marcus and his missing wife, Betsy. He paused before saying, "I hope they have been reunited at last. Let's take a moment of silence to remember them both."

After he spoke, people took turns climbing up and down the chair, exchanging the microphone, and sharing stories about Marcus. He sounded like he'd been a talented person who meant a lot to the community. I wish I'd known him.

Someone read a poem they had written, another person sang a song, while a third did a brief interpretive dance to a drummer. I suppose that when you're active in an artist's guild, it's not surprising to have seen the creative ways everyone grieved.

I felt a tap on my arm. Candles were being passed around, just as the sun was setting. As we stood there, along the boardwalk in the twilight, our candles glowed beautifully, stark against the darkening sky. Behind us, orange, pink, and purple created translucent waves from the setting sun, while to the east, it had already turned deep indigo. The first stars appeared, twinkling dully and then soon brightly above the blue-black waters.

A violin pierced with a near wail before settling into a mournful but gorgeous song. I wished I knew my classical music better, because I didn't recognize the piece, but the violin reflected the sense of grief coupled with the community comfort.

I stood there and closed my eyes, taking it all in. I didn't simply mourn Marcus Howard but all the people I had lost. My grandmother and grandfather, as well as the people whose cases I've become involved with since returning to Rose Mallow. The pain I felt here was because this place was so special to me.

"You doing okay?" Leo asked me.

I hadn't realized that I'd started crying. I wiped my eyes with my free hand. "I'll be fine. It's a lot to take in."

He nodded. "It's a big loss. And I'm sorry you're the one who found him."

One of the ones, but it wasn't worth correcting. Instead, I leaned against Leo, who put his arm around me. I felt him breathe and tried listening for his heartbeat, but there were too many sounds around us. I didn't mind. Having the moment was enough.

His phone pinged. He stood up and dug it out. "Annie texted. She wants to go over a few things about the grant. Can we catch up later?"

"Sure, of course. I'll be at your grandmother's for work tomorrow." I gave him a quick peck on the cheek.

# Chapter Fifteen

After the vigil ended, I headed back down the boardwalk towards the Wildflower Inn, only to be stopped by Luna Moray. I assumed she was there to cover the event for *The Chesapeake Chronicle*.

"You didn't respond to my calls," she said.

"Sorry, it's been a busy time." While that was true, I conveniently left out how much I did not want to be interviewed, especially by her. We had become cordial, but I didn't imagine we'd become friendly enough that I'd want to do favors for her.

"Will you consider being on my radio show tomorrow? Or interviewed for the paper?

Maybe both?" She looked at me expectantly.

"Luna, I'll be honest. I haven't forgotten the way you portrayed me last time you featured me. It wasn't exactly kind." When I'd been pulled into an investigation earlier in the summer, Luna had me do both, but she had given me the "villain edit." Since she had pushed, I felt that I needed to share why.

She waved her hands. "Water under the bridge. I wouldn't do that to you again. I promise."

I sighed. "I doubt that Detective Gupta wants me talking."

"She's not your boss," argued Luna.

"Well, to be fair, I doubt my boss wants me talking either." Although I no longer worked for the Calverton Foundation, I still worked for the Calvertons, now serving as the personal librarian to Dorothea "Dor" Calverton, the family matriarch—and Leo's grandmother. Since leaving the Foundation, I'd tried being more private about my work. With Dor's background in spycraft, I doubted she wanted me running around talking to the press, given my new connection with her.

Luna put a hand on my arm. "Look, if you chat with me, I'll share some inside information with you. I have a scoop."

"Oh, really?" That caught my attention. Did she have something useful to share?

"I heard it was official that Marcus was killed."

"Do you know how or by whom?" I should have been stunned that she already knew, but it was a small town and news traveled quickly, especially given that she was a reporter.  Maybe the detective or the police had announced it? Besides, I could almost hear Luna pointing out how I was involved. I could go the rest of my life without running into another body.

"Well, I figured if I mentioned the 'm' words to you…"

"The 'm' words?"

"You know…" She opened her hands wide.

"No, I don't know. What are you talking about?"

She came closer to me and whispered, "Murder and mystery."

I rolled my eyes.

"You'll be able to figure it out," Luna replied, surprisingly brightly.

"I'm not the town's resident investigator. I have a job. Which I need to go back to tomorrow morning, Luna."

"Right, right, working with Dor."

Now that shocked me. "How did you hear about that?"

Luna stared at me. "I am a reporter. I learn things."

"And I'm a rare books librarian.  That's my job.  Not playing detective. Besides, we have Detective Gupta, and she's very good at her work."

"Not as good as you, Juniper."

I rolled my eyes. Maybe not the most professional of answers, but I was getting tired of going back and forth with her.

"Besides, I heard another rumor."

"What's that?"

"Your buddy Nuri is a suspect."

I felt the life rush out of my body, like a wave pulling me down. "What?

Where did you hear that? Why do they think that?"

But Luna must have known she had caught my attention now. "Set up a meeting with me. On the record. At least partially. And then we can discuss further." She waved at me as she sauntered off.

I shook my head. Luna had found my weak spot. I still didn't understand what was going on with my friend. Was she even still my friend? I tried calling her again, but only got her voicemail. I considered going over to her apartment, but that seemed extreme. Instead, I headed back to the Wildflower Inn.

* * *

Still mulling everything over, I wandered the library in the Wildflower Inn. Nothing about the past twenty-four hours made any sense to me. I stared at the spines of the books, wishing that they could tell me something. Anything.

I realized I kept lingering on one of the books, although I couldn't say why. I pulled it off the shelf. A hardback edition of Jane Austen's *Pride and Prejudice*. Again, not a particularly old or rare printing. Probably dated back fifty years at most. But yet, something seemed strange about the book. I turned it over. No strange markings, although it showed signs of age and wear. Some of Nana Z's favorite pages were dog-eared.

So what was setting my librarian senses all a tingle?

I took the dust jacket off the book. Inside were letters. Jane Austen letters. The letters that Nuri had shown me in the car.

How? Why?

Realization dawned on me both slowly and quickly.

Nuri had been the one to break into The Wildflower Inn overnight. She hadn't been looking to steal anything it appeared, but to hide these. I stared at the letters. I knew I should call Detective Gupta, but my curiosity kept ringing like a loud bell in my ears.

Why had Nuri gone to such great lengths to hide these letters here? In our library? I turned them over and over again. I knew why.

She wanted me to keep them safe.

Did that mean she didn't feel that her place was safe?

I took them up to my room. I needed to talk to Nuri, but I couldn't leave them out. First, I put them under the bed, but come on, I'm an expert. I know that was a foolish idea. Then I tried the bottom of my dresser. It didn't feel any better. Where would be safe?

Eventually, I took a page from Edgar Allan Poe's *Murders of the Rue Morgue*, hiding them in plain sight. I put the letters with some others from my grandmother, which I had started organizing on the desk in my room, planning to read through.

# Chapter Sixteen

ownstairs, I found Azalea preparing dinner. She was also going through her grocery list to prepare for Rosh Hashanah dinner. She had the back door open, as Clover and Violet played on the verandah.

"Hey, do you want to tell me about that kick earlier?" I asked.

"What kick?"

I sat down with her at the kitchen table. Out of the corner of my eye, I spotted our kids—her two-legged and mine four—zooming past on the verandah. Clover barked happily.

"When I was talking to the detective, you gave me a kick. You obviously didn't want me to say something to her. But what?"

"Oh, that." She put down the list on the table and twisted her hands.

"Yes, that."

She sighed. "There's something I should tell you about Esme."

"What?"

She tapped a short tattoo on the table. "You know how the Wildflower Inn was going through a tough time financially."

"Yes, I remember finding the letters from the bank." The bank had almost repossessed the house based on the loans she'd taken out to restore the place and turn it into a hotel. Part of the reason I'd moved in was to become a regular resident of the inn and pay my sister rent. She had objected at first, but I saw it as doing my part to keep the business alive as it caught on and ensured the house stayed in our family. That's another reason I'd argued to the Calvertons about investing in the community, which paved the way for the grant program.

"It was even worse than what you saw."

"How could that be? Why didn't you tell me?"

Azalea put her hands on the table, palm side up. "I didn't want to tell anyone. Certainly not my successful sister in D.C."

"You thought of me as successful?" That would never have occurred to me. I had left college early and then spent years traveling, trying to figure out my left from my right. When I'd gone back and become a librarian, I'd been proud of my success, but I hadn't considered it anything noteworthy.

She smiled. "Of course! You worked at the Library of Congress. Had your own townhouse. How amazing was that? I was and still am very proud of you."

"Thank you, Azalea. You know I look up to you, too."

She nearly laughed. More of a sputter emanated from her mouth. "But I was estranged from my husband, and failing to make ends meet. I didn't want you to know how bad off I was. I didn't tell anyone. I was too prideful."

"I had no idea. I'm sorry." I came over and gave her a side hug.

"Thank you, but you need to hear this." She motioned for me to sit back down, which I did.

"How does this involve Esme?"

"Esme offered me money."

"Money? Why? How?"

Azalea shrugged. "I don't know how she got wind of my problems, but she did. I didn't know her well, but I knew she'd been in the Rose Mallow Artist's Guild with Nana Z, so I decided to listen to her. She offered me a lot of money. Like a lot of money."

"How successful is her cleaning business?" Maybe Esme was some sort of secret millionaire. That could explain her eccentric collection of expensive items.

"I don't know. I strongly considered taking the money."

"But you didn't, I take it?"

"At first I thought it was a simple loan."

"And it wasn't?"

She shook her head. "Keisha's sister Desiree warned me not to take it." Keisha was my sister's high school assistant. She wasn't able to work as frequently during the school year, though. Her older sister, Desiree Douglass, ran a small electronics and repair shop on the boardwalk. A real hole-in-the-wall place, but Desiree was a technical wizard. Her sister appeared to be following in her footsteps.

"Why?" I asked.

"She told me there would be strings attached. Esme had offered Desiree a similar loan to help with her store. But she wanted collateral."

"What kind of collateral?"

"She wanted Desiree's most prized possession: her Star Wars figurines."

"Wait, those belonged to Keisha's sister? You knew that?"

"Not at first. No. It wasn't until after learning it was Esme's unit that I put two and two together," Azalea replied. "But here's the thing."

"What?" I didn't like the sound of where this was going.

"After Esme got the Star Wars toys, she changed the conditions of her loan to Desiree."

"How did she change the conditions?"

Azalea sighed. "It was no longer a loan. It became…blackmail."

"Blackmail?" I repeated.

"Esme refused to give the Star Wars toys back to Desiree. She required more and more money on less and less favorable terms."

"So why didn't Desiree take Esme to court? Or at least call the police?" I asked.

"Well, she threatened to reveal something about Desiree if she did any of that. Something secret."

"What?"

Azalea shrugged. "That's not for me to share. But what I can say is that Desiree got locked up in a bad situation with Esme. She warned me not to accept her money. And I'm glad I didn't. You know why?"

"I'm afraid to ask."

"You should be. Because Esme wanted my most prized possession."

"Oh, no."

Azalea nodded. "That's right. The deed to the Wildflower Inn."

I gasped. "Are you serious?"

"Dead serious."

I sat back in my chair and considered the implications of what my sister told me. Esme hadn't purchased those toys. She had gotten them from Desiree and held them hostage, forcing the woman to pay more and more or risk a secret being revealed.

"You think she did this to other people?"

"Very much so."

"But why didn't you want me to tell the police?"

Azalea didn't answer at first. Instead, she stared out the back door. I followed her gaze. The kids—as I liked to think of Violet and Clover—were playing hide and seek. Neither were doing a great job hiding, but that didn't seem to matter.

"Because I recognized Nana Z's watercolors in one of the boxes," Azalea finally said. "And I took them with me."

"You did what?"

"I think that was the box that the detective was describing as having been left open. I didn't want to risk having to return them to the police."

"Oh, Azalea. Why didn't you tell me that?" I remembered thinking the box the detective showed me in the picture hadn't seemed right for holding Nuri's small letters. But they could have been right for our grandmother's watercolors. I never would have guessed that my sister had taken them. No wonder she didn't want me saying anything more.

She sucked on her lips. "I know. I should have. But I was already worried about what you had gotten into. I didn't want to make it worse."

I put my hand out, and Azalea grasped it. We held tight for a few moments. Then I released the grip. "Why do you think the watercolors were there? Do you think Esme had blackmailed Nana Z?"

"I don't know. I hope not."

I considered everything she had told me. So many pieces to figure out. Had Esme given Nana Z a so-called loan? It worried me that she would have needed one. It didn't make sense since my sister and I both got a generous inheritance after her passing, in sharing the inn, until my sister bought me out. So Esme hadn't taken that.

We now knew that the Star Wars toys belonged to Desiree. But she hadn't been anywhere near the unit that morning and had not participated in the auction.

I knew that Nuri had also taken something from the unit: the Jane Austen letters. And she had hidden them in our house, although I didn't know why. Hearing what my sister told me alarmed me as to how Esme had gotten the letters from Nuri in the first place. Had she also been under a predatory loan from Esme?

And how did Olivia's photographs fit in? They were artwork like Nana Z's, but were either—her photographs or Nana Z's watercolors—worth what the Star Wars toys, Jane Austen letters, or the deed to the Wildflower Inn was worth? Maybe, but I didn't know yet. I'd have to do some research into them.

Which led me to the biggest question of all: how and why was Marcus in the unit? Then I realized that wasn't the only big question left.

"Esme is missing," I said.

"What? I thought she was on some vacation."

"That's what a neighbor told me. But everyone at the Rose Mallow Artist's Guild had another story about where she might be. I heard everything from a silent retreat to rehab."

"Oh, wow."

"Now I'm wondering if any of those things are true."

Azalea's face lit up. "Because if Marcus is dead in her unit, and she's missing—"

"Exactly." Neither of us wanted to say the possibility out loud. Esme might also be dead. She'd obviously made some enemies across town, assuming she was enacting the same kind of predatory behavior on other people. And sadly, I'd seen people hurt for much less.

"Nuri," I whispered.

"What?"

"I'm worried about Nuri. Marcus is dead, Esme is missing, and Nuri knows more than she's willing to tell me. And I think she's in danger because of it."

"What do you mean?"

I explained about the incident with the car and revealed the truth about the letters. To say Azalea appeared shocked was an understatement.

"She stole letters…and they are in your room?" Azalea sounded like she was in a daze.

"Pretty much. You're not mad?" I asked.

"Furious. But that's not fair. I mean, I did it too. Plus, I think you're right. Nuri sounds like she's in trouble. What are you going to do?"

"I need to find her. And get her to talk to me. Then we can figure things out."

Azalea nodded. I knew she wanted to tell me to call the police, but she knew from experience that I was going to seek out my friend no matter what, especially if that friend was facing trouble.

"Keep me updated."

"I promise," I said.

# Chapter Seventeen

lthough it was dark, I jumped into KG and headed to Nuri's apartment. She didn't answer when I knocked on the door. I tried several times without success. I was about to give up and head down the stairs when I heard an odd tapping sound. As I looked around, I spotted Nuri hiding in the door of the stairwell, trying to get my attention. She crooked a finger and motioned for me to follow her.

She didn't say anything as we wandered down the stairs. She stopped every now and then to look around or listen for something. My friend, dressed all in black, struck me as being on the verge of paranoia, or maybe the start of a panic attack. Her strange actions since the auction appeared like someone desperate.

We ended up in a small courtyard behind the apartment building with high fences. There wasn't much growing there except weeds and tall grasses. It could have been a lovely, small park with some care, but the lack of care suggested it'd been forgotten for some time.

Nuri looked around, eyes darting every which way, before she finally seemed to decide it was safe here. With it being night with only the tiniest crescent of a moon and no lights working in the courtyard, it was easy to disappear into the shadows. At least it was still warm outside. It'd be a few more weeks before fall truly chilled the air.

I put my arms out for her. She appeared timid and uncertain, but when she finally gave in, she sank into my arms.

"I'm so sorry, Juniper. I can't believe I made you get out of my car. After everything you've done for me."

"Nuri, I'm sorry too. Something is going on, and I needed to listen to you the way you wanted, not just push myself on you," I replied.

"Thank you, but what I did was inexcusable." Her expression instantly shifted into terror. She obviously hadn't meant to let that slip.

"I know it was you who left the Jane Austen letters in the library." I was angry, but more than that, I was curious. Something had turned my logical friend completely irrational. But what?

"Oh, Juniper…I'm sorry."

"Why did you do that?"

She chewed on her thumb.

"Are they safe?" Nuri asked.

"The letters?"

I nodded.

"For now. Yes. But I wish you would have just talked to me."

She held her head with her hands. "I wish I had too. I was just so scared. I still am. I'm sorry. I should have explained everything."

"Look, it'll be water under the bridge, if you're willing to share what you can. And I'll tell you what I've learned." I put a reassuring hand on her upper arm. As upset as I was, my curiosity overwhelmed me. How could I help anything without knowing anything?

Nuri sighed. She led me to a bench hiding within the tall grasses of the courtyard, and we sat there. "This has been the worst weekend of my life. And that's saying something."

"What do you mean?" I asked.

Nuri breathed in deeply. "Have you ever wondered why I left graduate school right before graduation?"

"Yes, but I heard there was some sort of family emergency."

Nuri wiped her face. "Well, that's sort of true. There was a family emergency. It was me. I was the family emergency."

"What happened?"

Nuri stood up and paced in front of me. "See, I didn't have much money. Neither did my parents. They were both immigrants to America."

"Right, from Turkey and South Korea, right?"

She nodded. "They had spent all their money bringing our family here. They'd given me what they could for school, but it wasn't much. And sure, I could take out endless loans, but it's not like librarians make a lot of money. I'd be swimming in debt for the rest of my life."

"I understand."

"So, well, you see…" She made circles in the ground with her right foot. As usual, she was sporting thick black boots with metal tips. My punk rock friend. "I found a way to pay for my education."

"That's great!"

She shook her head. "Not great. Not at all."

"I don't follow."

"You know the Jane Austen letters," she said.

"The ones you left in the library."

She nodded. "Those ones. There's something you should know about them."

"What?"

She stared at the ground. "Well, here's the thing. They aren't actually from Jane Austen."

"I don't follow." Although as I said that, a sinking feeling pulled my stomach towards my

shoes.

"I paid for school by creating fake archival documents."

"You what?" Even sitting down, I felt like I was falling.

"I forged documents for unsuspecting buyers. Including those letters."

"Oh my goodness. Nuri. Are you serious?" My brain felt like it was exploding inside my cranium. How could this be possible? We went into librarianship because we loved books. We studied the preservation and maintenance of rare books because we wanted to ensure they were here for generations to come. Creating forgeries went against everything we valued. Or at least everything I valued.

Nuri began to cry. I felt torn between comforting my old friend and yelling at her. She had broken into my house and planted stolen fake letters in it. After she had kicked me out on the side of the road. My body shook, like a small earthquake trembled.

I stood up and walked in a circle. "How did you...do I even want to know...I..." I couldn't finish a single sentence. Everything had stopped making sense.

"Juniper, I'm so sorry."

Then another realization hit like a tidal wave. "You used my code."

"What?"

"For the front door. I gave you the code."

"I know. When we were working on projects for Broadway Books." After Nuri had taken over the store, we had worked together on updating the place. With the Wildflower Inn closer than her apartment, we'd used my sister's place to organize and store materials. Giving Nuri the door code had made the project easier to manage.

"I trusted you, Nuri." I knew she had been the one to break in, but this somehow made it all worse. Even with everything she was going through, I couldn't simply excuse it as water under the bridge.

"I can't apologize enough," she said.

"We thought we had a burglar. There were people staying in the house. What if one of the guests had run into you? We called the police!"

"I should have told you," she said between sobs.

"You should have told me," I repeated. My head pounded.

"I'll explain everything."

I wanted to know, but I couldn't do this now. I felt like I was on fire. She had forged documents, stolen them from the storage unit, and hid them in my house by breaking in with my code. The full weight of her confession began to dawn upon me.

"I need some space, Nuri."

"Juniper, please. Forgive me."

"Not yet," I said.

She nodded, even as she cried. "I can explain everything."

"And you will. You need to tell the police," I said.

Her face flushed. "No, no, I can't do that."

"Why not?"

She slumped. "It'll make everything worse."

"Because you might get in trouble?" I asked.

"No, it's not that. It's just that I'm in danger."

The whole reason I had come here in the first place.

"What's happening?" I asked.

"I can't stay here anymore. There are people after me. I need to get somewhere safe."

"Then call the police, Nuri."

She shook her head. "No, I can't do that. Not yet. I will. Once it's safe."

I sat down on the bench and put a hand to my forehead. Talking with her felt like it was going in circles. She had told me some horrible things, and yet, I had the feeling there was more she was withholding. Something critically important. I tried to put my exploding feelings aside for the moment.

"Do you have somewhere safe to go?" I asked. As upset as I felt with Nuri, I believed that she was terrified.

Nuri nodded. "Yeah, I'm figuring it out right now."

Part of me wanted to save her, offer the Wildflower Inn, but how could I do that? She had broken into our house with my code, planted stolen materials, and refused to go to the police. How could I subject our family to this? Or could I? Should I?

"I'm going to be okay, Juniper. And when I'm safe, I'll fix this. I promise."

"And you'll contact the police?"

She nodded. Her phone buzzed. She pulled it out. "Okay, my safe place is going to work out. I should head there. I'm sorry, Juniper."

"I'm sorry too, Nuri."

"I'm not a bad person, Juniper. I promise."

I wanted to believe her. So badly. But her actions indicated that at best she'd made bad choices. Many of them. When did enough bad choices mean someone wasn't good anymore? It was difficult to reconcile these feelings with our history. Besides being so close in graduate school, we'd worked so hard the past few weeks on her taking over Broadway Books. We'd been a good team. She was always cheerful, even when we hit snags on the project.

"Let me know you're okay, Nuri."

She breathed out deeply. "I will."

"We'll talk more."

She nodded vigorously. "Yes, yes, of course."

# Chapter Eighteen

After leaving Nuri, I drove around in KG in an attempt to settle my mind. "Attempt" being the key word. New questions kept popping up. What if the police discovered the letters? How did they get from Nuri into Esme's unit? And for that matter, how had she known about the auction? She had told me so many things that made my brain hurt that I'd neglected to ask her the most basic questions about her connection to Esme.

Plus, new thoughts formed. If she had lied about this much, were there other things she hadn't told me? I didn't want to believe she could be involved with Marcus's death, but maybe I should consider it? My stomach turned, and I pulled over to put my head down, fearing that I might throw up.

I wasn't ready to talk with Nuri again, so instead, I started driving again once my stomach settled. I probably should have headed home, but instead I found myself circling Esme's neighborhood. Eventually, I located her house. Having only been here once with Leo driving, I wasn't sure how I'd stumbled back upon it, but there I was.

I pulled up and parked on the street, cutting KG's lights. Where have you gone, Esme? A cruise, a retreat, rehab? Were any of these things true? Why did you have Nuri's letters? How did Marcus end up in your unit? And why was your unit abandoned?

While I never expected the house to answer me, it suddenly created a new question. There was a flashlight moving through the inside of the house. That was bizarre. I stared from KG, but I couldn't make out who was inside.

Sure, I should probably have called the police, but the intruder might have left before they arrived. Instead, I crept as silently as I could from the car and across the lawn. I snuck up to a window and peeked inside. Maybe I could get some photos or video?

Noah Danvers. And the woman from the auction.

They appeared to be searching for something. They moved through the house, disappearing from my view. I hid in the shrubs, trying to spot them. I considered again calling the police, but I didn't want to be heard by them. What were they up to?

They were gone for a few minutes. I was about to slink back to KG when the two came out a side door.

"I thought you'd paid the bills, Noah," the woman said.

Noah simply shrugged.

"How do we fix this?"

"I'll fix it. Just an oversight."

"But how? We don't even have—"

A twig had snapped under me. The woman had obviously heard. She looked around, aiming the flashlight erratically. Again, the dark, nearly moonless sky helped conceal me, even as close as I was to them.

"Susannah, you're being paranoid," Noah said. Ah, so the woman was Susannah, Esme's niece. This had to be his girlfriend. "Let's get in the car."

She sighed. "I'll rest easier once we find the logbook."

"Don't worry. We'll find it. And once it's all over, we'll get away. Just the two of us."

"Maybe to a sunny beach?"

"Anywhere you want, Susannah."

"You promise?"

He nodded and took her hand. She sported a sizable diamond ring. Had Olivia been right that the two had been arguing over a contract for an engagement photo session? I needed to find out more.

As the two walked away, Susannah stopped. "Wait, whose car is that?" She pointed to KG.

"It's just a car."

"But it wasn't there before."

"Look at how many cars are on this street. You think someone parked right in front of her house and is secretly spying on us? Wouldn't they have at least parked out of the way?" He shook his head, oblivious to how correct he was. "You're going to draw attention to us if we don't get going."

"So no one knows we're here?"

"Of course not. And even if they did, don't forget. You're Esme's niece. Plain and simple."

"Right," she replied, although her voice suggested she wasn't sure. So this was Susannah, the same supposedly lazy artist that Olivia had gossiped about. That made sense. If Victory Cleaners had the contract for the Chessie U-Store, then she would have been there for work when Noah came to surprise her with the flowers I nearly destroyed. Had she known that her aunt's unit was up for auction that morning? Or was it purely happenstance?

However, as Noah got into their car, I noticed him staring at KG in a way that made me uncomfortable. Did he somehow recognize it? I didn't drive to the Chessie U-Store, and I'd walked to the vigil. He couldn't have possibly known it belonged to me, right?

I waited for what felt like forever until after they left before returning to KG. Should I call the police? And say what? That Esme's niece was in her house? Was that illegal? From what I gathered, they had been living together. It was all strange and unsettling, but she was likely allowed there. Although if that was the case, then why was she sneaking around? I decided to make note and tell Detective Gupta tomorrow. It was late, and I was exhausted. It didn't help that I kept adding to my list of questions instead of answering any of them.

# Chapter Nineteen

The next morning, I went to work at my boss's home, deep in the rural countryside of southern Maryland. Like the so-called cottages lining the ocean view in Newport, Rhode Island, the word "cottage" was an oxymoron. Her home was actually a grand mansion. The nearly three-hundred-year-old home had been added on over the years, creating an eclectic mix of architectural styles jutting off of the original Georgian revival brick manor. Dor called the place "The Rabbit's Hole," but its official title was actually "Calverton's Delight." She made a sour face whenever anyone used that name.

I had asked her about the estate's name when I started working with her only a few weeks earlier.

"I doubt it was much of a delight to the hundreds of people forced to live and work here," she'd mused, referencing her ancestral family's use of enslaved labor. Dor was nearly ninety, but she remained unapologetically progressive in her views. Then again, she was unapologetic about everything she did or said.

"So why Rabbit's Hole?" I asked.

Dor smiled wistfully. "When I was a child, my grandparents lived here. Whenever I visited, I considered this place Wonderland."

"Like *Alice in Wonderland*?"

"Exactly. There are surprises hidden in every room. I always felt like I'd gone down the rabbit's hole. So when it became mine, I renamed it. Well, unofficially at least."

"That's lovely."

* * *

This morning, the house was abuzz with activity. In the library where I worked, Dor was having tea with another older lady, elegant and refined. Normally, I would frown on tea being served in a library with so many precious books and documents, but this was her home, so who was I to restrict her entertaining there? Dor smiled broadly when she saw me come in.

"Juniper, dear, I'm so pleased you're here. I wanted to introduce you to a darling friend of mine, Lillian Van Der Brook."

I put out my hand, but Lillian stood and wrapped me in a surprisingly strong bear hug. All of Dor's friends tended to catch me off guard. During my last case, I had become close with her neighbor, Hal. The two of them had retired from some three-letter government agency, and while they would never say it outright, it was clear they had both been spies. Was Lillian a former spy as well?

"Juniper, it is wonderful to meet you. Dor has told me everything about you," she said. While Dor was casual in nice jeans with a simple blue blouse, Lillian wore a tunic-like blouse covered in a myriad of flowers and birds. Her hair—as silvery white as Dor's—was braided into intricate patterns and spun around her head like a crown.

"I hope they were good things, Ms. Van Der Brook," I said, feeling somewhat shy in front of these two grand dames.

Lillian's laughter was like bells tinkling, while Dor roared like a donkey braying.

"Of course, my dear. But please call me, Lillian," she said.

"As you wish," I said.

"Join us, Juniper," Dor said, patting the available seat beside her on the settee. "Have some tea. A very lovely and rich Irish Breakfast that Lillian brought back from Dublin."

"Thank you," I said, happily filling up an antique teacup. The china was so thin, and yet it had survived generations.

"I heard you had quite the weekend," Dor said.

"Oh no." My eyes closed. I should have expected her to hear about the incidents, but foolishly, I hadn't considered it until now.

"Are you okay?" Lillian asked with concern.

"Yes, it's just been trying."

"I can only imagine."

"Dor, you know everyone, it seems. Did you know Marcus? Or Esme?"

Dor nodded. "Oh yes, although not well. They were all in the Rose Mallow Artist's Guild, right?"

"Yes, that's right. Seems to be the connecting thread."

"I never had much artistic talent myself, but I always liked going to their shows and supporting local artists. Wasn't your grandmother a member?"

"She was a past president," I replied.

Dor smiled. "Of course she was. That was Zinnia. Always such a good civic servant. I miss her."

"I miss her too."

"Your grandmother was Zinnia? Zinnia Blume?" Lillian asked.

I nodded.

"Oh, she was a wonderful talent. I have a few pieces by her."

"So do I for that matter." Dor jumped up. We followed her into the hallway. "Ah ha. Look at this beautiful garden scene. Probably of your Wildflower Inn." She pointed to a gorgeous watercolor framed and hanging.

"That is quite lovely," Lillian added.

"Thank you for sharing this with me." I couldn't help my eyes smarting. Knowing that my grandmother's artwork was treasured by so many touched me.

"You know, I think I've got something by Marcus, too…" Dor continued down the hallway. We made a few turns—left and right—before she abruptly stopped. "Here we go!"

I had expected something made out of wood or at least sculptural. This was completely different. "He did calligraphy?"

"A true Renaissance man. You know he was also a painter. That's one of his over there." She turned and pointed to a surprisingly large oil painting. It had an old masters feel to it.

"He could do everything," Lillian murmured. I agreed. I hadn't realized how gifted he was in so many media.

"That painting reminds me of Rembrandt. Yet this calligraphic piece looks like something East Asian," I said.

"Chinese?" Lillian asked.

"Japanese," Dor replied. "Although using kanji, Chinese letters, so it has that feel. It says, 'What is your original face, the face you had before you were born?'"

"That's fascinating," I said. "But the guild members said he was a woodworker. It was in his bio at the gallery as well as in the brochure they gave out during the vigil."

Dor nodded. She walked back towards the library, while we followed. "I think he switched after Betsy disappeared. At least around then."

"Oh, Betsy," Lillian said.

Dor paused in her steps and turned back to her friend. "I'm sorry. I forgot how close you two were."

Lillian nodded. "My house is full of works she found for me. Her eye has always been excellent."

"She was also in the arts?" I asked.

"No, antiques dealer. We became dear friends over a shared love for antiques."

"We probably would have spent more time together if my house wasn't already overflowing with historical pieces. My family have been collectors for generations," Dor said, as we found our way back into the library. This was true. The first time I met Leo over the summer, he showed me the collections areas at the Calverton family offices, which were chock full of material culture brought back from every corner of the world by various generations of grandparents. Their love of history had inspired him to become an archaeologist and support digs in Italy and England.

"Do you know what happened with Betsy?" I asked Lillian as we retook our seats.

"How much I wish I did. She vanished. Eventually, Marcus claimed she had died, but there was never a funeral."

"No funeral?" I repeated.

Lillian shook her head. "I wished I could have said goodbye."

"That is unusual," Dor agreed. She turned to me. "I turned to my own old network to see if I could find out what happened to Betsy. But I guess I'd been out of the service for too long. I didn't have access to what I used to. And from my limited attempts, I found nothing. It was as if she simply stopped existing."

"Sort of like Esme now," I said.

"What do you mean, Juniper?" Dor asked.

I explained all the various theories about where she might have gone. But no one really seemed to have a full explanation.

"But something happened. She stopped paying rent on the storage unit. And apparently on her electricity as well," I said, before explaining what I had seen last night.

"You went to her house?" Lillian asked, sounding surprised.

I probably should have been more careful with what I said. Although Dor was a former spy, she was also my boss and entertaining a friend. I didn't want to appear like I was messed up in everything. I kept my mouth shut about Nuri. At least for now.

"Juniper is quite the sleuth." Dor sounded proud. "She's solved multiple cases since joining us here in Rose Mallow."

"I can't wait to hear all about them," Lillian replied.

"She reminds me of myself when I was her age," Dor said.

"That's a high honor," I replied, feeling genuinely touched.

"So, what did you find out?" Lillian moved up on her seat. I explained about the flashlights and how Esme's niece Susannah had come up out of the house with her boyfriend—and possibly fiancé—Noah Danvers.

"Have you told the police about this?" Dor asked.

"Not yet."

"Why not?"

"Because I only have little bits and pieces. Nothing concrete."

Dor laughed. "Oh, Juniper. That's how investigations go. Whether you're with the police, an agency, or doing it on your own. Things don't get handed to you on a silver platter."

"Well, yeah…"

"Look, go to the police. You can come back to work if there's time. And if not, don't fret. My books aren't going anywhere in a day," she said.

"Thank you." I stood up. She was right, and I knew I needed to listen to her. Before leaving, I asked, "Can you reach out to your networks and see if you hear anything about Esme?"

Dor nodded. "I haven't had much success with Betsy's disappearance, but it can't hurt to ask around. Especially if we have two women missing."

"And Marcus dead," Lillian added with a sad sigh. "I've heard he was murdered."

"As have I," said Dor.

"Something connects those three people together," I said. "I don't know what. Or who."

"See, Lillian, this is why I wanted you to meet Juniper. If she hadn't become a librarian, I think she would have made an excellent agent," Dor said.

"You still could switch careers," Lillian suggested. "Many mid-career switchers. Or so I hear." She winked at Dor. It increased my curiosity if she had also been at an agency. We were close enough to Washington, D.C. that it wasn't uncommon to have people from the CIA, FBI, and NSA retire around here.

"I love my books," I said.

"That's fair. I love them too," Lillian replied. "Good luck, Juniper. It was a pleasure meeting you."

# Chapter Twenty

I headed to the Purple Oyster Coffee Shop to meet with Detective Lakshmi Gupta. Dor had been right. The detective was eager to hear whatever "bits and pieces" I had uncovered. I asked her to join me at the cafe because I didn't want to risk bringing the detective back to the Wildflower Inn. I still wasn't sure how to handle the forged letters and Nuri's part in this escapade.

Speaking of which, I walked past Boardwalk Books. It was still closed with the lights off and the door locked. The same sign as I saw yesterday was taped to the door, proclaiming a "family emergency." I wondered how deep Nuri's role went in all this. And in what ways was she involved? As much as she had told me, there was obviously more to the story. I still felt conflicted on how much sympathy I had for her versus concern over her bad choices. I wanted the sympathy to win.

The detective was already waiting for me inside the Purple Oyster. She raised a hand to acknowledge me as I walked inside.

However, before I could join her, Luna Moray caught my arm.

"I've been trying to contact you," she said.

"I know, but it hasn't been a good time."

"You promised you'd work with me."

"And I will, but I'm about to talk with Detective Gupta."

Luna followed my gaze to where the detective watched us both with obvious interest. Luna stiffened immediately. "Look, get in touch with me. Anytime. I'm a night owl, so it can be as late as you want. But I have something important to tell you. Very important."

"Have you told the detective?" I asked.

"You first. Trust me, it's worth your while." She released my arm and jetted off, leaving me curious. I didn't want to be interviewed, but I might have to put up with it to find out what Luna was holding back. Was it information that would put more pieces together?

"Juniper? You okay?"

The detective was right in front of me.

"Sorry, I guess I spaced out for a moment."

"What did Luna want?" she asked.

"She asked me to contact her later. She didn't say about what, though. Probably to do an interview." That wasn't untrue. Luna had made it clear she wanted me for a newspaper article and maybe a radio show interview.

The detective shook her head. "Luna published this morning that Marcus's death was a murder. I wish she would have waited."

"I don't think Luna likes to work on the police's schedule," I said.

"Agreed. Come on, I have a table for us." She walked back while I followed. "Oh, but feel free to order first."

"Sure. Maybe just a tea." And probably a scone. Or two.

Within a few minutes, I sat with Detective Gupta with my hot tea and an orange scone. She had made the far healthier selection of a harvest salad. It did look really appetizing. I'd see if I had room left after the scone.

I caught her up on my late-night visit, where I spotted Susannah Vienna and Noah Danvers. I paused, wondering if Susannah's last name was Vienna. She was a niece, so it could have been different. But the detective confirmed that I was correct.

"Okay, so you went by Esme's house," the detective said, repeating back part of my story to her. "And you went there, why exactly?"

"I'm not really sure. I felt weird about everything. I told you how everyone thinks Esme is somewhere different. So many rumors."

"And I'm going to look into all of them."

"Thank you. It's just her missing…"

"You think she's actually missing?"

"I don't know, but maybe. Especially after Betsy—Marcus's wife—went missing. It was some time ago, but still…"

"And you think the two disappearances—assuming they are both disappearances—are related somehow?" she asked.

"Well, I probably wouldn't except for Marcus's body being in Esme's unit," I answered. "Maybe Esme killed Marcus and ran away? Maybe she killed Betsy, too?"

The detective nodded. "Trust those instincts, Juniper. You may be onto something here."

"I just don't know how it all fits together."

"We'll find out. But there's something else, isn't there?"

I nearly spit out my tea. Did she know about Nuri? Or maybe it was about the blackmail. I hadn't yet caught her up on that.

"Oh?" I asked.

"How this all fits in with your break-in?"

"Oh, right." I knew exactly how it fit in, but all I could hear in my mind was Nuri pleading with me not to go to the police, promising she would as soon as she was safe. Would I put her in further danger if I said something now?

"It's a lot to sort out."

"Yes, it is," I said. Then I realized that with everything that had transpired, I had left something else important out. "There's something more about Esme you should know."

"What is that?"

I gave her a quick run-down of what my sister had said about Esme offering generous loans that turned into blackmail. Including how she wanted the deed for the Wildflower Inn. "All those items in the unit might have been collateral for blackmail."

The detective whistled at that. "You think that's why Esme may have killed Marcus and Betsy?"

"I don't know for sure, of course. And I don't know who they all belong to. But I've been thinking. When Noah and Susannah came out of her house, they mentioned looking for a ledger. Or was it a logbook? Either way, what if that book was how Esme recorded everything in the unit? Who owed money to her, what they had given, and who knows what else?"

"It would make sense she tracked that somewhere. But we don't know if that's what they were referencing," Detective Gupta replied.

"At this point, I don't think it would surprise me to learn there were even more loop de loops to this mystery."

"Loop de loops?"

"Oh, sorry. Like on a rollercoaster ride." I made a circle with my fingers.

She nodded. Then she paused before saying, "You know, you've mentioned a lot of people to me. Esme and Betsy, both possibly missing. Or maybe Esme having killed Betsy and Marcus. Noah and Susannah searching for something in Esme's house. How Esme tried to blackmail your own sister. But I can't help noticing one name missing from this otherwise exhaustive list." Her face was cold.

"What do you mean?"

"Your friend Nuri. Wasn't she with you on Saturday morning at the auction?"

"Yes, she was."

"And her store has been closed up since then." She nodded in the direction of the store.

"Has it been?" I asked, although I knew it had.

"How is she involved with all this? Is she involved with all this?"

"You'll have to ask her," I replied.

"Well, I would, but you see, I have been having trouble reaching her," the detective said. "She hasn't been answering my calls. And she hasn't been at her apartment. So with her store being closed, I must admit I'm getting a bit concerned."

"That does sound off."

She nodded. "If you happen to hear from her, will you tell her to get in touch with me?"

"Of course."

# Chapter Twenty-One

Back at the Wildflower Inn, my sister was unloading groceries. I gave Azalea a hand, bringing bags into the kitchen from her minivan. She explained that Violet was with Rory. He had worked yesterday at the car dealership, so he had the day off. They were having a daddy-daughter day. But Violet hadn't wanted to go without Clover, so all three were together. She thought they'd gone to a new playground in the area. That sounded lovely. I was glad they were having a good time together.

"Wasn't expecting to see you, Juniper. Aren't you supposed to be at work?"

"Dor told me to take my time with the case. She wanted me to speak to the police," I said.

"Dor wants you to investigate? That surprises me."

"I don't think she wanted me to be foolish but to work with the authorities."

Azalea pulled several varieties of apples from the bag. "Well, she was a spy at a time when few women were spies, right?"

"I don't think she'll ever say officially." My bag had a couple of different types of honey inside, including, of course, wildflower. I was excited to see so many options. "But yes. She was some sort of agent."

"So maybe she sees you as following in her trailblazing path."

"That could be," I agreed. "So what's on the menu?"

"Well, I have a few apple and honey cake recipes I want to test out."

"I'm happy to taste test."

Azalea laughed. "No surprise there. But you have to help if you want to be my guinea pig."

I made a face. "Are you sure? I'm not good at these things."

"You can peel." She stuck a peeler into my right hand.

"Great." My voice dripped with sarcasm.

"So you were out late last night. And then right off to work this morning," Azalea said, as we worked prepping the apples.

"Finally, someone I can tell everything to," I said with what was undoubtedly an overly dramatic sigh.

"What do you mean by that?"

"I need to tell you about Nuri."

"Is she okay?"

"Not really." Long strips of apple spiraled from my peeler into a ceramic bowl that Azalea provided. "It's a long story."

"I have time."

I nodded. "Well, uh, I don't know where to start. You know that Nuri and I have been friends for years."

"Right, you were in school together."

"Until she abruptly left, not long before graduation."

"I didn't realize that." Azalea waltzed around the kitchen, making sure everything was put away properly, while also pulling out more supplies for cake baking.

"It turns out she had needed money for school. So she ended up creating forged historic documents." I winced, waiting for my sister's reaction.

"That is…" She stopped, obviously trying to find the right word. "Unusual. I'm not sure what I think about that. Obviously, it's bad, but I'd need to know more." That was extremely generous of Azalea. Far more so than I felt.

"One of the things she created were faked letters from Jane Austen."

"Really?" Her eyebrows lifted.

"That's what was in Esme's unit."

"Those were the letters you said she stole, though?" Azalea asked. "The ones we now have here somewhere?"

"In my room. Yes, those are the same letters," I replied.

"Okay. That makes sense."

"That makes sense?" I repeated. "How does any of that make sense?"

She stopped looking for ingredients and sat down at the kitchen table beside me. I put down the peeler, curious about what she would say. "I told you about how Esme treated Desiree and what she wanted from me. She must have taken those letters as collateral from Nuri."

"You think that Esme gave Nuri a big loan? But for what?"

My sister looked at me with the same high and mighty stare she used to give when we were teenagers, and she thought I was being dense. "You can't think of a big project Nuri has recently undertaken that involves a lot of money?"

"Oh." I was dense. "Broadway Books."

She nodded. "She took over the used bookstore and acquired the space next to it. She's doing major renovations. You just told me that she created fake documents because she needed money for school, so it doesn't sound like she's swimming in funds, now does it?"

"So Esme must have given her one of those blackmail loans. And took the letters in return. Do you think she knew they were fake?"

Azalea shrugged. "Probably not. Sounds like your friend duped her into getting the money."

"Only for Esme to turn the tables and require whatever terms on her so-called loan."

"Exactly." Azalea stood back up. But just as she was going to resume working on the cakes, she stopped and twirled back around to me. "Wait a second. Nuri knew those letters were in that unit for sale, didn't she? Is that why she was there?"

"I think so."

She picked up a spatula and waved it at me. "Is that why you spent so much money?"

My cheeks burned. "Yes. I didn't know it was for forged letters, though. I just knew that it was important to Nuri. That was enough for me."

"Oh, Juniper." She shook her head but was smiling. "You'll do whatever you can to help a friend in need, won't you?"

"When I can," I said sheepishly.

"But how did Nuri know the unit was abandoned and going up for sale?"

"I honestly don't know."

"And did she know that Marcus Howard's body was in there?" Now, Azalea appeared alarmed.

"I don't know, but I don't think so. She seemed just as shocked as the rest of us." I didn't want to add my concerns that my friend could have been the reason he was there. Why would she have hurt him? That seemed ludicrous. It was more likely that Esme had.

"True. If she was faking it, that was an impressive performance."

"She's really scared right now. She's not acting like herself. She's the one who broke into the Wildflower Inn the other night. Not to steal anything but to hide the letters," I explained.

"What? Why wouldn't she simply give them to you?"

"She thinks someone is out to get her. I don't think she trusts anyone right now. I'm guessing she hoped we wouldn't have noticed the letters hidden here. I must have caught her right after she put them into Nana Z's copy of *Pride and Prejudice* in the library. I found them and have taken them up to my room," I explained.

Azalea sat back down. She tapped the spatula on the table. "She sounds like she's having some sort of mental breakdown."

"I saw her last night, and she was terrified. She apparently set up some sort of safe house to go to."

"You said you talked with the police. What did Detective Gupta say about all this?"

I gaped like a fish out of water.

Azalea's head dropped. "You didn't tell her, did you?"

"I thought I was only going to make it worse for Nuri."

"Juniper. You have to tell her. Everything."

"Nuri's scared enough that it's made me nervous. She begged me not to say anything to the police. She promised she would when she's safe," I said.

"She doesn't sound like she's in a good place. She needs help. More than you or I can give her."

"That's true. There's just so many strange things happening. Multiple women missing. It's left me feeling rattled," I said truthfully.

"Multiple women missing?"

I told her about Betsy, Marcus's missing wife, and how we still didn't know where Esme had gone. "Did you know Betsy?"

"A bit. I shopped at her antique store before it closed."

"But you didn't know Marcus?" I asked.

Azalea shook her head. "Never saw him there when I was shopping, so I didn't know what he looked like."

"Why did her shop close?"

"She told me that the space was getting too expensive. So she moved online and into more personal shopping. Concierge, I think she called it. Still focusing on antiques. She could get some amazing things. Such a good eye," Azalea said with admiration.

I rubbed the apple gunk off on a nearby cloth. Curious, I looked up Betsy on my phone. Azalea sighed, wondering aloud how I could find much on there. I shrugged. I didn't need to do much digging.

"Elizabeth 'Betsy' Howard," I read in one of the articles about her antique store. There was a photo. She was a beautiful brunette. Maybe in her fifties or sixties. In the picture, she sported a similar retro vibe to our grandmother's mid-century clothes I loved to wear. "She's really lovely looking."

"Quite the beauty," Azalea agreed.

"This article is all about her hot streak for amazing discoveries," I said. "Oh my goodness..."

"What?" Azalea rushed over to me and peered over my shoulder.

"You're not going to believe this."

"Believe what?"

"One of the items mentioned in the article. It's about how Betsy discovered a rare letter from Jane Austen."

"No," Azalea said. "When is the article from?"

I scrolled back up to find the date. "It's back when Nuri and I were still in graduate school. So several years ago." I paused. "It has to be a coincidence. Right? It couldn't possibly be one of Nuri's, could it?"

Azalea shrugged, but her face suggested that my friend might be guilty of selling a fake letter to Betsy Howard. The same woman who was now missing and whose husband was dead in a storage unit, where the fake letter had ended back up. I knew that coincidences sometimes happened, but this seemed extraordinary to be one.

I looked for more articles about Betsy, finding several from when she disappeared. There were pictures of her with Marcus. She had a pleasant smile but sad eyes. "Marcus said she went on a work trip to England. Searching for more unexpected discoveries."

"What happened?" Azalea asked.

"She never came back. Except, wait a second…" I read more. "Oh, the police say she never went there to begin with. She had booked flights and hotels, but she never checked into any of them. No one ever saw her again."

Azalea gulped. "A missing woman. Maybe two missing women, with Esme. And a dead man. Your friend is somehow involved."

I nodded. "I'm scared too. Really scared. For Nuri."

"Are you sure you shouldn't be scared of Nuri?" Azalea asked.

I didn't have an answer to that.

# Chapter Twenty-Two

My calls to Nuri's cell phone went unanswered. After dinner, I headed back up to Boardwalk Books, but not surprisingly, it was closed. I called again, but still no answer.

Should I drive back to her place? Even if I did, it seemed doubtful she'd be there, given her discussion of a safe house. I hoped she was safe.

As I wandered back down the boardwalk, I spotted the lights on in Desiree Douglass's electronics and repair shop, The Reboot. Well, half the lights on. For being a place focused on fixing things, I wasn't sure if the overheads were broken, or if Desiree just didn't bother with them.

While the place resembled someone's unorganized basement, overflowing with techy things, Desiree ran it like an apothecary, somehow knowing which magical electronic treasure each drawer and jar held, mixing and matching to repair almost everything. As with the last time I was here, I couldn't help wondering why she also had so many clipboards.

Not much younger than me, she looked like an adult version of her teenage sister Keisha, except while Keisha wore locs with different colors, Desiree sported beautiful beaded braids.

"Juniper, this is a pleasant surprise," said Desiree when I entered. She was wiping down the countertop. "Keisha is always talking about you and Azalea. I hope she's working out well with you both at the Wildflower Inn."

"She's the best. We only wish she was older and could do more hours," I replied.

Desiree smiled. "Yeah, her high school schedule keeps her busy."

"Agreed. I think she was studying for some big exam this weekend?" I didn't remember the exact reason that Keisha hadn't been on the schedule, but with everything happening, I was relieved that she had stayed out of this escalating melee. If nothing else, I wouldn't want all the stress impacting her schoolwork.

"Yes, the SATs. Getting ready for college applications soon." Desiree shook her head, but the smile on her face shone bright. She was obviously proud of her little sister.

"She's a gifted young woman. I can only imagine her having a bright future."

"Thank you. I hope she will too. Do more than I have done."

"Better than you? You have a successful store and a great reputation. A little birdy told me that the Calvertons have wanted to hire you for your technological skills. Anytime you want."

Desiree waved a hand, smoothing away my offer. "That's generous of them, but I'd rather have a simple life. A simple store. Being available for my parents. Let Keisha take on the world. I'm content with this."

"I understand. You have something special here," I replied.

"Rose Mallow is a special place."

I paused, unsure of how to say the next thing, but with no other segue popping into my head, I barreled on ahead. "Azalea told me how you helped her."

"What do you mean?"

"You advised her not to take money from Esme."

"Ah." Desiree came out from behind the counter. We found mix-matched seats beside an architect's table towards the back of the shop. "I heard about what happened this weekend. I'm so sorry."

"Thank you."

"And yeah, I heard you found my *Star Wars* figurines." Her voice was surprisingly timid.

"Once I get them back, they'll return to you."

She sighed deeply. Her shoulders slunk back like a big weight had been lifted. "I can't wait. I've missed them."

"Did you want to talk about what happened with Esme?"

Desiree looked away. "Not really. But given that you're in the middle of everything, you deserve more information."

"I appreciate that."

"Anything that Azalea told you is true. Esme is a shark. I thought she was being generous, keeping everything between friends. But then she changed everything. She demanded more money. So much more." Desiree shook her head. Her expression was steely.

"Why didn't you tell the police?"

Desiree considered her words. "She knew my secret. I don't know how she found out, but she made it clear that she wasn't afraid to reveal it."

"I'm so sorry. Had she revealed other people's secrets?"

"I don't really want to answer that. It's bad enough that I don't want to gossip further. I'm sorry, Juniper."

I put a hand on her arm. "No, no, I'm sorry for pushing you. In Judaism, we have this concept of 'lashon hara'—not sharing speech that damages others."

"I like that."

"But we also value life above all else. And with Marcus dead…Well, I'm worried. Esme is missing. Betty went missing. And I have another friend who is scared."

Desiree stood up. She paced her store. She looked into boxes stacked atop one another, before pulling out bits of wire. She moved them into another box. I had no idea what she was doing, but she seemed to be on a mission.

Then she turned back to me. "You should talk to Olivia."

"The wedding photographer?"

Desiree nodded.

"Why?"

"Look, that's all I'm comfortable saying. You found some of her works in that unit, didn't you?"

I nodded.

"And I spotted you talking together at the vigil."

"Okay. I didn't see you. I'm sorry."

"Don't worry about it. That was crowded. But it'd make sense to talk to her more," Desiree said.

"Oh, of course. Esme had blackmailed Olivia."

"I didn't say anything. And I'm not suggesting anything. Except that you two connect." Desiree's expression was stern.

"I understand. Thank you, Desiree."

She nodded and headed back to the counter.

"Wait, I have another question."

She paused on the balls of her feet and turned to me. The look of fear was clear across her face. She must have been worried I was going to ask her to reveal her secret.

"Do you know why the boxes were coded the way they were?" I asked.

Her body relaxed. "Unfortunately, no."

"It must all be part of her system. How she tracked everyone."

"Were there a lot of boxes in her unit?"

I nodded.

"How many people did she blackmail?" Desiree asked.

"Looked like half the town," I replied.

"Seriously. It sounds like it."

"Did you know Marcus well?" I asked.

"The man found dead in the unit? No, not really. I saw him on the boardwalk, since the gallery is nearby, but I can't say the artsy crowd was the one I ran with frequently."

"Or Betsy?"

"His wife, who disappeared. That was such a strange story. Sorry, no. I wish I could tell you more," Desiree replied.

"Thank you, Desiree."

"Good luck, Juniper. I hope you can get it resolved. And thank you for bringing home my *Star Wars* figurines. It may sound silly, but they mean a lot to me. My dad gave them to me. He had gotten them when he saw the movies in theaters. We watched them so many times together. It's just not how much they're worth, but they mean family to me. You know?" she said.

"I understand completely," I said.

* * *

After finishing up with Desiree, I tried Nuri again. Not surprisingly, the call went to voicemail, and her shop remained dark. Not sure why I thought that might have changed. I guess I'm an eternal optimist.

# Chapter Twenty-Three

I had probably been asleep for an hour when my phone pinged. Having always been a light sleeper, I jolted up, worried that it might be something from Nuri. Clover popped up from across my feet, looking sleepy and confused.

"It's okay, Clover. Go back to bed," I said. He didn't need to be told twice.

Instead, it was from Luna. I had completely forgotten that I was supposed to call her. Not that I had been crazy about being interviewed, but she deserved to hear back from me.

"Can you meet up?" Luna texted.

"Now? It's after midnight," I replied.

"I promise it'll be worth your time."

What did that mean? As always, my curiosity won over. Even though I was in my pajamas and sported some serious bedhead, I climbed out of my cozy, comfy bed. This better be good.

"Where?" I typed.

"*Chesapeake Chronicle* office. ASAP."

I grumbled, but I still pulled out my clothes and found a brush. Clover lifted his head a few times, but he didn't seem to care much about getting up. Lucky dog. The things I did for curiosity's sake.

After getting halfway decent, I responded, "On my way."

* * *

Located on the third and top floors of an otherwise unobtrusive office building, *The Chesapeake Chronicle* was half newspaper office and half cat sanctuary, since Luna—the only full-time employee at the newspaper these days—also worked with the Rose Mallow Feline Rescue Society. An untold number of cats wandered around the offices, taking up residence on desktops, beside stacks of paper, and, of course, in any open banker boxes. Cat toys littered the surfaces. Last time I was here, there were seven cats hanging out. I wondered if that number had gone up or down.

As with before, there were various paper structures around the grounds, as if someone's kid had been let loose to create art projects. But this time I knew they were for the cats. This was their home first, and a newspaper office second.

A familiar gray cat wandered up to me.

"Tabitha!" I cried, kneeling down to pet her. She happily brushed up beside me and purred as I stroked her back.

"Juniper, glad you could make it," said Luna, appearing from seemingly nowhere.

"You sure this isn't too late?"

She shrugged. "Newspapers run on strange schedules."

Honestly, I assumed that it was just her who did, but who was I to argue?

"Besides, the cats are nocturnal, so they'd be running around anyway. They love when I'm here overnight. Follow me." Luna zig-zagged around the towers of papers, dancing over various cats along the way. Tabitha followed us into Luna's office.

"I'm glad you're not allergic," Luna said as she moved an orange cat from a desk chair to sit down.

"Me too. Have you been able to find homes for some of the cats?"

"Many of them actually. But I have more than enough foster fails here. Including Tabitha there. How could I resist this sweetie?" She smiled as I sat in the faux leather chair and Tabitha popped into my lap. "Although she does seem to be a fan of yours as well."

"Not sure that Clover would be such a friend though," I said.

She slid her head side to side. "I feel that they might be buddies. But also that he has enough with his current best friend. A little girl?"

"Violet. My niece."

"Azalea's daughter. That's right." Luna touched her forehead. She claimed to be "a touch psychic." I wasn't sure how true that was, but she wasn't wrong about Clover and Violet being close.

"So, what did you want to tell me?" I asked.

"Nuh uh. You first."

"What?" Were we back in elementary school?

"You share first, and then I'll catch you up. I know you, Juniper. You're investigating."

"Not on purpose," I protested. "And I'm not sharing anything about that with anyone but the police." Maybe I should have crossed my fingers. I had shared plenty already and not told the police enough. But Luna ran the newspaper and radio station. I needed to be judicious with what I told her.

She rolled her eyes. They were gray, like Tabitha's. "Fine. Then at least tell me about your bidding war on the storage unit."

"What do you want to know?"

"Why spend so much money? I heard that you'd never done anything like that before."

"I'm sorry, but I can't tell you anything."

"Why not, Juniper?"

"Well, because…I don't know."

Luna threw her head back. She was clearly frustrated with me. "Fine, fine. It's for the best you didn't say anything anyway." She spoke as if she begrudgingly agreed with herself.

"What do you mean, Luna?"

"You're a good friend, Juniper. Thank you for holding my secrets."

I turned to the doorway. To my shock, Nuri stood there. I jumped up, knocking poor Tabitha to the ground.

"Are you okay?" I asked Nuri.

She nodded. "Yes, thanks to Luna. She's been hiding me."

"Hiding you? Here?"

"Where better than here?" Luna asked. "No one would ever expect someone to be in a newspaper office. The media is the last place anyone would look." She appeared smug at the thought.

"Luna has been helping me out. She promised to keep my secrets," Nuri said.

"How can you trust her? She's a reporter?" I asked.

Luna looked hurt by my accusation, but if Nuri wouldn't trust me, then I didn't know why she would believe in someone she only recently met.

"Well, there's a good reason I can trust her," Nuri said. She looked over at Luna. She shrugged and nodded. "Remember those comic books in the storage unit?"

"The something *Spider-Man?*"

"*The Amazing Fantasy #15.* First appearance of Spider-Man," Luna replied.

"Yeah, that one. Wait, is that yours?" I asked.

"It was my father's. I don't know how it ended up in there. I thought it disappeared years ago," she replied.

"I see. So you share the storage unit in common," I said.

Nuri and Luna's heads bobbed in unison.

"And in return?" I looked between the two women. "You want something, Luna. I know you do."

Luna cracked her neck. "And in return, Nuri will give us an exclusive. Once everything is settled down."

"Of course," I said, unsurprised.

"No, I'm happy to do so," Nuri said. "She's been amazing to me. She's keeping me safe."

"What is going on, Nuri? Who is trying to hurt you?"

Nuri sighed. She came further into the office and leaned against the desk. "Someone is trying to hurt me. To make me disappear. Just like Esme and Betsy."

"What can you tell me?" I asked.

"Like I said, when I was in school with you, I didn't have enough money, so I started crafting forged letters and documents. I thought it was a victimless crime." She shook her head. "What I didn't tell you was that Marcus had been the one to teach me everything."

"Marcus?" I thought back. "That's right. He taught at our school. But in arts, not library science."

She nodded. "I took a few art classes with him. I especially loved the classes on historic methods and materials. Learning how our ancestors made artwork. Everything from Chinese calligraphy ink to egg tempera to even mosaics. He could do anything." She spoke with a reverence that caught me off guard.

"I've seen that he mastered several different media," I said.

Nuri nodded. "He recognized my talents. Nurtured them in a way no one else had. And not just him, but Betsy too. They became like surrogate parents to me. We talked for hours about authors and artists."

"Nuri's parents didn't want her to become an artist," Luna added.

"They accepted me going to library school. Although they didn't have much money to give me for it," Nuri explained.

"I remember you saying," I replied. "Tell me more."

"Marcus and Betsy really encouraged my art. Then, one day, Marcus told me he was struggling. He had arthritis and couldn't create the way he used to." She walked from the desk and found a folding chair to sit on. Perhaps annoyed at how I'd dropped her, Tabitha waltzed over and jumped onto Nuri's lap.

"I'm sorry to hear that."

"The two of them explained creating letters like an artistic challenge. One that incorporated art and history. In the beginning, I thought it was fun."

"Fun?" I repeated.

"Well, from a technical challenge, yes. It seemed like a way to combine my librarian and artistic skills. Plus, they reassured me that they'd been doing this for a long time. That no one was ever really hurt, and that this was just part of how the artistic system operated. Not only was I naive, but by this point, I'd do anything for them."

"Because they had done so much for you," I said quietly.

"Exactly. So we came up with plans. I'd create something new that looked really old, and Betsy would magically find my creations. My documents would also provide the proper provenance while she found the creations new homes," Nuri said.

"Oh, because she's an antiques dealer," I said, recalling.

"Yes, that's right."

"But then…she disappeared."

Nuri sighed. "Yes, except there was something that happened before she disappeared." She turned to Luna. "Something not in any of the media reports."

"What?" we both asked.

"We had been discovered," Nuri said quietly.

"Discovered?"

Nuri nodded. "Someone had figured out our little ring. They knew Betsy was selling fake documents to up the value of her antiques."

"Who?" I asked.

"How?" asked Luna.

"Marcus told us. He'd gotten some notes or something. All anonymous. He reassured me that the notes only mentioned Betsy and him. The person must not have known about me," Nuri told us. "But they were worried for me. They said they had gotten me into this mess and figured it was only time before the person discovered my role."

"What did you do?" Luna asked.

"At first, we decided we'd hang low. See what happened. I dropped out of school. Betsy decided to go out of the country to hide. Just until things chilled over, she said. She promised I'd go back to school then, too. We'd start back up. They both promised me everything would be okay."

"But then Betsy never returned," I said.

Nuri nodded with a deep sadness.

"Did you figure out who discovered your ring?" I asked.

"Not immediately," she said. "Things quieted down after Betsy disappeared. It was like everything just went silent. I had foolishly wondered if the situation was over. I didn't think I was safe exactly, but I thought I could at least give another try at life."

"Is that when you came to Rose Mallow?" Luna asked.

Nuri nodded. "Marcus actually helped me get the job at Boardwalk Books. He felt bad about everything that happened, so he figured that this could help me get restarted."

Given that the previous owner had also been a criminal, I shouldn't have been surprised that he and Marcus had been buddies.

"Wow. And now you run the place," Luna added.

"After I took it over, this woman came in."

I held my breath. I suspected I knew where this was going.

"Was it Esme Vienna?" I asked.

"The very same. Somehow, she knew I was struggling. She offered me a loan. All the money I could ever want. At an amazing rate. And all off the books. No one needed to know about it." Nuri looked close to tears. "I thought she was a gift."

"But things went sour?" I asked.

Nuri nodded. "She was so patronizing. At first, I thought she just assumed that a young adult taking over a bookstore and looking to expand would need financial help. But then she mentioned things. It became clear she knew things about me that were unsettling. Details that no one knew. And then…"

She closed her eyes before covering her face with her hands.

"Esme knew about the letters. She knew I had them. She required them as collateral for the loan. I had to give them to her. What if she told people what she knew?"

"You believe Esme was the one who uncovered your ring?" Luna asked.

Nuri lifted her head and shrugged. "Maybe. I don't know. But it made sense. She knew all these things about what I done with forging documents." Her whole body shivered. "And if she knew that, then maybe she knew more about what happened with Betsy. I had to find out more."

"What did you discover?" I asked.

"I tracked her…" Nuri replied with a sheepish tone.

"You spied on her?" I repeated.

"Really, Juniper? As if you haven't. I have reported on your cases," Luna replied. I had to concede the point. I wasn't any better.

"I learned about her storage unit. That's where she kept everything. Nothing in her house. I had to get in it. See if there was more information about Betsy there."

"That's why the sale was so important to you. That and your letters," I said. "But how did you find out it was happening?"

Nuri massaged the bridge of her nose. "I'm not proud of this, but I noticed that Esme's mail began piling up. She had gone. Just up and vanished."

"Like Betsy?"

"Maybe. People suggested different things. Someone thought she was visiting a sick relative in Canada," Nuri said. That wasn't one I had heard yet. But it added to the list of theories of where Esme had gone.

"So you figured she was out of town?" Luna asked.

"I spotted the notices in her mail. It wasn't just bills for the storage unit, but for her utilities. A notice from her bank. All sorts of bills asking for money right now. I didn't open them, but it was clear they were urgent. So I started hanging around the storage unit, checking when the sales were being held," she explained.

"You wanted to be there when Esme's unit went up for auction," I said.

She nodded. "Look, I know I did some awful things. And when I saw Marcus dead in that unit, I freaked. Absolutely panicked. His wife disappeared. Esme disappeared. And Marcus was obviously murdered. I've been beyond terrified that I'm next."

"Oh, Nuri." I walked over to her and put my hands on her shoulders. No wonder she had acted so irrationally. "So that's why you stole the letters and then put them in my house."

"Those letters have to be involved. Otherwise, why would Esme have wanted them? And she's missing, so I've assumed I'm the only one left. That's why I needed to get away from my apartment. Fortunately, Luna agreed to hide me. No one else knows I'm here. Just you and the cats."

And they weren't talking.

"We'll keep it that way," Luna reassured her.

"But why haven't you gone to the police?" I asked.

Nuri curled up into a small ball in her chair. "Because I'm a criminal."

"You're in danger."

"I won't be safer locked up."

I paced around the office. "I can't promise not to tell Detective Gupta. She needs to know about you. About everything you've told me."

"Juniper…" Nuri pleaded.

"Because what you told me suggests that not just Marcus, but Betsy and maybe even Esme have both been murdered too."

"I hate to admit it, but Juniper is right," Luna said. "We should go to the police."

"No, I trusted you both," Nuri nearly screamed.

"Wait, wait." Luna put up her hands. "I know what you're saying, Nuri. And I'm not giving up your trust. Juniper, Nuri has made it abundantly clear that she will run away if we tell the police. She has said that she'll disappear before someone can make her disappear."

"That's the fear talking," I argued.

"Well, yeah, I know," Nuri replied, "But I don't want to be the fourth one killed. And Luna is right. If I believe you've gone to the police, I'm going. Far, far away. And I'm not coming back."

I wiped my hands across my face. "That's an impossible request, Nuri."

"Maybe. But it's what I'm offering. Take it or leave it." She crossed her arms.

I didn't like it. Honestly, I should have told Detective Gupta everything already. But I hadn't, and if I did now, I would destroy Nuri's trust and send her running. No one could help her then. I'd need to find a creative way to keep her feeling safe and bring in as many reinforcements as I could manage. Or if not, figure out what had happened. Were Betsy and Esme also dead? Who was involved? And how could I save Nuri?

"Fine. I understand and agree." I put out a hand, and Nuri shook it. Then I turned to Luna. "Thank you."

"For what?"

"Giving Nuri somewhere safe to be. For not printing anything."

"Of course. I won't endanger someone. But as I've made clear, once this is all over—I expect an exclusive. From both of you." She pointed her index finger at each of us.

# Chapter Twenty-Four

Tuesday morning came far too soon. I called Dor to let her know I had a lead I wanted to follow. She told me to take my time and how her library could wait a day or two. With her permission, I headed out to Olivia Grover's photography studio.

Olivia knew something about Esme, maybe even if she didn't realize it. But given what Desiree said, and after seeing her photographs in the unit, I needed to know more. Was she also being blackmailed? It seemed likely, but for what? Could it involve that camera lens-shaped flask she whipped out? Who would want to hire a drunk wedding photographer? But I wasn't sure if that was the right lead. I needed to know more.

I expected a modern, black and white space, but to my surprise, her studio was housed in a rustic, refurbished barn, surrounded by late summer flowers. Two of the old wooden walls had been replaced with large, perfectly cleaned glass windows. Inside was a receptionist's desk with a young woman, distracted by her phone.

"Excuse me?"

The young woman's head popped up, obviously shocked that someone had come in. "Oh, uh, hi." Then she held up a finger. I figured she was telling me to wait for her phone, but instead, she let out the loudest sneeze. Followed by a second one. "Sorry about that. How may I help you?"

"Can I schedule a photoshoot?"

She pulled out a large desk calendar. "When?"

I should have thought about this more. Leo and I only started dating recently, so it would be uncomfortable to pose for engagement pictures, even undercover. Was there something else I could muster a reason for? Oh, wait…

"My family is coming in for Rosh Hashanah this week. So I'm wondering if there is any last-minute availability?" I asked.

Sneezy flipped through the desk calendar. It was a beautiful calendar with Chesapeake Bay images. Maybe it was made from Olivia's photography? That would make sense. Large framed photos hung on the other walls, including colorful ones of happy families, weddings, and maternity shoots. Interspersed were various black and white nature images, including several of the Bay.

I inched closer to the desk, hoping to get a peek at the calendar. Were there any other interesting appointments coming up? However, just as I had positioned myself, Sneezy put it in her lap, put her nose in her elbow, and sneezed again, very loudly. I stepped back.

"Are you okay?" I asked.

"Yes, it's just that I'm allergic to the new cat." Sneezy reached for some tissues. "I told Olivia about my allergy, but she basically told me to take some antihistamines."

"Oh no. I'm sorry. Is she normally so unaccommodating?"

Sneezy shook her head. "She can be great, but she's fickle. You know how artists are. Her moods change like the clouds." She paused to sneeze again. "She can be incredibly generous but also really vindictive."

Sneezy paused, as if realizing how unrestrained she had been. "I shouldn't be saying any of this. I'm sorry. It's not professional. But the allergy medication is making me a bit weezy in the brain."

As she spoke, she leaned across the desk calendar. I couldn't catch much, but there was one name that caught my eye: Susannah. Noah's girlfriend and Esme's niece. What was she doing here? Was this involving the photoshoot with Noah and the argument I overheard him have with Olivia?

"I'll put you down for an appointment, but…" She sneezed again. "Sorry. Anyway, you'll need to do a consultation first."

"A consultation? What is that?"

"A chance for you and Olivia to go over your vision for the shoot, discuss what you were, scenery, all that sort of thing."

"Oh, I see."

"Anyway, with Rosh Hashanah coming so soon, we need to get you in with Olivia like yesterday. Are you available this afternoon?" Sneezy asked.

"I'll make myself available."

She smiled and marked me down for an afternoon consultation.

* * *

Walking back to KG, I noticed a bench along the sidewalk. Splashed across the back was a large sign for Noah Danvers' realty office. His overly bright white teeth smiled as he promised that the "Danvers Team is your True Dream Team." It was only a block away. Not that I should have been surprised. Nothing in Rose Mallow was far from one another. I decided to make an unannounced visit there as well.

A matching sign greeted me outside a mid-century townhouse with large bay windows. Early fall flowers overflowed beyond the tiny stamp of the yard out front. A bell tingled as I went through the double set of front doors.

"Welcome to Danvers Realty, Home of the True Dream Team," said a young man from behind the desk. He sported tiny curls crowning his head and a retro-style suit in neutral browns. He popped up and thrust a hand out.

"Thank you." I accepted the hand. "I'm interested in homes in the area." As I said this, I wondered if this was true. I kept thinking about how I assumed I'd pay myself back the five grand on the auction when I sold my D.C. townhome. Was I seriously thinking about moving out of the Wildflower Inn, though?

"Perfect." His voice was chipper. "Do you have an idea what neighborhood you're looking at? And what kind of budget you're thinking about? Oh, and do you know if you want a condo, townhome, single-family? Square footage?"

If I held up a mirror, I'd probably see the color draining from my face. "I…I hadn't thought about that yet."

"No worries, no worries. The Danvers Team is your Dream Team. We'll make your dreams happen!" His teeth are as ice white as Noah's picture on

137

the bench sign.

"Well, I…" I still wasn't sure where to begin.

"Daniel, who do we have here?" Noah Danvers entered from a back office. He was all smiles until realizing it was me who entered.

"Juniper. Juniper Blume."

"Noah Danvers."

"What brings you here?"

The young man piped in. "She's considering buying a place in the area."

"Oh, is that so? Shall we meet in my office?" He stretched out a hand, and I followed his lead. The young man picked up a notepad and followed suit until Noah turned and said, "Privately."

Dejected, the man dropped back into his seat. "I started talking with her first, Mr. Danvers."

"Next time. Trust me." He gave a cheesy fake smile. I didn't think either of us appeared convinced, but there was nothing the young man could do.

I followed Noah into his personal office. Unlike the overflowing one at *The Chesapeake Chronicle*, his office was pristine, as if out of an architectural magazine. Most walls were a boring gray, but the one behind his desk was a dark hunter green with light burled wood shelves, lined with maritime-themed antiques.

Outside his window was a tree with three or four bird feeders. Even with the bounty of early fall, the feeders welcomed a variety of birds darting back and forth.

When Noah closed the door, I spoke up, "I have so many questions."

At the same time, he said, "What are you doing here?"

Realizing we were speaking at the same time, I held up my hand. We took a beat. He motioned for me to take a seat in one of the matching warm brown leather seats. It wasn't particularly comfortable.

"You go first," I said.

"Why did you bid so much at the auction?"

"Why did you?"

"Oh, come on. We both know, don't we?" he asked.

"Did you know who the unit belonged to?" I knew full well he did.

Noah pursed his lips.

"Or what was inside?" That I wasn't as sure about.

"Did you, Juniper?"

I shook my head. "We're going in circles here."

Daniel sat down behind the desk and crossed his arms on top of it. "Neither of us are willing to share anything, are we?"

"No, I guess not," I agreed.

"Then perhaps we make a deal?"

"What kind of deal, Noah?"

"You sell me the unit…" He paused. Maybe for dramatic impact? "You told my assistant that you want a home in Rose Mallow? I'll make that happen."

"In return for the storage unit?" Was he suggesting a trade? Or was this a bribe? And given everything else, was it even worse? Yet, the idea of a trade was tempting. Should I consider what he was saying as being truthful?

"If you just give me ownership of the unit, no questions asked, we'll work it out."

"But the police have it cordoned off," I said. "I couldn't give it to you, even if I wanted to."

Noah nodded. "I know. But when they're done. I can wait till then."

That surprised me. He wasn't in a rush to get in there? Didn't I just see him and Susannah breaking into Esme's house? That certainly suggested a rush.

"Why is the unit so important to you?" I asked. Then I decided to push things. "Do you or did you know Esme or Marcus? I saw you know Olivia Grover."

"Well, of course, I know all of them. I'm a realtor. It's my business to know everyone. Plus, I had the pleasure of helping all of them."

"Help them? How?" I asked.

"Well, Olivia wanted to expand her photography business, so I helped her get her place. Marcus wanted to downsize in his retirement, so I helped sell his old house. I'm really sorry he wasn't able to enjoy that," he said, taking a pause. "And Esme, well, she wanted something bigger, grander."

Was it just me, or did his voice develop an edge to it?

"She wanted something bigger?"

He nodded. "Her place didn't have enough room for a real artist's studio. Her current place is a little cottage. Not much room to do anything."

It sounded like he was unaware that I'd seen her house. "Do you know where she is?"

"On a cruise through the Panama Canal."

"That's nice." That was a new one. I hadn't heard that explanation before. Added it to the list. "Sounds like her cleaning business must be doing well. Guess she's moving up in the world." I kept my voice cheery.

Noah nodded.

"But if that's the case, why did she stop paying for her unit? How did it go up for auction?" I asked.

He simply shrugged. "I'm just a realtor, not a personal finance consultant." He threw me another one of those fake uber-bright teethy smiles. I managed to meet his fake smile with one of my own. "Now, Juniper, did you actually want to buy a house?"

"I have a lot to think about." I stood up, prepping to leave.

"Look, if you're serious, I'll be happy to show you some places." He puts a business card out. I took it with my continued fake smile. Even if I did decide to move out, I wasn't going to use him. But he didn't know that.

As I walked back out of the office, I felt a strange shiver. Looking over my shoulder, Noah watched me from the large bay window.

# Chapter Twenty-Five

Trying to figure out my next move, I grabbed some lunch. Leo agreed to meet me, although he said he couldn't stay long.

We shared sandwiches from the Purple Oyster while sitting on benches overlooking the Chesapeake Bay. Being early October, the weather was some of the best Maryland offered. Not too hot or humid, and not yet cold and dreary either. When Leo caught me glancing over at him, he winked at me. My heart fluttered. I wanted to pocket this moment forever.

"How are the archaeology projects going?" I asked.

His face lit up. "Pretty amazing. I've got several in the works right now across Italy and England. I'm looking forward to returning to the field in a few weeks."

"That's great."

"Want to join me? I'm sure I can convince Grandma to let you loose for a little bit."

"Yes, but I can't."

"Why not?" he asked.

"Well, besides work, I've got various family things. You're still on for Rosh Hashanah dinner, yes?" I asked.

He nodded. "Excited to meet your parents."

"Will I meet yours at some point?" I practically choked out the question. While Dor was fantastic, I was freaked out at even the thought of meeting Leo's parents. They ran the multi-national eponymous company. What if they didn't think I was good enough for him? What if I hated them? My body tensed with anxiety.

"At some point. But they're in…wait, what day is it?" He checked his watch. "I think they're in Switzerland right now. Davos." He rolled his eyes.

"Impressive." The only thing I knew about the town was that it hosted the World Economic Forum. It seemed like a good guess that's why they were there. Then I recalled his sister getting a call from Zurich. His family seemed to have a lot of connections with the Swiss. That reminded me of how Annie had invited me to participate in the grants committee.

"I'm thinking about going to the grants committee meeting tonight," I said.

"Still only thinking about it? I figured you'd jump all over the idea."

"I want to help Rose Mallow, but I think you can understand my reticence after dealing with the Foundation board." I shivered, remembering my meetings with them during my short-lived tenure for the family's library and museum project.

"This won't be anything like that," he promised.

"Who is on the committee?"

"Townspeople."

"No one from the company?"

"Not no one. Annie, of course. But most of the committee are residents. Like you. I was clear that this would be local-driven. It's also much smaller than the Foundation board," Leo said.

"Okay, then yes, I'll check it out. Thank you."

"But you never answered my first question. Come with me to one of the digs," he said.

I wanted to go. Especially with Leo. But I also wasn't ready to jet set quite yet. I had done a lot of globe-trotting before graduate school, so I knew how exciting it could be, as well as how disruptive. I had finally started to get a rhythm going. How could I explain to him that I was just getting settled here? I needed a little more time.

"Can I go in the spring?" I asked.

"Whenever you want. Simply say the word."

"You're like a wizard. Or a genie."

He laughed. "Happy to grant you three wishes."

"How about a kiss?"

He leaned in, and we shared a sweet kiss. It felt magical.

"Two more wishes," he said.

"Two more kisses?"

"Your wish is my command." Afterwards, Leo asked, "So tell me what to expect from your parents."

"Oh, uh, I'm not sure. What have I told you so far? That they're professors at Johns Hopkins—"

"And they play in a klezmer band? Am I saying that word correctly?" he asked.

I nodded. "I'll send you a playlist of their songs, so you can familiarize yourself. Klezmer is incredible. My dad plays clarinet, and my mom sings. Although sometimes she'll play other instruments, including the tsimbaloms."

"The what now?"

"A hammer dulcimer. It's really beautiful. She used to play lullabies on it when Azalea and I were little kids. She'd sing these lovely Yiddish songs. I never knew what they meant, but it didn't matter. They were full of heart. I always slept amazingly after she sang to us." Our family wasn't particularly religious, but our cultural traditions had remained important. My Nana Z had taught us that, and my parents reinforced how critical our heritage was. Whether it was through food, stories, or music, we never forgot where we came from.

"That sounds very special," Leo said. "Do you know how to play any instruments or speak the language?"

I shook my head. "No, I never learned Yiddish or to play an instrument. It's probably too late now."

"Pshaw. It's never too late."

"Do you really believe that?" I asked.

He wrapped an arm around my shoulders. "Completely. I also believe that Juniper Blume can do anything she sets her mind to achieving."

I could feel my face blush. I curled closer into him.

* * *

After my lunch date, I decided to do what the cliche says and return to the scene of the crime. Not surprisingly, the storage unit was still blocked off, so I'm not sure what I had expected to uncover.

As I wandered the labyrinthine place, I ran into Lizzy, the staff member whom I'd talked with the morning of the auction. She was on a small ladder, changing a light bulb. For some reason, she again wore sunglasses. Not sure how she could see anything in here, let alone fix a light bulb. People definitely had their quirks sometimes.

"Hey, it's you. The one who won the unit. It isn't available yet." Lizzy climbed down.

"Juniper," I said, putting out my hand. She took it with a light grip. "Thanks for the heads up." I wasn't sure what to say about what pulled me here. Telling people you wanted to know more about why someone died tended to be a bit too blunt. But then again, everyone was naturally curious about such tragedies. Maybe I could play on that? "Such a sad situation. Did you know the guy found inside? Or the person who owned the unit?"

"I haven't been in town long."

"You recently moved to Rose Mallow?"

"To the States. I've been abroad for a while," Lizzy said.

"What brought you here?"

She laughed. "Thought it would be all peaceful and quiet in a small town like this. Could have used that for a change. But guess I'm out of luck."

"For a change?"

Lizzy waved me off. "I shouldn't have said that. Talking without thinking."

"Guess that's why you got a job at a storage facility. I imagine it'd normally be very peaceful and quiet," I said.

Lizzy nodded. "*Normally* is the right word. This should be a place of order, an oasis in the chaos of the outer world. Most people don't understand, but it's a mess out there. This is a refuge. A home."

"I understand. I view libraries the same way," I said, although I didn't have such a strong negative feeling about "the chaos of the outer world." That sounded a bit paranoid to me. Maybe something had happened to her, and the Chessie U-Store provided some sort of solace? That might explain her strange habit of wearing sunglasses in the darkened place.

"We're kindred, aren't we?" she asked with a smile. I wasn't sure I agreed, but I didn't contradict her. Instead, I nodded along, encouraging her to continue. "We both love the stories of things. You with books, me with objects. They're permanent and don't disappoint the way people do."

"Someone disappointed you?"

She laughed. "So many. You know, my dad used to tell me not to trust anyone. I thought he was overly cautious, but it turned out he was right. It would be a good lesson for you to learn, too." She wagged a finger at me. Did she think she was providing some matronly advice? I rolled with it, nodding along.

"Sounds like your dad really cared about you," I replied.

Lizzy shrugged. "He did, until his own demons got the best of him. He skipped out on my mom and me when I was a teenager. Men." She spat at the ground. "My husband wasn't any better. I finally thought I'd found someone I could trust and then, he…" She paused. "Well, let's just say that he disappointed me, too. That's why I like objects."

It sounded like she had some of her own demons to deal with. But this conversation wasn't helping me figure out who killed Marcus. I decided to switch tactics.

"Have you heard any more about what happened here?" I asked.

"Not really. But it's scary. Killers on the loose where I work." Her shoulders tensed up towards her ears. "I had thought this would be a quiet retirement job."

"Peaceful and quiet," I repeated.

"Exactly."

"Did you see anyone acting strange around here before the…incident?"

She considered my question. "Why are you asking?"

"I've ended up in the middle of all this. I think it's scary, too." Not untrue.

"Well, there's one couple I've seen a bunch recently. They're a bit off."

"A couple?" I asked.

Lizzy nodded, brushing her long blond ponytail over her shoulder. Something about the texture of her hair made me wonder if it was real.

Between the sunglasses and possible wig, could she have been in an accident? Maybe that was the stress she wanted to escape.

"Young couple. The girl cleans here sometimes. But she doesn't do a good job. Pretty awful, actually. Honestly, I think they just come here to have trysts."

"Trysts? Why do you say that?" I asked.

She half-smiled. "Because they seem to avoid the security cameras. I think they know where all of them are."

"Was that the couple at the auction?"

Lizzy shrugged. "I didn't stick around. So maybe? Busy with lots of work to do. Speaking of which, I need to get back to it. But I will say this much:…They were both here the night before the auction happened."

* * *

I headed to the general manager's office. Gary's nostrils flared when he saw me come in. "Unit's not ready yet. Police still popping all over the place. Scaring off renters."

How was this my fault? But I didn't want to annoy him further, especially as I had a favor to ask. "Do you know how Marcus ended up in my unit?"

"Look, missy, I gave everything to the police. All the security footage, key timings, you name it."

"Could I see the security footage, too?"

He laughed almost like a growl. "No way."

"Could you tell me if it showed anything suspicious?"

Gary looked ready to decline me again, so I interrupted to say, "What if I rent another unit?"

"Another unit?" His thick eyebrows lifted.

"I have a lot of stuff in my D.C. townhouse that I want to bring down here. And there's not enough room in my sister's unit." That much was true. There might have been space in the Wildflower Inn, but when my choices were a hot, humid attic, or the gross, unfinished basement, I didn't want to risk putting things in either. Plus, it'd taken my family this long to get all of Nana

Z's items out of the Carriage House. Honestly, I should rent a unit here.

"How about this? You rent a deluxe, pay three months up front, and I'll share."

I put out my hand. "You have a deal."

When we shook, his heavy hand was somehow rough, dry, and slimy.

"Gladys! Hey, Gladys!"

His sister trekked into the office. Gladys smiled at me before turning back to her brother. "Before you ask for another task…" She rolled her eyes. "Do you know where the new girl is?"

Gary shrugged.

"She's barely shown up lately." She tsked.

"Do you mean Lizzy?" I asked.

"I think that's her name. Lizzy, Liza, Eliza…something like that," Gary said.

"You need to be better at details. Not even knowing your employee's names." She sighed dramatically. They probably had this conversation daily.

"I talked with her in the hallway," I said. "She was fixing a lightbulb."

"Well, see, there you go. She's here today," Gary said to Gladys.

"Not like she's reported in."

"Anyway, I need you to pull up the security footage from last Friday night," Gary said.

"I've shown you how to do that a million times, Gary."

"Once more. Please." He batted his eyes.

"You're lucky I'm your sister. And a pushover." She laughed and adjusted her glasses. She pushed him out of the way and went to work on his computer. "Here you go. See, easy."

We scrolled through the videos. For a long time, nothing happened, but then Marcus appeared, entering the facility. The quality wasn't great, but I could identify him by his height. He showed up in different hallways. Was he looking for something? Probably Esme's unit.

Then he's spotted in front of the unit. He had stopped, not opening it. His back was to the camera. He stood there for a long time. At first, I wondered if the video had frozen, but then I realized he was moving a little. His arms swayed slightly, and it looked like his attention was entirely on something just out of screen. Was he talking with someone? Who? If there was someone there, they were out of frame. They must have known where the camera was.

"Is there sound?" I asked.

"Nope," Gary replied.

I suspected that the person he was speaking to knew that too. Whoever it was seemed to have been perfectly placed to stay out of view and not be heard. That couldn't be a mistake. Would Esme have known all that? Who would have figured out such minute details in a storage facility? I wasn't a detective, but this struck me as meticulously planned.

Marcus gestured a few times. His movements grew bigger. He stepped away with his arms out wide, like he was going to hug someone. But then he steps backward. The attempted hug turned into a flail. He moved in and out of frame, appearing agitated.

Then his arms dropped to his side, seeming to surrender. He turned away from the unseen person, and we got a decent visual of Marcus's face. Even with the graininess, his expression radiated sadness. He stood there for a while, maybe listening?

Then he turned and gesticulated urgently. He moved back and forth wildly. An argument? Hard to say, but if Luna had been here, she'd probably comment on his aura being inflamed or something.

The unit suddenly opened.

"Wait, how is that happening?" I asked.

"No idea," Gary answered.

"Guess someone had the code," Gladys added.

"Esme?" I asked. Gary shrugged.

"Or someone who knew her code," Gladys replied.

We didn't see him get hit with the unknown murder weapon, but we watched him stumble into the storage unit, grabbing at his head. Even with the poor film quality, I could make out the seriousness of his wound. He needed medical assistance, but instead, he teetered, falling out of frame inside the unit.

"Can we see inside the unit?" I asked.

Gary laughed sourly. "We don't have cameras inside those."

I still couldn't see the other person. How had they managed to stay off camera? Who would know all this? My thoughts went to the young couple with their trysts. That had to be Noah and Susannah. Could it have been one or both of them unseen here? Or was it someone else?

The door to the unit closed. A gloved hand locked it back in place. Marcus never came back out.

"Any idea what he was hit with?" I asked.

The siblings shook their heads.

"It was also cleaned up. There was no blood outside that unit," Gary said.

"So someone who not only knew where the cameras were but also how to clean up their mess?" This had to be Noah and Susannah. They knew about the cameras to hide their get-togethers, and she was cleaning here for her aunt's company. They had to be involved.

"Do you know who he was talking to before he was hurt?" I asked.

"Couldn't say," Gary said with a shrug.

"Not a clue. No one saw or heard anything. I went through the footage earlier with the detective. We looked at everyone who came in and out during that day. Nothing strange." Gladys leaned closer to me. "I think it's a ghost."

Gary rolled his eyes. "Well, I held up my end of the bargain. Let's get that contract signed."

# Chapter Twenty-Six

That evening, I found myself sitting on an uncomfortable metal folding chair in the town's historical society for the grants committee meeting. The historical society was housed in a decommissioned brick church, going back centuries. Inside, the pews were long gone, replaced by various exhibits about the town's history under vitrines atop rolling display cases. Most of the displays had been pushed to the sides to make room for a small half-circle of chairs and a portable screen. Just beyond the semi-circle was a six-foot table covered in a plastic red tablecloth with pastries and water. I wished there had been tea. I could have used some caffeine.

Unfortunately, my old friend Harold wasn't there as I had hoped, given that he volunteered for the society and was close with Dor. Still, there were a few faces I recognized, including Maria Gutierrez, who owned the local panaderia La Artesa, Desta Martin, who oversaw marketing for the Calvertons, and my friends Desiree Douglass and Luna Moray. I hoped that if Luna was here that it meant Nuri was okay.

"Juniper Blume, good to see you again." Desta thrust a hand out towards me. Her wrist jingled with a dozen mismatched, brightly colored bangles. Always fashionable, she sported a close-cut bleached fade and teal cat's eye glasses that sparkled against her dark skin. I loved her sense of style.

"Desta, how are you doing?" I kept my eyes focused on her, but I could feel Luna watching me.

"Hanging in there. Did you hear that Florence has taken over the museum and library project?" she asked. Florence Dowd was a long-time librarian for the Calverton Foundation's collection—not to be confused with the personal family collection I managed at Dor's mansion. This one was their "public" collection. For one short week, I had run the project, before murder and mayhem pushed me to go in a different direction. Being in charge of such a large project had also felt beyond my capabilities at this time, and I wasn't being self-deprecating. Rather, I recognized that my strengths were more in working with books, not so much managing a staff of people, or even worse, the Foundation board. I shuddered thinking about how frustrating they had been.

Desta had been one of the bright spots that week. She was smart, quick, and worked with my team to pull together a small exhibit incredibly fast. I enjoyed working with her.

"I'm sure Florence is doing a great job. She's meticulous and dedicated." There were many other words I could use for my crabby former employee, but she did believe in the work passionately. She had worked for the collections for years—single-handedly—and knew the best practices in the field. She was well-suited to take it on. Far more than me, and I was happy to see her make it happen.

"And Eric is there still, too," said Maria, coming up to join us. She was the proud mother of the young library tech I had worked with so briefly. He had been another highlight, given his enthusiasm and resourcefulness. "He will be so happy to hear that I ran into you."

"Please give him my best," I said, taking her hands in mine.

"I brought treats for everyone." Maria motioned to a platter full of goodies on a nearby table. Desiree Douglass was enjoying one as we looked over. She gave a big thumbs up.

"Can't wait to try them." I worked my way over to the table. As I did, Luna pulled up alongside me. "How's it going?" I whispered the words.

"The same. She's still scared. But I think having all the cats with her helps. They're healing. I can tell."

"That's good," I replied non-committally before picking up a delectable-looking pastry. Maria had brought many goodies: honey-drenched sopapillas, thick slices of pastel de tres leches, and a plate filled with pan dulce.

Somehow, everything tasted even better than it looked.

A whistle blew. We all turned on our heels. Annie stood at the front of the room with the whistle still in her mouth. Her bright purple fingernails rapped against a metal folding chair.

"Thank you all for attending tonight. If you wouldn't mind finding your seats," she announced. I exchanged a glance with Luna, whose eyebrows were about as sky-high as mine. I hadn't expected our gothic-princess lawyer to also be a drill sergeant. She was full of surprises.

There were ten of us in the room, including Annie, Desta, Luna, Desiree, Maria, and myself. The other four people were strangers, all men. At least strangers for the time being, although I looked forward to getting to know everyone. I sat between Luna and Desta.

Annie passed out green folders embossed with the Calverton family logo. While I opened my packet, Annie rolled in a screechy A/V cart, setting it up in the middle of the chair half-circle to face the portable screen. She prepped the projector before trotting over in her Doc Martens to flip off half the lights. The room became very dark, save the light of the projector screen.

"Alright, let's see if we can get this slideshow running." Her laptop connected, and we could see her background photo. To my surprise, it was a family picture of the Calverton siblings, including Leo, their younger brother Cecil, herself, and the others I hadn't yet met. I hadn't expected her to be so nostalgic, but it was nice seeing the kids with their arms around each other's shoulders. They were all dressed up. Maybe at one of their family's galas? I'd have to ask Leo.

"Need a hand?" Desiree asked.

"Yes, please," Annie replied. Desiree worked her electronic magic, and soon, the slideshow took up the screen. The title screen simply said Grants Committee Introduction, but had a sleek, professional style.

"I designed the slides," Desta whispered to me.

"No wonder they look so fabulous," I replied.

Desta winked.

"Okay, team. Again, thank you for joining our Grants Committee. I'm going to go over the program in this brief slideshow. You also have a copy of the slides in your folders," she said.

I pulled out the stapled copy. Was this her version of brief? Because mine had 52 pages. How long were we going to be there? I really wished we had tea right then. And a few more of Maria's treats.

Over the next ninety minutes, Annie outlined all the details of the grants program, including eligibility for participants, priorities for the grantmakers, our scoring rubric, timelines and deadlines, and a host of other logistics. I tried to remain focused, but between the dark room and the late hour, I came close to dozing off multiple times. Luna elbowed me gently, so maybe I had fallen asleep completely. Oops. I hoped I hadn't snored.

"The application window ends after Halloween, so take some time to review all the materials. We'll meet again in November for our first round of reviews. Depending on how many applications we receive, you may be put into teams to review a selection. But everyone will help determine the overall winners," Annie finished up. She turned off the projector and flipped back on the lights.

Hands shot up across the room.

"How many applicants will be funded?" Desiree asked. Several heads nodded in curiosity.

"As many as we can."

"Can we apply for our own businesses?" Maria asked.

Annie nodded. "Yes, although you will not be allowed to vote on your own application."

I thumbed through the slides. Also in my packet was a copy of the grant application, Annie's contact information, and other sheets. I'd have to review this all more closely soon, but it'd likely have to wait until after Rosh Hashanah. However, if we weren't meeting again until November, I had time.

"And how much money will be awarded per grant?" Luna asked. Everyone's necks appeared to stretch an extra three inches.

"You'll get to decide. Some will need more, others will need less. Remember, I'm simply helping manage the process. You all are the decision-makers." She smiled, but there was something off about the way she looked at us. For some reason, it felt strange to hear her describe us as the decision-makers. Not that I could put my finger on why. However, when I looked around the room, I only saw nodding heads and beaming smiles. Apparently, no one else felt strange about it, so I chalked it up to having a difficult week.

# Chapter Twenty-Seven

The next day, Azalea agreed to join me at Olivia's office for a consultation over our planned family holiday photo. We traded notes before heading inside the strange rustic barn slash modern glass-filled photo studio.

"If you work out logistics with Olivia, I'm going to excuse myself to snoop around," I said.

Azalea made a face. "I'm not comfortable with that."

"Just going to look a tiny bit. Nothing outrageous. I'm hopeful I can find out more about what's going on with Olivia and how she's connected to all this."

"I know. And I'll help you. But don't cross any lines, okay?"

"Of course not," I replied, although I was mentally crossing my fingers behind my back.

Inside the studio, Sneezy greeted us, but before she could introduce herself, Olivia waltzed in with wide-open arms. "Juniper, Azalea, I'm so pleased you could join me." Her words slurred, and there was a strange odor to her. Was she drunk? It was only the morning.

I glanced at my sister, whose eyebrows had popped up her forehead. Sneezy didn't look thrilled with Olivia either, but she kept her face down, looking through some notepads, and kept her back to her boss.

"Follow me…" Olivia led us to the back room, barely walking a straight line. We took seats on highly uncomfortable white and translucent chairs. I got the sense that Olivia was hoping to fuse the rustic barn with a modern aesthetic, but honestly, everything felt more cobbled and half-thought than synchronicity. Like these hard chairs.

"I'm so excited to do your photoshoot," she said. "Normally, people have to book months out in advance. You know how schedules are. But we did happen have to a last-minute booking available this week. Assuming you're available, tomorrow afternoon?"

"What's the cost?" Azalea asked.

Olivia waved her hand like a symphony conductor. "Creating such memories is priceless, really. My assistant will go over the various packages with you. I have to head out to a photo shoot. Art waits for no photographer."

To my shock, Olivia picked up several items, gave a quick "Ta-ta," and disappeared out the door. I hoped she wasn't driving anywhere.

"What was that?" Azalea asked.

I shook my head. "No idea. But it wasn't a consultation."

"And we didn't approve anything."

Sneezy coughed from the door. "I can help you."

"Is she worth it?" Azalea asked us both.

I put up my hands in uncertainty while Sneezy sighed. "She's incredibly talented, for what it's worth. She's like this sometimes, but her photos are good. I can show you some examples." She pulls out some photo albums for us to leaf through. Like everything else, some had that traditional, weathered leather feel, while others gave slick gray and white modern vibes. It was as if she couldn't make up her mind as to her branding: old school or contemporary. Maybe she just wanted the best of both worlds?

"They are lovely photos," Azalea murmured. I agreed.

Sneezy pulled out a laminated sheet of paper: the price package menu. She handed it to Azalea, who nearly dropped it in alarm. "What? That's outrageous."

I picked up the sheet. She wasn't kidding. Olivia's prices were worse than in Washington, D.C.

"People pay this?" Azalea asked Sneezy.

"Well, she upped them recently. Upped them a lot actually."

"Business going that well?" I asked.

Sneezy shook her head. "It was going great, but in recent months, not so much. There's a lot less work. My hours have been cut." Her eyes dampened.

"What happened?" I asked.

"Well, uh…" She bit her lower lip. "You saw her."

"She dropped a camera-shaped flask at the vigil for Marcus," I said.

Sneezy closed her eyes and shook her head. "It's bad. Really bad. I shouldn't tell clients that. But she's hinted at my job ending, so what does it matter?"

"Olivia upped her prices because she's not getting enough work?" Azalea asked.

Sneezy nodded. "She thinks that those prices demonstrate her quality as a photographer, which will encourage more people to hire her. But then she'll turn on a dime and ask me to run these crazy flash sales, reducing prices by a lot, because she's not getting enough work. Honestly, neither idea is working."

"You said this started a few months ago? Any chance it was after this person visited her?" I pulled up a photo of Esme Vienna on my phone to show Sneezy.

"Oh yeah, I remember her. They had a big fight. I didn't know what it was about, but I thought they were going to really punch each other. It was bad. I was this close to calling the police that day." She shivered.

"And after that, did Olivia's drink…I mean, behavior change?"

Sneezy nodded. "You know, I hadn't put those two things together before, but you're right. That's when Olivia really started to go downhill."

"I'm sorry," I said.

"Thanks. I'm looking for other jobs. Hope to open my own studio one day, but I'm not there yet."

"Wishing you all the best," I said.

"If you ever need a family for your portfolio," Azalea added. "I have the most adorable four-year-old."

"And her cutest best friend dog."

"That would be awesome. Thank you. You know, I did put together a business card. I thought it was just a flight of fancy, but still…" She pulled two out and gave them to us.

Sneezy's real name was Sarah.

# Chapter Twenty-Eight

After the strange experience at Olivia's studio, I was happy to go to work. I needed somewhere else to funnel my focus. That day, I worked on condition checking, scanning, and cataloging old photo albums. The process was laborious, but it was delightful looking at Dor's family over the years.

At the moment, I flipped through an album of Dor and friends at Ocean City, Maryland in the mid-1960s. Although most of the photos were in black and white, I could tell that the bathing suits must have been bright and colorful. She sported an "itty bitty teenie weenie" bikini with polka dots. I wondered if it was yellow like the song.

"That was a great summer," Dor said, popping up behind me. I startled, nearly jumping out of my seat. She laughed with a voice like a ringing bell. "Sorry about that, Juniper. You know they used to call me 'The Cat' because of how quietly I moved."

"That's amazing. It looks like you all had a great time together. Who is with you?" I asked, planning to take notes on each photo in the database.

"Well, you know Hal of course." She pointed to the young man with the classic All-American smile. I hadn't recognized my elderly friend from the local historical society, but as soon as she pointed him out, it was clearly him. What was amazing was how, even today, they continued to be vibrant, even being well into their eighties.

"Did the two of you ever date?" I hoped I wasn't pushing things with my question. We had a good relationship, but I wasn't sure if Dor wanted to be that personal.

She laughed again. "A few times, but never anything serious. We were always better as friends. Still are. I did marry that young man—for a few years." She pointed to another man, whom I didn't recognize. "Johnny O'Henry was a good guy, but he wasn't crazy about how often I was away from home, which could be months at a time. Or longer. He thought that once we married, I'd give up my service to become a mom and stay home. My sister loved being a stay-at-home parent, but it wasn't for me."

"Wait, but how does that work? You were born a Calverton, but you married an O'Henry? How did your kids stay Calvertons?"

"Kid, not kids. Johnny and I had one son together. That's Leo's dad. But when I didn't want to stay at home with him, Johnny got upset. Not just about that, though. He had lots of odd thoughts. Became convinced the government was out to get us. He didn't simply want me to give up my job, but he wanted us to move away from the area and live off the grid. Before that was even a phrase people talked about." She shook her head. I suspected there was a lot more to the story than she was telling me, but I appreciated her candidness. "Granted, it was the time of the Cold War, and maybe I told him a bit too many things that should have stayed secret. Loose lips sink ships, you know."

"That's a phrase from World War II."

She shrugged. "Still applied. When we first started dating, he thought what I did was fascinating and tried to get as much intel as he could from me. I didn't tell him much, but it was still too much. My work fed into his worst fears."

"What did you do?" I asked.

"We got divorced, and I got sole custody of our son. That wasn't easy, even with all the resources at our family's disposal," she explained.

"You changed your son's name to Calverton?"

Dor nodded. "It wasn't easy to make sure my son kept my last name, especially in a family as old and traditionally focused as this one. But what helped is that my father despised Johnny. He thought Johnny had lost his marbles. Definitely not good enough for his little girl. So he helped me fight tooth and nail for my son to remain a Calverton."

"What happened to Johnny?"

"He wasn't happy, of course, but eventually he found a new girl to share his paranoia with and left us both alone. They got married and had their own daughter." She snapped her fingers, apparently trying to recall something. "Elizabeth? I think that was the daughter's name. After she was born, he dropped out of our lives entirely. Not that I kept track. I had enough other distractions with my job and raising my family as a single mom. At least for a little while."

"A little while? Did you marry again?" I asked.

Dor nodded. "You know, I married three times. None stuck. I liked the idea of marriage, but honestly, I'm not good at it. Not sure I turned out to be such a great parent either. My sister raised my kid more than I did. Never had another child."

"Leo's parents seem to have become very successful," I said.

"True, true. His father was a wild child growing up, but amazingly, as an adult, he was able to channel that energy into running so many businesses. I can barely keep up." She sighed. "But we're not close. Sure, we have family functions together, but he and I never get to sit here and chat, like you and I are doing. I should have encouraged that more."

"It was a different time," I said.

She shrugged. "People use that as an excuse. It was a different time, yes, but it's not like that stopped me. I did quite a lot of unconventional things for women. Granted, I'm lucky that my father supported my ambitions. And loved his grandkids."

"You clearly love yours."

"That's true. Being a grandmother is much easier. You get to spoil the little ones rotten and then return them home at the end of the day." She laughed.

"Like me and my niece."

"Violet is adorable," she said. "I love the videos you show me of her with your dog. They are a hoot."

"Are you going to join us for Rosh Hashanah dinner?" I asked.

"I wish I could, but unfortunately, I have another obligation that evening. Will Leo be escorting you?" she asked.

"He told me he's looking forward to it. Oh, and I met his sister Annie."

Dor's smile broadened. "Yes, I've seen her a few times. She's a riot. Reminds me a lot of her dad with all that wild child energy. She doesn't let anything stop her."

"Sounds like you," I said.

"Well, thank you. I hope I'm in there somewhere when she's off saving the world," she replied.

"She's in town focusing on the grants from the family to neighborhood businesses," I explained.

"I had heard a little bit about that. Including that it was your idea?"

I blushed. "I wouldn't go that far, but I'm glad they went in this direction instead of Port Chesapeake."

Dor stuck out her tongue. "Can you imagine? Bulldozing everything down to build some bland luxury development. I was never a fan. But they didn't listen to me. I'm the so-called matriarch, but my son and daughter-in-law wield all the real power. I try to stay out of it. So I'm glad you proposed something that's working better. Is your sister's inn benefiting, I hope?"

"She's submitting a grant application."

"Good, good. It makes me happy that you're here, Juniper. You've been a good influence on Leo. He's been spending more time in Rose Mallow lately, and that's because of you, you know? I get to see him more often, too, which is nice."

"Thank you. He invited me to join him on a dig," I told her.

"What did you say?"

"Maybe in the spring."

"Not now?"

I sucked in my breath. I hadn't planned on sharing so many personal details with my employer, especially since she was my boyfriend's grandmother. "At the moment, I just want to get through the week. It's been jarring and disorienting."

"Have you figured out more of what happened?" she asked, sounding concerned.

"Nothing conclusive. I feel like every time I learn one thing, more questions spring up."

Dor laughed. "It was like that all the time during my service days. You would have been a good intelligence officer, Juniper."

"Thank you, but I'd rather stick to my books and archives. These have enough excitement. I mean, how amazing is it that I can learn all the stories behind each one of these photographs?" I tapped gently on the photo album.

"I love your enthusiasm. It's a real gift."

My cheeks burned again. "I'm grateful for it as well. And for this opportunity. Leaving the Library of Congress wasn't an easy decision to make, so I'm glad I've ended up somewhere where I can still work with such great wonders."

"That's kind of you to say, Juniper. Well, I hope you and Leo do get to go on some adventures together, maybe add on to the library here."

I nodded. "I hope so too. This may be strange to say, but part of the reason I want to wait until the spring to take that trip is because, well, I don't feel like there is a need to rush. My connection to Leo feels strong. So whether it's now or later, it doesn't matter."

"Oh, my girl. That's lovely. I think he feels the same about you. I wouldn't rush you so much myself, but I'm not a spring chicken anymore, and it's good to see my grandchildren finding people they care about. Wouldn't mind a few great-grandchildren either."

"Dor," I blurted out. She had encouraged me to always use her first name, but I hadn't meant to sound so informal and blunt.

She laughed and winked at me. "Alright, as much as I'd love to go on more of a stroll down memory lane with these photos, I have some other things needing me. Will you be okay for a bit?"

"Of course, thank you," I said and went back to work. My relationship with Leo was still fairly fresh, but looking at these photos, I wondered if we'd be sharing our own photos together with another generation sixty or more years from now.

# Chapter Twenty-Nine

That night, I returned to *The Chesapeake Chronicle* to check in on Nuri. I found her in the main office with Luna. The gray cat Tabitha stretched out across the desk before cuddling up between a few stacks of papers.

"Juniper, you came back." Nuri popped up. Her face was pale, and there were heavy circles under her eyes. Her dark hair jutted out in different directions, but even with as punk rock as my friend tended to dress, this look didn't seem on purpose.

"Of course, I came back. Did you think I wouldn't?"

She ran over and hugged me. "I wasn't sure after everything I had done."

Luna put a hand on Nuri's back as my friend relaxed her grip. "Don't be so hard on yourself. Juniper understands, don't you?"

"It's a lot to take in, but Nuri, we've been friends for years. You were there for me with everything that happened at Labor Day. I'm not going to abandon you. Not now. Not ever." If kicking me out of her car, breaking into my house, and revealing that she had been a forger hadn't scared me away, obviously nothing was going to. Friendship can be fiery, but ours had been forged into steel.

I also thought about Luna, who had not been so helpful during my last incident. The woman had nearly destroyed my reputation with her newspaper articles and radio shows, but we had made it through. And she was helping Nuri now. People had needed to forgive me for my poor choices, so it was only fair for me to forgive Luna and Nuri.

"I was at Olivia Grover's this afternoon," I said. "She's going through a tough time. One that started a few months ago when she met with Esme Vienna. Any chance you know what Esme has on her?"

Nuri shook her head. "Not a clue. Sorry."

But Luna took off, disappearing out the office door. Nuri and I exchanged looks and then followed her. We traipsed through the jungle of papers and felines, weaving our way around the box towers to a locked door. "This is the newspaper's institutional archives," Luna said.

She unlocked the door, revealing a small room. Unlike the disheveled mess outside, inside was shockingly ordered. There were well-maintained black shelves with acid-free archival boxes and bound copies of past newspapers. "The cats aren't allowed back here," Luna said as she flipped on a light switch and shut the door behind us.

I reviewed the large, leatherbound copies of newspapers. Some went back eighty, ninety years. I pulled one open at random and searched through, perusing life in Rose Mallow in the 1960s.

"It'll be our centennial soon. Exciting times!" Luna glided through the shelves, apparently searching for a specific edition. As she did, I went through the pages of this one.

"Oh, hey, look, it's an ad for the Chessie U-Store," I said.

"Really?" Nuri looked over my shoulder.

"The Chessie U-Store for All Your Family Stores," I read the headline of the advertisement. It showed a family carrying boxes, including what appeared to be a husband and wife with a young girl. The man looked familiar. Where had I seen his face before?

"Found it!" Luna called out. She pulled out another bound copy of newspapers from only a few years earlier.

"These aren't all digitized?" I asked.

Luna laughed. "How I wish. Don't have the funding or manpower for it, though. So I still have these issues produced to keep a decent record of the newspaper." She carried the oversized book to an empty desk, before clicking on the lamp. She ran through the pages with ease until she found what she sought. "Lookie here."

Nuri and I peered over her shoulder. Luna pointed to an article. "Hit and run several years ago. The person survived, fortunately, but the driver fled the scene. The victim described how the car swerved, not slowing down, before crashing into them."

"Sounds like the driver was drunk," I said. Luna nodded.

"Do they know who the driver was?" Nuri asked.

"Didn't get a good look, but the vic thought it was a woman. Car was red. That much they were certain of." Luna then flipped to another edition of the newspaper. "Few days later. The red car was discovered. Abandoned a few miles away. Guess who it belonged to?"

"Olivia Grover?" Nuri and I asked in unison.

"Ding ding ding. But Olivia claimed someone stole it from her the day of the accident. See, she's quoted about how the thief must have gone joy-riding and things about 'kids these days.'" Luna shook her head.

"You think Olivia was actually the drunk driver?" Nuri asked.

Luna didn't respond. Instead, she flipped to yet another edition, earlier in the book. She pointed to the crime report. "Public drunkenness." Then she closed the book, swung around, and searched out another one. Luna carried it over and plopped it on top of the first one. With a few agile page turns, she landed on another crime report. "And here again…"

"Neither of those articles lists names," I argued.

"I know, but it's Olivia." She tapped the side of her forehead. "I remember." She went to another section of the book and again pointed to the crime report. Then she turned on her heels, obviously ready to grab another book.

I raised my hands. "I think we get the point."

Nuri nodded. "She clearly has a drinking problem."

"Esme must have figured out she was lying about the hit-and-run accident," Luna said.

"Maybe she even had some proof," Nuri added.

"Definitely possible. But whatever she said scared Olivia." I counted on my fingers. "Okay, so Esme knew that Marcus and you were involved in a forgery ring. She also knew that Olivia had been a drunk driver, nearly killing someone. She obviously had something on her own niece and future nephew-in-law. And…" I almost mentioned Desiree, but caught myself at the last moment. No reason to involve her. Or at least not now. I also didn't want to say anything about my grandmother's paintings being included. The idea that she may have been blackmailed as well absolutely chilled me. It was not a thought I would seriously entertain. "…And she had others, too, given the number of boxes in that unit. Each box's code must have connected it to the person she had blackmailed."

"That makes sense," Nuri agreed. "A filing system. Just like we learned in library school."

"I saw her niece Susannah and her boyfriend Daniel at Esme's house. They were searching for a logbook. I'm guessing that's where Esme tracked everything."

"Do you think she recorded people's secrets in there?" Luna asked.

"Maybe. And who knows, maybe she had something on Daniel and Susannah, too."

"Or maybe they were planning to take over the family business," Luna suggested.

"I hadn't considered that. But that would make sense." A dreadful feeling crept down my spine. "If that's the case, though, do you think they might have gotten Esme out of the way?" I had already suspected they were involved with Marcus's death, but what if they started with Esme? Susannah's very own aunt?

"You mean like…" Luna ran her right index finger across her neck.

"I don't know. But we have several people involved that might have wanted to hurt Esme," I said.

Nuri piped up. "Wait, do you think of me as one of those people?"

"Never, Nuri." I went over and put my arms around her.

Luna followed suit. "We know you got wrapped up in something difficult."

"Marcus and Betsy took advantage of a grad student," I said. "They knew you had a skillset they needed and recognized a weakness in needing to pay for school. They dragged you into this mess."

Luna nodded. "Juniper's right. We're here for you."

"Agreed. And we're going to keep you safe."

I went to put back the copy I had been paging through earlier. Curious about the photo, I flipped through more newspaper editions. I frequently found the same ad, but sometimes there were different versions, including other photos of the family. As I studied them, I tried to figure out why he had rung a bell for me. Not only that, but his wife and daughter struck me as familiar as well. Why was that? Did I know them from somewhere? It had been around sixty years since these photos were taken, and I wouldn't be born for decades after them, so who were they? How strange.

# Chapter Thirty

The next morning, I woke up to something amazing smelling. I followed my nose down the stairs to discover my sister working in the kitchen. A veritable feast spread across the kitchen table: apple crisp topped kugel casseroles, a round raisin challah, green beans bathed in butter and spices, a fragrant carrot and chickpea tagine with delicious Moroccan scents, a bright red beet soup, and a platter covered in various apple varieties, dates, and pomegranates. Beside that was what appeared to be a flight of different honeys to taste.

"These are all vegetarian dishes," I said in happy shock.

Azalea smiled. "It was supposed to be a surprise, but yes, I'm planning an entirely vegetarian meal for Rosh Hashanah. I figured that would be fun for you. Plus, by going vegetarian, I can make it a dairy meal. Well, except for some vegan options for Leo. "

"You're making these kosher?" Being a not-so-religious family, we had never kept strict kosher anywhere. By being vegetarian, I already never mixed milk and meat products, but I also never went further, not requiring my food to be prepared under any rabbinic supervision.

"Not strictly. But pretty close. I'm hoping no one misses the brisket."

I knew I wouldn't, but looking around, I suspected no one would either.

I wrapped her up in my arms. "You are the best sister ever. Thank you."

"Yes, I am, aren't I?" she replied with a laugh. "But seriously, it's a fun challenge. I'm enjoying trying all these recipes out. And these are just the savory dishes. Wait till you try the desserts."

"I can't wait. And you really went in on the symbolism, didn't you?" I asked.

She nodded. "Apples, honey, and raisins for a sweet new year, green beans for a fruitful one, carrots for increased blessings, chickpeas for prosperity, and pomegranates for abundance and renewal." She pointed to an open cookbook on a counter. My sister loved her cookbooks. "I learned a lot. Such a great experiment."

"Let me know if you need a taste tester," I said.

"Obviously. I can't try all these alone." Azalea winked at me. "Dig in. And be brutally honest."

"Happy to help."

The only problem was I couldn't find a single critique. Everything was absolutely perfectly delicious. Azalea didn't seem to believe me, but I loved all her culinary creations.

"Where's Rory?" I asked in between mouthfuls. "He's going to want to try this too."

"He'll be back soon. He took Violet and Clover to the playground for a bit."

"That was nice of him to take them both."

"They're a package deal," Azalea said.

"True. Thick as thieves." I had eaten more than my fill of food. I couldn't find room for another bite. "Can I help clean up?"

Azalea squirmed. "Thanks, but no thanks."

I don't know why I could handle the incredibly fragile documents and books in collections with the proper care, but a plate always seemed to slip to its doom in my hands. Azalea was probably right to be concerned.

"Is there something else I can do to help?" I asked.

"Well, when Mom and Dad get in, could you pick them up from the airport?"

"I'll need to take your Mom-mobile. KG won't fit more than one more person. Let alone their luggage. And instruments. And who knows what else they have brought back from their tour." My vintage Karmann-Ghia was fun to drive, but it wasn't particularly practical for carpooling purposes.

Azalea made a face. She obviously didn't appreciate me calling her minivan a Mom-mobile, even if it's what we had called our parents' car as kids. "That would be great. Thank you, Juniper."

I looked at my watch. "And there's the photoshoot today."

"You're still going to that? After her leaving drunk yesterday? I really don't want to expose Violet to her…uh…shenanigans." That was a polite word to describe her actions.

I figured it wouldn't help to mention what Nuri, Luna, and I had discussed about Olivia's background last night. But Azalea was right. As much as I'd love to get a nice photo of Azalea, Violet, and me for our parents, it was unsafe to have them near Olivia. What if she was the killer? I shuddered at the thought.

"What if I take Leo instead?" I asked.

Azalea nodded. "If he can join you, I think that would be good. I'd feel safer than you being there by yourself."

"I'll text him and see if he's available."

"Keep me updated."

"Thanks, sis."

* * *

I was about to drive to Dor's for work, but as I turned on KG, my phone rang. It was Noah Danvers. I hesitated at picking up the phone, but I couldn't resist finding out why he was calling me.

"Hey, Juniper, are you still thinking about getting a place in Rose Mallow?" Noah asked.

"Sure," I said, hoping the uncertainty was more in my head than in my voice.

"Then I have the perfect place to show you."

"Oh yeah?

"Could you come now?" he asked.

"Well, I'm about to head into work."

"Okay, then come afterwards." He gave me the street address and a time. I acknowledged receiving them before he hung up.

I stared at my phone. Did I just make plans to meet up with a murderer? Or given the photoshoot, had I made them with two killers in one day?

# Chapter Thirty-One

I tried to focus on work, but unlike yesterday when work proved a valuable distraction, today, my mind ping-ponged from worry to worry. I had to re-enter an entry into the database three times before getting the information correct.

Unable to keep my head straight, I walked around the library. Dor had several Jane Austen books in her collection. Unlike my grandmother's, these were actual first editions. I pulled out *Pride and Prejudice* gingerly, just to hold it in my hands. How must have Jane felt when it was published? I wondered about this book's story. Who had owned it, loved the story, maybe thrown it at a wall during reading a few times? I chuckled before carefully sliding it back into place.

I checked my phone yet again. Leo still hadn't responded to my text about meeting at Olivia's studio. I knew I shouldn't go by myself, but was there someone I could take with me? I didn't want to pass up the opportunity to find out more about Olivia.

After another fifteen minutes of distraction, I decided a bigger walk was in order. I wandered the hallways, looking for artworks by Marcus. Staring at one of the calligraphic works, I mentally asked it if it could tell me anything. Did it somehow know where Marcus's wife, Betsy, went? Or how deeply enmeshed they were with Esme? Why did you have to involve Nuri? She was a young woman, and you took advantage of her.

Not surprisingly, the artwork didn't answer me.

In between short bouts of work, I continued my research. Dor had access to all sorts of databases, so I searched for more information about Marcus,

Betsy, and Esme. I found a photo of the three of them at the grand opening of the gallery for the Rose Mallow Artist's Guild from a few years earlier. They were front and certain with their arms around each other's shoulders. Their smiles were bright and genuine. This must have pre-dated any issues amongst them, or at least before Esme knew about Marcus and Betsy's forgery ring with Nuri. I shook my head. All three of them were or would soon be criminals. Yet, you would never know it to look at them.

I zoomed in on the photo. What happened to you, Betsy? Where did you go? My skin prickled. I had seen her before. But when or how? Maybe when I was a teenager, coming here in the summertime? That didn't seem right.

* * *

The day dragged on. Leo didn't respond to my text. I tried calling him at lunchtime, but it went straight to voicemail. I would have asked Dor, but she was out doing who knew what that day, so I was on my own.

Was I willing to meet Olivia by myself? And what about Noah?

"Let's try something else for a bit," I said to myself. I'd brought the folder that Annie had given us at the grants committee meeting. While it wasn't work for Dor, I figured it was her family's work, and she wouldn't mind me perusing it for a bit.

Most of the information was as detailed and boring as it had been during her presentation, but I knew it was important and could make a difference in the community. Still, there was that strange sensation I had left the meeting with plaguing my stomach. What had bothered me? I flipped through the materials, scanning the pages, when something caught my eye. It was in small italicized type in a footnote.

"No. That can't be right?" I had good vision, but this tiny text was hard to read even for me. I pulled the page closer to my face. "What? No. That's not..."

I put the sheet down. Should I call Annie? No, because she obviously knew what was in there. She had tried to hide it. I attempted Leo again, but not surprisingly, I didn't hear anything.

Unsure of what to do, I tried calling Luna. Had she read what I'd just read? And maybe she could join me in visiting Olivia and Noah. Two for two?

"Oh, Juniper, I would be glad to join you, but I'm back on the air in fifteen seconds," she replied.

"Your radio show?"

"Yes, when am I getting you on? Answer later. I'll reach out when it's over." She abruptly hung up. I hadn't had a chance to tell what I'd seen in the grants information.

At least that meant another person knew where I'd be if Olivia or Noah turned out to be a killer. That was some solace, wasn't it? I figured I should alert Detective Gupta, too, but she'd put a stop to my investigating immediately. I'd have to hope I had warned enough people that a murderer wouldn't risk hurting me.

# Chapter Thirty-Two

That afternoon, I drove over to Olivia's studio. I wish I had studied the parking lot before, as I had no idea what Olivia drove. Not surprisingly, there wasn't a red car in sight. The hit-and-run car was likely long gone.

Once more, I tried Leo and Luna. Voicemail both times.

At least Sneezy was inside. No, wait, what was her actual name? Sarah. It was Sarah.

I headed inside, where Sneezy…Sarah was building a house of cards on her desk. Not with a deck of cards but out of various business cards. She carefully placed another one on top before releasing a steady breath.

"Hi, Sarah?"

"Juniper!" The house somehow stayed steady. "I'm sorry. I forgot to call you."

"Everything okay?"

Sarah stood up. This time, the house collapsed, and the business cards flew every which way. I scooped down to pick some up. Victory Cleaners. Not surprising.

"Olivia isn't feeling well. She's sorry, but she has to reschedule," Sarah said.

I handed the small stack of cards I had collected to her.

"Sorry, I know it's not the most professional thing," she said.

"Don't worry about it." I pointed to the stash in her hands. "Did Victory Cleaners come here often?"

"Used to come every week at the old place."

"Old place? How long have you been here?" I asked.

Sarah counted on her fingers. "A couple months, maybe. Not long. This is much nicer than the tiny and bland office park we used to be in."

"And Victory Cleaners came to both the old studio and this one?"

"Right. Except lately. At first, I thought Olivia had cut back on the cleaning company, but honestly, I'm not sure. The new girl either doesn't show up or she does a poor job." Sarah rolled her eyes. She must have meant Esme's niece Susannah.

"Did Esme use to clean?" I pulled up my photo again to jog her memory.

She shrugged. "Maybe. I didn't pay much attention, to be honest. Well, not until the new girl." Her face reflected how much she didn't like Susannah's work ethic. Assuming it was her. I didn't have a photo of Susannah to show her, but it had to be her. I remembered Olivia describing her as being lazy. Could that be true?

Even if Olivia wasn't here, I wondered if I could get some use out of my visit.

"I left something in Olivia's office yesterday. Would it be okay if I poked inside real quick?" I asked.

Sarah shrugged. "Have at it. Honestly, I'm not planning to stay much longer."

"Today, or in general?"

She sighed deeply. "Both?"

"What would you rather be doing right now?"

Sarah smiled. "It's a gorgeous day outside. I'd love to take photos. All the autumnal colors. I'm not into Olivia's moody grayscale stuff. I mean, it's pretty, but it's not me. I want color."

"If you left, would Olivia know?" I asked. I knew I was pushing buttons, but at least I'd be safe if Olivia wasn't here.

"Well, no. But I should let you get your...what did you leave?"

"A bag," I lied. It was scary how quickly the words popped out. "But I don't want you waiting on me."

Sarah considered my suggestion. "Well, maybe just for a little bit. The light is really golden and lush and perfect right now."

"Carpe diem."

She nodded. "Okay, I'll do it. Seize the day."

* * *

Left alone, I pulled on my always-ready pair of purple nitrile gloves, an archivist's favorite tool. I had promised Azalea I wouldn't do anything more than look, but couldn't that include peering inside file folders? My sister would have berated my logic, but my curiosity won out.

I tackled different drawers and attempted to log into Sarah's and then Olivia's computers. Maybe I shouldn't have been surprised that they were locked down tight. I wished that Keisha or Desiree were here. They might have been able to help me. Not that I should be leading a teenager into illegal acts. Hmmm. I was definitely pushing the lines right now, wasn't I? I needed to get my head back on straight. This was going too far.

Instead, I wandered through the studio. In the back room where we met so briefly with Olivia yesterday, I explored the staging area. The place was littered with various plinths, drapery, chairs, and a big black backdrop. Nothing looked out of the ordinary.

"What are you doing here?"

I turned and put my gloved hands behind my back, quickly taking the purple nitrile gloves off and stashing them into my right fist. It was Olivia. She wobbled into the room. Drunk again? I stepped backwards, knocking over one of the plinths.

"Now, why did you have to do that, Juniper? It took me forever to get it just perfect." Olivia zig-zagged across the room. She reached down to get the fallen column, but she couldn't pull it and herself back up.

"Olivia, you need help."

"No, I'm fine. One hundred percent fine."

I shook my head. I pocketed my gloves and leaned over to give her a hand. She pushed them away, but it was a gentle attempt, so I persevered, and she was standing. But it didn't look like it'd last, so I guided her into a seat.

"I wanted to talk to you." I sat in a nearby chair.

"What about?"

"Why did you tell me Esme Vienna was at a rehab center?"

Olivia's brow furrowed. She looked like a child caught with their hand in the proverbial cookie jar. "I don't know where she is."

"So why lie?"

"People asking makes me nervous. So I spouted the first idea off the top of my head."

Was she projecting her own issues? Maybe she knew deep down that she needed help herself? I hoped that thought would work its way up.

"You don't like Esme missing, do you?"

Olivia blew a raspberry. "Marc is dead. Esme is missing. That can't be a coin…coin…" She struggled to get the word out.

"I don't think it's a coincidence either. Olivia, are you afraid that Esme will tell everyone your secret?"

Her face reddened. "What secret? I have no secret." She jumped up from her seat.

I put my hands up. "I know that Esme was collecting people's secrets. It sounds like she was blackmailing people to keep them quiet."

Olivia must have thought I didn't know hers, because she relaxed. But only for a moment. She collapsed back into her seat. She appeared on the verge of tears. "I can't take it anymore."

"Take what?"

"All this pressure. It's too much."

"Tell me," I said quietly.

Olivia nodded. "I didn't know what Esme knew. Her company had been cleaning for me for years. Sometimes she came herself. We'd catch up. She seemed like a good friend."

"But something changed?"

She nodded. "Esme knew I wanted to grow my business. We were friends. In the same artist's guild, too." I didn't bother reminding her that I already knew this. Instead, I listened intently, silently encouraging her to continue. "When she offered to help me expand, I was appreciative. She helped me get this place."

"But after you moved in, something changed, didn't it?"

"Yeah…" Her voice trailed off. Then she said, "Years ago, I had a problem. There was an accident. Someone got hurt. But they survived. Thankfully."

"And Esme found out?"

"She said she'd reveal the truth if I didn't pay her more money. I didn't have enough to meet her demands. So I gave her my artwork. I gave her everything I could." Olivia sobbed in between words.

"But it wasn't enough?"

"Nothing was enough. Ever enough." She wiped her eyes with her sleeve. "Worst of all, I had to keep pretending we were close friends. I couldn't let anyone know the truth."

"So when Esme disappeared…" I nudged her, hoping I wasn't being too strong.

"I had imagined her disappearing. That all my problems would vanish. But when she actually did, I didn't feel relieved. I felt scared. Deeply scared. When you found her unit with my artwork inside…with Marc inside…I turned back to drinking. Too much. I need help."

I took Olivia's hands in my own. They trembled. "We'll make sure you get the help you need."

"Really?" Her voice was so small.

"Really," I promised.

# Chapter Thirty-Three

After wrapping up with Olivia, I headed back to my car. Nothing on my phone from Luna or Leo. I needed to meet with Noah soon. Well, I'd come this far. I could go a little longer, right? I texted both of them the address where I was headed.

Turned out it was a new development of townhomes, not far from the Chessie U-Store. Noah stood outside the model home, waving as I pulled up.

"I think you're going to love this place," he said as I walked up the path. It looked fresh and trendy, but he obviously had the wrong idea about me if he thought a monotonous row of matching new homes was up my alley. Being a rare books librarian who lived in a century-old Queen Anne style house, I was all about history and character—not uniform modernity.

"Looks lovely," I said as we entered the house. Noah slammed the door behind me. Was that a sign? Should I run out the back door?

"Sorry, that door is heavy," he said with a smile. "Great for storms and winter. Will definitely keep the heat inside."

"Oh, come on, Noah. You know she's not really interested."

Susannah entered the foyer. She led me down the hallway to a dining room. Being the model home, it was furnished with a glass table and black metal chairs with heavy white cushions. She pulled one out for me. I obeyed.

I scanned the room, trying to decide if I could break through a window or race to a nearby door. But with Noah and Susannah there, I knew I wouldn't win. Two against one was never great odds.

"You've been asking a lot of questions," Susannah said. "It's our turn to ask you some."

"What do you want to know?"

"No holding back, do you understand?" she asked.

I nodded in agreement.

"Okay, now that we have that settled. Why did you buy my aunt's storage unit?"

"Well, because—"

"No, for real. No making up stuff," she said with a strong tap on the glass table. "What do you have in that unit that you wanted back so badly? Hmmm?"

"Nothing," I answered truthfully.

Noah laughed. "That can't possibly be true. You have something in there. Something Esme had against you. Didn't you? Something tying you to all this."

They didn't believe that I didn't have anything. That could only mean one thing. They still didn't know who Esme had been blackmailing. "You don't have the ledger yet, do you?"

Susannah's face stretched. "What do you know about the ledger?"

"It's the book that ties everything in that unit together. It connects each box in the unit to a specific person that Esme had worked out an arrangement with." I didn't want to say the word 'blackmail' to her niece. Especially when I didn't know if they had taken over the family business. "I'm guessing you haven't found it yet?"

Susannah pulled a book from a bag on the floor beside her. "Actually, we did. Here it is." She put the book on the table and opened it to a random page.

"I'm surprised you're showing this to me," I said.

"We don't know what any of this means. It's all random numbers and letters. I can't figure it out. We're hoping you can help us."

"Help you?" My voice struck a high note.

Susannah nodded. Noah came behind her and put his hands on her shoulders. She sighed. "My aunt did some bad things. Very bad things. We're trying to figure out who all she has hurt."

"You're not trying to blackmail people?" My hands flew to my mouth, not having meant to blurt that out.

"Blackmail people? No, not at all," she said.

"We want to clean up Aunt Esme's messes, not make more," Noah said. Susannah looked up at him with a grateful smile.

"Wait, so…" My brain hurt like an ice cream headache. I had thought the two of them were out to possibly hurt people, but instead, it seemed I had them all wrong. "Do you know where Esme is?"

"She's in a nursing home. Memory care unit," Susannah explained.

"Her memory really went downhill. First slowly, but then rapidly. It's getting worse," Noah added.

"She didn't want us to tell anyone, so we've been keeping it a secret. I don't think she necessarily understands anymore, but she deserves her dignity."

"What about the police? Why haven't you told them where she's been?" I asked.

Susannah looked up at Noah again. He shrugged. "I guess we wanted to get a better sense of how deep into everything she was. We thought we could fix it all first," he said. "But it was far messier than we ever expected."

"Aunt Esme had begun forgetting and messing things up. She inadvertently began revealing secrets. It put her in danger."

Not to mention all the people she had blackmailed.

"We realized too late. Way too late." Susannah's eyes watered. "Her gardens became overgrown, her bills piled up, and I just wish I had realized sooner."

"Her bills," I repeated. "So that's why she lost the storage unit." I remembered what Nuri had said about checking her mail.

The two of them nodded in unison.

"And why the electricity was out at her house?" I knew the answer already from Nuri, but I wanted to confirm.

"How did you know that?" Noah asked.

I gulped. I hadn't meant to play my hand. But it was too late now. "I saw you there with flashlights. When I was trying to figure out whose unit I had bought."

Noah's shoulder slumped. "We didn't want her going to jail."

"She wouldn't survive there," Susannah said. "My aunt did some awful things, but what's happening to her now…it's not pretty. I hope others will accept it as justice."

"How did she learn all these people's secrets? She seemed to learn things no one else knew," I asked.

Susannah laughed dryly. "We're cleaners. Background people. No one paid attention to us. They are always blabbing about things they shouldn't."

"Esme used that intel to her advantage," Noah added.

That made sense. How many times had I seen Victory Cleaners come up recently? They had been everywhere. And even where they weren't, they likely heard gossip about those places.

"So why didn't you keep going at the auction?" I asked. "You let me win."

It was Noah's turn to laugh. "I would have. I would have spent every penny I had. But Susannah talked me out of it. She saw how much the cost had run up. She figured you were someone her aunt had hurt. We hoped we would be able to figure out your story and work out from there how to take care of things."

"Which is why you offered me the house?" I asked.

"You offered her a house?" Susannah repeated in shock.

"I wasn't really going to do that," he mumbled.

"And I wasn't really going to accept it either," I added. "It sounds like we were essentially investigating each other."

"Yeah, pretty much," Noah agreed.

"So, tell me, why were you arguing with Olivia Grover at Marcus's vigil?" I asked Noah.

He rolled his lips. "I didn't need a ledger to tell me that Olivia has been drinking too much. I told her that she needed to get help. She pushed back, saying she was fine. But unfortunately, she's not."

"I hope she gets help too," I said.

I took in a deep breath. It was time to ask the truly difficult question.

"What about Marcus?" I asked quietly.

Susannah's tears started in earnest. "I don't know how Marc ended up in there. Aunt Esme adored him. She never ever would have killed him."

"She couldn't have. She's been in the nursing unit. She wouldn't have the strength or mind to do it," Noah added.

"But she knew something about him, didn't she?" I asked, not wanting to give up the forgery ring to them. What if they didn't know about it? I'd hate to put Nuri in danger like that.

"She had to have. But I don't know the details since I can't crack this ledger code." She hit the ledger with her fist. The table reverberated, but the glass remained intact.

Noah massaged her upper arms. She put a hand on one of his to stop him, but it was a kind gesture. He nodded in understanding.

"I don't want her going to jail. She's in such poor health. We figured we could end her schemes. Let her pass with dignity."

"Ah, so all the different rumors about where she had gone…"

Susannah nodded. "We spread those."

"The cruise, silent retreat, a cousin, rehab…" I counted on my fingers, trying to remember them all. I was pretty sure I'd forgotten a few.

"Rehab? We didn't say that one. But yes, we told different things to different people. It didn't take long for the rumors to catch on like wildfire."

"My turn to ask a question," Noah interjected.

"Anything you want," I replied.

"You know our story, but you claim not to have been impacted by Esme. So how did you know about the storage unit?" he asked.

"Oh." I sucked on my bottom lip. "A friend wanted it. And I wanted to help my friend." I shrugged. "But my friend is scared now. Esme knew their secret. And with Marcus dead and Betsy missing and Esme having seemingly vanished…"

"Wait, what does Betsy have to do with anything?" Susannah asked. "That was a long time ago."

"I don't know, but it was enough to have scared them."

"We're sorry," Susannah said. "We didn't want anyone to be scared. Like I said, we simply wanted to clean up my aunt's messes."

I nodded. I hoped that when the ledger was decoded, we'd figure everything out somehow. Maybe find out why Nana Z's paintings were in there? The idea that she had a secret sat like a heavy weight at the bottom of my stomach. Thank goodness her mind stayed sharp until the end, but if things had been different, I would have done anything in the world to help her. I understood where Susannah and Noah were coming from.

I got up to leave. Neither of them tried to stop me.

"The offer still stands, you know," Noah said.

"The house?" I was shocked.

"Well, no, I can't actually give you a house. But if you ever want to buy a place, I'd be happy to help you out."

I smiled. Ever the realtor. "Thank you. But if you want to help me, go to the police."

He and Susannah shared a look. "Yeah, we know. We held off too long. We will."

# Chapter Thirty-Four

Being near the storage unit facility, I decided to stop by the Chessie U-Store before heading home. Maybe I could find something else out? Or finally figure out how to navigate that maze of a campus? Not that I had much luck. When walking through the building, I couldn't determine if I was on the correct floor. Everything was so dark, and the mildew odor was so strong that I quickly got disoriented. Where was I heading anyway? What did I think I would find? This had been a bad idea. I decided to turn around and head home.

Suddenly, there were hands on me, pushing me from behind. I stumbled into an open unit, falling to the cold, concrete floor. I scraped my knees and palms, but at least I didn't hit my head. Still, by the time I turned to see who had pushed me, the door swung shut. I was trapped inside.

I pounded on the door, but no one responded. Worse, I heard a sound. A code being punched in. But it wasn't opening my door. I was locked inside.

Digging my phone out of my pocket, I tried calling 911, but there was no reception in this dark closet. Text messages remained stuck in my outbox.

"Let me out! Let me out!" I yelled over and over again, but instead of responding, I heard footsteps clattering away down the hallway. The culprit had run away. Who were they? Why had they locked me in here?

Panic set in. I tried jumping out, although there were no windows, and the ceiling was high. All I did was add to the bumps and bruises on my arms and legs.

I shoved my body at the door like in the movies, but nothing. I ran backwards and flung myself at it, but all I got for my efforts was a jolt of pain surging through my system.

In the darkness, I felt around the floor and walls, but my efforts proved futile. Nothing there. With the darkness, I couldn't tell if I missed anything, so I tried several more times, but only found dust.

What was I going to do? Yelling didn't work. Kicking and pushing failed. My body hurt. I slumped down to the cold, hard ground. After a few minutes, the panic subsided.

Stuck in here, I had time to think about everything that had transpired. Especially my conversation with Susannah and Noah. And Olivia earlier. I wanted to believe I was a good judge of character. And as much as I wanted to know who had killed Marcus, I didn't think it was any of the three of them. It certainly wasn't Esme.

So who had killed Marcus? Had he been pushed into a unit like I had? Was I going to be found dead? My stomach lurched at the thought. Then it growled loudly because, of course, I was hungry now. I tried ignoring it and focusing instead on my list of suspects. Who was even left to consider?

A thought trickled into my head. It didn't make much sense, but then again, neither did much of anything else right now. But what if it was true? I tried to calm my nerves and focus on thinking through the puzzle.

A flash of inspiration hit me. I knew why I recognized the faces in the old 1960s ad for the Chessie U-Store. And why the photo of Marcus, Betsy, and Esme at the opening of the gallery of the Rose Mallow Artist's Guild had given me prickles up and down my skin.

Of course. It all made sense now.

I knew who had murdered Marcus.

"Juniper! Juniper!"

"I'm in here," I shouted as loudly as I could muster.

"She's there." Someone pounded on my unit. I pounded back.

"We found her. Thank goodness."

The door creaked open. Nuri and Luna stood with Gary and Gladys. I rushed out of the dark, cold room to where my friends waited with open arms. We hugged and cried while I got my bearings back. All in all, I had been in that room for less than an hour, but the dark solitude had been torturous. At least I now knew what had happened.

"How did you find me?" I asked.

Luna held up her phone. "I got your messages about seeing Olivia and then Noah and Susannah. You sounded scared, so when we couldn't reach you, we drove after you. Olivia's studio was closed, so we went to the development, but they told us how you'd already left a while ago. Then Nuri noticed how close we were to the Chessie U-Store. She knew you wouldn't turn up an opportunity to investigate further."

"I said 'research,' actually," Nuri explained. We laughed. "But you weren't at the unit you bought. Or your sister's one. So we went to the office."

"I pulled up the camera footage to find you," Gary said, sounding proud.

Gladys shook her head. "You did no such thing. You know how he is. He wouldn't let these ladies anywhere near the footage."

"Until I threatened an expose in *The Chesapeake Chronicle*," Luna said.

"And then he changed his tune," Nuri added.

"Well, we found you. That's what's important," Gary muttered.

"How did you locate me?" I asked. "Did you see who locked me in here?"

The ladies shook their heads. "We saw you coming in. No problems there," Gladys said.

"And we could see that you were pushed in there," said Nuri, pointing to my temporary jail.

"But whoever did it kept out of sight of the camera," Luna finished off.

I nodded my head, not surprised anymore. "They knew where the cameras were and how to stay out of frame." I tapped my chin. "Is Lizzy here today?"

"The new employee?" Gary asked.

"Yes, she should be here somewhere," I replied.

"I can never reach her," Gladys replied with a shake of her head.

"But she does her job well," Gary added.

Gladys made a face. "How would you know?"

"Well, because…I…uh…" He scratched the stubble on his chin. Then he shrugged. Gladys rolled her eyes at her brother. He obviously had no clue.

"Do you have a picture of her?" I asked. "One without her hat and sunglasses preferably."

"Why?" Gary asked.

"In the personnel files," Gladys said to me, ignoring him.

I turned to Nuri. "Go with Gladys. I want you to look at that picture. Really study it."

"But why do you want me looking at a picture of some employee named Lizzy?" Nuri asked.

"If I'm right, you'll recognize her. Or at least if you imagine her with dark gray hair."

# Chapter Thirty-Five

I switched to face Luna. "I need you to call the police."

"Wait, are you going somewhere?" she asked.

"I'm going to find Lizzy."

"Not by yourself, you're not. Not if you think she pushed you in there!"

"Luna, go with Nuri. If I'm right, then she needs more protection than I do." There was a small part of me that wanted to stop and ask her about the grants information, but that would have to wait. We could go over the details once everyone was safe.

"Then, Gary, you take the girls. I'll go with Juniper here," Gladys said. "You think you can figure out where the personnel files are?"

He grumbled but nodded. Nuri and Luna followed him down the hallway.

"Thanks for coming with me," I said to Gladys.

"Sure thing, kiddo. I've worked here the longest and know this place like the back of my hand. Well, assuming you don't look too close at my manicure. Time for an update." She held up her leopard print purple and gold nails. They appeared spotless to me. I liked Gladys' retro style, although I suspect it wasn't so much retro for her as having never left the 80s.

"How long have you worked here?" I asked.

She counted her nails. "Ten years we've owned the place. Give or take."

"Did you buy it from Johnny O'Henry?" I asked.

She stopped. "Where did you hear that name?"

"Wasn't this originally his place?"

"Whoo. That's going back. No. I mean, yes, he did start this place. Way back in the 1960s. But no, we bought it from someone else. He was long gone before we got involved," Gladys replied.

She had confirmed my thinking. The ads I'd seen in the bound copies of the newspaper had been of Johnny O'Henry and his family back in the 1960s. After he and Dor divorced, he must have remarried and had a kid, just like she had said. What she hadn't mentioned was his constructing this place. Still, the pieces were falling into place.

"So, where are we going?" she asked.

"To the grated door," I said.

"Why there?"

However, before I could answer, all the lights shut off. Gladys shrieked in surprise. "Oh, no, no, no. I hate the dark. Absolutely hate it. Get me out of here."

"It's going to be okay." I put a hand out in the darkness and touched her upper arm. I turned on the flashlight on my cell phone. "See?"

"That's not much. And the auxiliaries aren't even coming on. Why is it so dark? Did the power go out?"

"If you hate the dark, why work in such a cavernous place?" I asked.

"Because the lights normally go on automatically. And there are the backup lights. But why aren't they working?" Her voice rose in fear.

"Hey, stay with me. Take my hand. You said you've worked here for over a decade. Tap into that muscle memory," I said, using my phone flashlight to find her again. She gripped my hand fiercely, and we walked onward.

We made seemingly random turns, but I followed Gladys, lighting our path with my cell phone's tiny light. We ended up by the elevators, but perhaps not surprisingly, they weren't working. Instead, we had to use my little flashlight and feel our way through the darkness to the stairwell. It was colder and damper than the main hallways. We held tightly to the handrails as we descended. How many levels did this place go down?

"Tell me about the history of the facility," I said, hoping to keep Gladys distracted.

"Back in the 60s, it became a storage unit facility. Early pioneer. You know, I heard that the owners originally built this as a fallout shelter when everyone was worried about Cuba and Russia and the missile crisis."

"That was Johnny O'Henry?"

"Yep, exactly."

This wasn't surprising. From what I remembered of Dor describing her former husband, he had sounded paranoid, which was probably exacerbated by the Cold War crisis. Unfortunately, it sounded like his daughter inherited his tendencies.

"Does that fallout shelter still exist?" I asked.

"Maybe. It'd be down in the sub-basement."

"I thought you knew this place like the back of your hand."

"Well, the above-ground parts, yes. But not the tunnels."

"Tunnels?" Did she say tunnels?

"It was an emergency shelter, but Johnny expanded it in several ways to keep his family safe down here. At least, that's my understanding. I've never seen that part," Gladys answered.

Oh boy. Johnny's concerns were even worse than I had realized. It sounded like he had constructed his own personal subterranean fortress down here. I hoped I hadn't made a mistake.

We exited the stairwell onto the first floor and headed back into the building. She took me down the hallway to the grated door. Then she stopped. "I'm not going any further."

"Gladys, I need you. I don't want to get lost back there."

"I'm going back to the office. I'm going to get help."

"How about we simply wait here?" I asked, hoping I could convince her to change her mind. But she was resolute.

"No, I'm not staying here. I'm going back."

"That would have been a smart move, Gladys." A voice spoke behind us.

"Who said that?"

I turned my phone flashlight around in the darkness. It was Lizzy. Except she wasn't Lizzy. She'd taken off the sunglasses, hat, and even the blonde wig. Her long hair was graying but still dark, falling well past her shoulders. She flicked on a camping lamp, which illuminated her face, revealing an evil smile. And a gun in her other hand.

"Betsy, leave her alone," I warned.

"Betsy? Who's Betsy?" Gladys asked. "That's Lizzy."

"Betsy Howard. Marcus Howard's missing wife. But she was born Elizabeth O'Henry, daughter of Johnny," I explained.

"Well, now, that's impressive. How did you figure all that out?" Lizzy said. No, not Lizzy. She was Betsy.

"I did the research. I found pictures of you from before you disappeared. But not just pictures of you. Also, the ads your family ran in the newspaper for the Chessie U-Store, starting back in the 1960s."

"But I was just a little girl then," she said.

"You look so much like your mother," I said.

She shrugged. "Well, she wasn't a natural blonde either. Box bleacher. She hated being a brunette. Was so upset that I turned out to be too."

"Sounds like neither of your parents treated you well." I hoped to keep her talking. Maybe we could stall long enough to figure out a solution.

Her evil grin soured. "At least my mother stayed. Unlike my father. I never thought he'd abandon this place, though. It was his real baby. But I guess he wanted to go even more off-grid. Somewhere where not even his family could find him. But how did you find all that?"

"I'm a librarian."

Betsy laughed. "A librarian. Like Nuri Cho was going to be?"

I nodded. "Exactly like Nuri."

"Hmmph. Okay, let's get moving," she said, motioning us to the door with her gun.

"Please, don't hurt us," Gladys said. "I'm scared."

Betsy rolled her eyes. "I only need one of you as a hostage. Two of you is too much. You, troublemaker, come with me." She waved her gun at me.

"Don't hurt her," Gladys pleaded.

"Gladys, it's going to be okay. I'll be fine." I hoped I was telling her the truth.

"Shush. Both of you. You," Betsy waved the gun at Gladys. "Stay put. Or I will very much hurt the librarian."

Gladys's eyes widened. "Of course. I won't go anywhere."

"Don't tell anyone anything."

I took it as a good sign that Betsy hadn't hurt Gladys. Yet at least. I wanted to believe that her threats were idle, but I also knew she could kill. No one was safe.

We entered through the old door and went down another set of stairs, using her lamp and my cell phone flashlight to shine the way. Not surprisingly, I didn't get any reception all the way down here. I guess that's why she didn't bother to take my phone.

As we descended, I hoped that Gladys hadn't been too scared to run away. And tell someone where we were and what was happening.

"Thank you for not hurting Gladys," I said.

"Psh. It wouldn't have mattered. She doesn't ever come in these tunnels. Such a scaredy cat. She'll never find us," Betsy replied with arrogance.

I gulped, hoping that she couldn't hear me.

"What's your name again, librarian?"

"Juniper."

"Okay, Juniper, keep going. Over there. We'll enter the tunnels there." She pointed to another door, which opened with a thud. Inside was the entrance to a large tunnel. Not huge, but there was enough space for us both to walk through. It wasn't all cleanly cut or polished like the other walls, but still reflected the jaggy, rocky ground we were exploring. The walls of the tunnel had been spackled various times, creating a strange, not quite smooth texture.

"Why did you pull Nuri into your operation with Marcus?" I asked, hoping to keep her talking, as we moved inside. The tunnel floor dropped, deeper and deeper.

"Aren't you the curious one?" she asked.

"I'm a librarian. Of course I'm curious," I said.

She laughed, apparently amused. "Nuri had your same sense of humor. I always liked her. She was very good at her work."

"That's why you used her?" I asked.

"Used her? No, we gave her the opportunity of a lifetime. Marc's hands were giving way from arthritis. He couldn't do the detailed work he used to be able to do for our forgeries. So, we needed someone young but also well-versed in historical documents. Plus, they had to be artistic. Nuri met all the requirements."

"You took advantage of a young woman in need," I said.

Betsy scoffed. "She was an adult. She could make her own decisions. She certainly didn't seem to mind the money we made."

"You know the tunnels well?" I changed tactics.

"I should. My father built this place." She occasionally told me to make a turn, as the tunnels branched multiple times. That made my heart drop, worried that we'd get truly lost down here.

"How big is this place?"

"Enormous. My father taught us to be ready for anything. Invasions, government coups, anarchy. We were always prepared," Betsy answered.

"Is this where you've been hiding all this time?" I asked.

She laughed bitterly. "Hah. I wish. No, I was somewhere much, much smaller. In prison overseas."

"In England?" I asked.

She laughed again, which somehow sounded even worse. "Is that what Marc told everyone?" She sighed dramatically. "No, I had gone to many countries on his behalf, picking up goods fenced for us. But Marc didn't do his job well. I got caught. And imprisoned. Where my darling husband promptly abandoned me."

"He never came to get you?" I asked.

"Never. I spent years in prison in a country few people have even heard of. Instead, when I was finally released, I discovered how he'd told people I'd vanished. Even that I'd died."

"How heartbreaking."

"Exactly. Turn here." We moved into yet another branch. She hadn't been wrong when she said this place was enormous. "Not only that, but he'd started taking up with Esme Vienna." Betsy spat the name. "The same witch who tried blackmailing us. And how he was courting her."

# Chapter Thirty-Six

We entered a small, nearly circular underground room. No windows. Betsy put the lamp on the wooden table in the middle and flicked on other lamps around the edges, creating a strangely warm glow to the subterranean lair. It was like a time capsule or a museum display. Around the edges were bookcases filled with books and low cabinets, including some ominously marked with skull and crossbones. We stood atop a small woven rug worn with time and dust, and to one side stood a makeshift kitchen with a bucket sink, cabinets, and a hot plate.

A faded photograph of a family hung on the wall. Looked like it was taken in the 70s or 80s; the photo featured a man and woman with a young girl. Sure enough, it was Johnny O'Henry. Did Betsy have any idea that her father had been previously married to Dor Calverton? Or that the Calvertons were her family?

But there were other questions to focus on first.

"So you stopped things between Marcus and Esme?" I asked.

Lizzy shook her head and rolled her eyes. "I didn't need to bother. It was clear that Esme wasn't doing well." She tapped her head with one hand but kept the gun trained on me with the other. "I found out she's now in some old ladies' home. So I don't need to worry about her."

"But Marcus was another issue?"

She scrunched up her face. "I got a job here to hide out right under his nose."

"Claiming to be Lizzy," I pointed out.

She scrunched her face. "Lizzy is just a nickname for Elizabeth. So is Betsy.

Are you slow? Did you not know that?"

I didn't respond, but she continued on, "My father called me Lizzy. Mother called me Betsy. They could never agree on anything. Except that neither ever called me Elizabeth." She laughed at her joke.

"You knew that Marcus would come here?" I asked.

"Well, of course. I found out that Esme had a unit here, so it wasn't hard to lure Marc to it. Just pretended to be Esme in my note." She wiggled her eyebrows.

"You know where every camera is."

"Of course. I know everything about this place. Every nook and cranny." She looked smug.

"You killed him there," I said quietly.

Her face lit up. "It was easy. A well-placed thwack with a metal pipe from my father's collection of materials to build this place."

"What if he had survived that? You left him locked in the unit." I was aghast.

Betsy was unmoved. "Don't worry. I gave him a little injection to ensure he didn't last long."

"You poisoned him, too?"

"Father kept many things down here in case of emergency. Including a few vials of poison. Quick death when the enemy invaded. Even had the syringes at the ready." She waved the gun towards a series of cabinets with a skull and crossbones painted on top. I briefly wondered if poison degraded over decades, but it wasn't something I wanted to find out firsthand. Then she put down the gun on top of them to open the cabinets up. "He was ready for anything and everything."

She was obviously proud to show off his display of medicinal-looking bottles, filled with various powdery substances. Betsy picked through them and pulled out one short, squat bottle. I couldn't make out its label in the dim light.

She opened the other cabinet, which contained a variety of supplies: gauze, scissors, hot pads, and syringes. She brought one out and held it up.

"You know, Juniper, I don't actually need you to be alive to be a hostage.

I just need anyone out there to think you are." The camp lights flickered in her eyes, while the shadows danced across her face. So that's why she hadn't cared about whether Gladys had run away or not. She didn't think it mattered. That either of us did.

"I thought you said we were kindred. How we both loved books and objects." I backed away from her, edging to the other side of the room, since she was near the doorway.

"Oh, Juniper. Who knows? We might be. But I'm not going to wait to see if you disappoint me, too," she replied. "You won't be allowed to abandon me."

I picked up my pace, now running from her, trying to keep as much space as possible between us.

"There's nowhere to go, Juniper," Betsy said in a sing-song voice.

I didn't look back but kept running around, trying not to smash into the room's oddly shaped walls or uneven ceiling, which dropped precipitously in places. I headed towards the bookshelf. Books had always been my superpower. Maybe they could help me again?

"This is the end of the line," she continued in the same creepy voice.

Betsy lunged at me with the needle. I darted out of the way, just in time for her to crash into the bookshelf. A series of old hardbacks fell atop her.

"Yes," I said while making my way to the door. I didn't bother looking to see if she was okay or if she had recovered. There wasn't time. I needed to escape.

I raced through the tunnels, trying desperately to remember the circuitous route we had taken. People have called me "Encyclopedia Blume" for my strong memory, but sadly, it wasn't eidetic. I wish I possessed the so-called "photographic memory" right now, though.

But more than anything, I kept running, unsure of how far ahead of Betsy I'd gotten. What if the tunnels fed into each other, and I ended up back where I started? I couldn't think of that now. Nor could I consider getting stuck down here for eternity. Right? I shook my head and instead focused on the pain in my legs building, and how hard I was breathing. My chest felt like it would explode. If I ever got out of here, I knew one New Year's resolution would be to increase my exercise. I could use endurance training.

The tunnels branched, and I chose without thinking. If one looked dark, I headed away, hoping to stay in the light.

There were sometimes doors that I didn't remember seeing before, although maybe they had been there. I tried them a few times, but each was locked.

I switched directions, ending up in a tunnel so narrow that I needed to crawl. Was Betsy going to catch me? Would she find me? We hadn't gone through these before. I turned around and headed back, hoping against hope that I'd find my way home.

* * *

I wasn't sure how long I'd been trying to escape. Eventually, I heard voices. Footsteps. Betsy must have caught up to me. But even with all my adrenaline, I couldn't keep going. My body felt like it was going to burst. I looked for somewhere to hide, but there was nothing. It was just tunnel everywhere. I'd never been claustrophobic before, but in the moment, I felt the walls would cave in at any time.

I turned again, falling right into her.

Wait, no, it wasn't Betsy.

"Juniper! I have Juniper!"

"Leo!"

I grabbed him so tightly, I heard him struggle to breathe. He didn't complain. Instead, he held me back. Then I loosened my grip and looked up at him to say, "It's Betsy. Lizzy is Betsy Howard." I struggled to get my words in order. "She's after me."

He nodded. "We've got her."

From behind him in the tunnel came more people. Including Dor Calverton. What was she doing down here? I released Leo and went over to hug her.

"How did you find me?" I asked them both.

"I got your messages and connected with your friends," he said.

"When Leo told me what was happening and where you were, I wondered if you had ended up down in these caves," Dor said.

"How did you know about them?" I asked. "Weren't you and Johnny divorced?"

She put a hand to my cheek and smoothed it. Her touch reminded me of Nana Z. "I told you that Johnny had odd thoughts. He believed the government was out to get us. He wanted me to move down into his grand plan with him, but I wouldn't have it. But to get him off my back, I helped fund this shelter. Part of the settlement."

"Grandma found the blueprints in our papers," Leo said.

"Family archives for the win," I replied.

"Building these was such a headache. Especially dealing with the water tables around here. I'm amazed they didn't flood years ago," she said, sounding impressed.

Behind them was a medic, who came to check on me. Besides my heart rate beating through the roof and a few scrapes, I was in good shape physically. As he tended to me, Detective Lakshmi Gupta and Deputy John Torres appeared. It had become quite crowded in the tunnels.

"You caught her?" I asked.

"We caught her," the detective responded with a confident smile. "How are you doing?"

"I've been worse."

She laughed. "Let's get you out of here. Then you can catch me up on everything. And I mean everything, Juniper." She wagged a finger at me. I gulped, realizing that she must have figured out how much I had yet to divulge. Had she spoken to Nuri already?

We wound our way through the tunnels, finally returning to the stairs leading up to the sub-basement and the grated door. On the ground floor, Gladys and Gary waited for me, alongside Nuri and Luna.

After many hugs and reassurances that I was okay, Nuri said, "You were right, Juniper. I recognized Betsy as soon as I saw the photo."

"And we called the police immediately," Gladys added.

Nuri took my hands in hers. "Does this mean it's over?"

Tears formed in my eyes. "Yes, Nuri. It's over. Betsy had been overseas in prison for crimes related to her and Marcus's forgery ring. When he abandoned her there, she grew angry and despondent." I knew that Detective Gupta needed to know about Nuri's involvement, but I didn't need to reveal that at this moment. Besides, watching the two exchange glances, I realized they must have already started talking.

"When Betsy returned," I continued, "She found he had actually taken up with Esme Vienna, even though she had been the one to blackmail them in the first place."

"Did you find out where Esme is?" Luna asked.

I nodded. "She's not doing well, but she's safe. Her memory has gone, so she's in a nursing home now. Betsy seemed to recognize that she wasn't a threat anymore, but she was still angry at Marcus, so she lured him to the unit and killed him with some poison her family had stored down here decades ago."

"What is this place?" Nuri asked.

"Emergency shelter slash off-the-grid underground compound. Betsy's family had it constructed because they believed the world was out to get them."

"That is one extensive set of tunnels," Deputy Torres said.

"That's my fault," Dor replied. "I helped fund them. I had no idea that it would be used to hurt people, though."

"It was decades ago," I told her. "I don't think that was Johnny's intent."

She nodded in agreement. Leo put an arm around his grandmother's shoulders.

"What about Esme's blackmailing? Was her niece going to take it over?" Luna asked.

I shook my head. "No, Susannah and Noah discovered what her aunt had been up to after she went into memory care. They've been trying to figure out what all happened so they could undo everything. They wanted to stop the blackmail."

Nuri sighed. "So that's why he was bidding so high at the auction. I wish I had known."

"How could you have? None of us knew. I don't think even Noah and Susannah realized how complicated Esme's plans were," I said.

Now it was my turn for questions. I turned to Detective Gupta and asked, "Can we return all the materials in Esme's storage unit to the people she took them from?"

"It's your storage unit. So once everything is cleared, you'll be able to do with what you wish," she replied.

"I'll reach out to Noah and Susannah and work with them on it," I promised. "But what will happen to the people Esme hurt otherwise?"

The detective made a face. "It depends. I guess they can look into filing claims, but that's beyond my pay grade to know the details of what people will or should do. But we can still help them if they seek support. I can direct them to others who know more."

"That sounds promising," I said. "Thank you."

# Chapter Thirty-Seven

Finally, Friday had arrived along with Rosh Hashanah dinner. I spent the morning heading up to the airport to pick up my parents, who finally arrived after nearly a week of delays and changes. Miraculously, their luggage and instruments arrived as well, including my father's prized clarinet, which had been in our family for generations. According to Nana Z, her father had managed to bring it from Ukraine when he immigrated to America during the Great Migration at the beginning of the twentieth century.

"Juniper, darling, it's so good to see you," my mother Iris said, squeezing me tight. Yes, even though she wasn't born a Blume, she also had the requisite floral name. I had a feeling it was a requirement for marrying into the family.

"We heard you had quite the week," my father, Asher, added, with a pat on my shoulder. His name was a tribute to both the Ash tree and one of the Twelve Tribes of Israel. "Even more chaotic than ours."

"Oh, honey, are you doing okay?" Mom asked.

"Much better now that you're both here," I said truthfully. We piled into Azalea's minivan and headed back down to Rose Mallow. As we drove, I updated them on everything that happened with Esme Vienna.

"Wait, I'm confused," Mom said. "Is Nuri in trouble or not?"

"And what about that photographer, Olivia Something or Another?" my dad asked.

"Yes, they are. But Nuri's talking to a lawyer who thinks it's going to be okay, especially if she agrees to testify against Betsy. Hopefully, she'll face probation, especially since she hasn't done anything else. As for Olivia, that's up to the police and courts to determine, but they're aware of her hit and run," I explained. "I don't think she'll get off quite so easily." We hit traffic on Route 2 going south, so there was more time to explain. But also to ask questions back.

"How is the tour going, Mom and Dad?"

"Great, really. A few bumps this week, but nothing we can't handle," Dad said.

"Bumps? More like a few mountains," my mom replied with a laugh. My dad grabbed her hand tightly. It was beautiful to see how much in love they were, even after all these years. I hoped that Leo and I would enjoy the same joy over the years. "The band sounds amazing. Oh, hon, did you bring the CD?"

"CD? Does this minivan even have a CD player?" I asked. My car was too old for one, and I wasn't sure if modern ones still had them. Honestly, I couldn't remember the last time I'd purchased a CD.

"Right here," my dad responded. He found the slot and plopped in their latest album. The first song opened with a long, high-pitched note from my dad's clarinet. It almost sounded like a funeral wail before shifting into something surprisingly jubilant and alive. I loved every note performed.

* * *

As we pulled up at The Wildflower Inn, other friends had already begun arriving. Leo waved from the porch, where he played with Violet and Clover, while chatting with Rory. Aunt Harmony walked over from the boardwalk behind the house, carrying a salad from the Purple Oyster. Desiree drove up with her little sister Keisha, jumping out of the car behind us to race over to the house. They were followed by Nuri and Luna, who parked right behind their car.

I couldn't help noticing Nuri and Desiree sharing a few glances and blushes. Was there something between the two of them? I looked forward to asking Nuri about it later. Really, I looked forward to talking to her about anything besides this week, although I hoped she knew she could trust me if anything strange happened ever again. And I hoped she knew I would trust her implicitly.

Azalea opened the doors wide and called out, "I know it's a beautiful October day, but you should see how gorgeous this meal is."

Everyone clamored to get inside, rushing to find seats at the dining room table. We all oohed and ahhed after my sister's culinary masterpieces. She had brought all the dishes I had taste-tested, but there were several more surprises in store. No one would be going hungry here tonight, for which we were all grateful.

As we sat down to the meal, I tapped my knife against my glass, getting everyone's attention. Standing up, I said, "Thank you all for joining us at this special meal. Congratulations to Azalea for a stunning array of delicious options." I paused as everyone clapped, hooted, and whistled in appreciation. "As many of you know, tonight heralds a new year in the Jewish calendar, which is why we call it Rosh Hashanah, or Head of the Year. It's a time to be together, reflect on the year past, and hope for a better future ahead. I couldn't imagine—"

Before I could continue my speech, there was a knock on the door. I looked at Azalea, but she shook her head, as everyone invited had arrived. Putting down my glass, I walked out to the foyer and opened the front door to discover Detective Gupta and Deputy Torres waiting outside.

"Is everything okay?" I asked.

To my shock, Detective Gupta erupted in a large smile. "I brought an apple pie." She held up the aluminum-foiled offering. "And John here…"

"Well, I know apples are traditional, but I hope you won't mind sweet potato pie instead."

I hadn't expected either of them, but not wanting to be a rude host, I welcomed them into the inn warmly. We'd have to find more chairs, but it's not like we were hurting for food. "These look great. Thank you so much."

Expressions ranged when they entered. My sister looked briefly concerned before putting on her hosting game face and finding more plates and silverware. Leo helped adjust the seating so we could make room.

Rory followed his wife, appearing worried at the sight of Deputy John

Torres, although Azalea had assured me that she had chosen her husband one hundred percent. To each man's credit, the deputy greeted Rory cordially, and they shook hands. When Azalea put her arm around her husband's waist, Deputy Torres didn't blink, only smiled politely. If there had been a romantic triangle once in the works, it appeared to be firmly over.

"Did you forget you invited us?" Detective Gupta whispered to me.

"Uhm, I guess so," I said honestly.

She laughed. "We're happy to simply pop by and say hello."

"No, no, please stay. We've got enough room and food. So much food. We could feed a small army. The more the merrier, Detective," I said.

"Juniper, please. We're not on a case. Call me Lakshmi."

I nodded. "Sure thing, Lakshmi." Boy, that felt weird to only use her first name. It was like calling an elementary school teacher by their first name.

Soon, we were all digging into the incredible meal that Azalea had made. For once, words failed me to aptly describe how delicious each dish was. Then I noticed there was a strange quiet that had descended across the dinner table. Looking up from my plate, I realized that the quiet wasn't because anything unusual had suddenly occurred but because everyone else was also absolutely absorbed in their meals. I looked down the table to see Azalea with her hand over her heart, smiling so brightly she might start crying. We locked eyes, and I gave her a firm nod. Somehow, her smile grew even stronger.

Nana Z would have been so proud of her. I was honored to have her as my sister.

# Chapter Thirty-Eight

After eating, I helped Azalea with cleaning up. A few others joined me, and while I told most of them to go relax, Luna refused, so I gave in and let her give me a hand.

"Juniper, wasn't there something else you wanted to ask me?" Luna asked after I came back into the dining room. I knew that Azalea would want to set up coffee and tea for dessert soon. Luna joined me as I went into the kitchen to help prepare the hot water for tea. She worked on readying the coffee.

"A couple things actually…"

"Like what?" she asked. She dumped a bunch of coffee beans into a grinder. The grinding was loud but quick. Thank goodness she was handling it. As someone who didn't enjoy coffee, you never wanted me preparing it.

"Well, first, did you ever find out why your dad's comic book was in Esme's unit?" I asked.

She nodded with a sad face. "Apparently, he was one of her first victims."

"Oh no!"

Luna crossed her arms. "The newspaper hasn't always been easy to keep up. Subscriptions and ad revenue have been down for a long time. Like pretty much everywhere. You already know that I'm the only staff person left." Her face clouded. "Some time ago, Esme offered him a loan."

"And took the book as collateral?"

"That one comic book is probably worth more than the rest of the unit combined," Luna replied. I remembered what Torres had said about it being worth nearly a million dollars. She might be right.

"Did she…" How could I ask this question?

"Did Esme have something on my dad?" Luna filled in my gaps. "No, she didn't. Like I said, he was an early victim. That must have been before she realized she needed blackmail fodder."

"So why didn't you get the comic book back?" I asked.

"My dad died, and I didn't know anything about the loan. Esme tried asking me a few times, but I told her to get in line with everyone else who wanted to get paid. There was a lot to figure out with the estate. I didn't know that she had the book either. She must have realized that and then left me alone."

Wheels turned in my head. "You think she knew how valuable it was?"

"Undoubtedly. She probably realized she could make more money from selling it than she could bugging me and a struggling newspaper. That's why I am excited about the grant."

"Yes, about the grant. That was the other thing I wanted to talk to you about." I looked around. I needed to discuss this with Leo, but I hadn't had a chance to catch up with him yet. Still, Luna was on the committee, so I was curious what she thought.

"What about it?"

"Did you see the footnote on page…what was it? Thirty-four?"

"Can't say that I did." She shrugged before resuming her coffee prepping duties.

"I took a picture of it." I pulled out my phone and scrolled through the gallery.

"You took a picture of something in our folders?" she asked, sounding uncertain.

I nodded and held it up. "Read this." I had made the image as large as I could and turned it to landscape mode.

"In return for receiving a grant from the Calverton Foundation, the recipient agrees to give…" Her voice stopped. "To give Calverton Incorporated a ten percent share of their business?"

"Annie never mentioned that, did she?"

"No, she did not." Luna appeared dumbfounded. "What does your boyfriend have to say about this?"

"Well, I haven't told him yet—"

"Told me what?" Leo entered the kitchen.

"You guys are really tricky. You know that? I had thought I was doing something good, but that is low. Even for a Calverton." Luna wagged a finger in his face.

"What did I do?" he asked, obviously blindsided.

Luna grabbed my phone from my hands and held it to his face, far too close for anyone to read anything. "You're taking percentages of all the businesses in Rose Mallow."

"I'm doing what?"

"Luna, please, let me tell him. I'm sure there's a reasonable explanation for this," I said.

"What are you two talking about?" Leo asked.

"We're both on the grants committee. There's a small…"

"Microscopic," Luna interjected.

"There's a small footnote here. In return for the grants, the recipients are giving your family a ten percent stake in their businesses," I said.

Leo's eyes opened and shut, and his mouth gaped. It wasn't his best look. He took the phone and read it closely several times. Then he handed it back to me and rubbed the bridge of his nose. "I'll talk to Annie."

"And you'll talk to the press?" Luna asked.

"I'm sure it's a misunderstanding," he said.

"I want a full court interview," she pressed. "You're lucky we have some other major news to break first." Luna turned to me. "Like your exclusive interview about Betsy Howard?"

"Of course. As I promised," I said.

"And on my radio show?"

"And on your radio show."

"Great. Okay, Leo. I will be in touch about this." Luna carted the coffee urn to the dining room.

"Did you really not know about this?" I asked.

"Not a clue. But I shouldn't be surprised. No wonder everyone in the family was so keen to change from the development project to the grants program. They can never not look for money. But I'll get to the bottom of it," he said with a disappointed sigh.

"We will together," I said, putting my arms around him. However, as I did, the tea kettle began to sing.

* * *

After pouring my tea, I went over to the library, where Nuri and Desiree sat on the couch chatting. When I came up closer, their hands flew away from one another, and they each giggled like blushing teenagers. Didn't I have enough of that with my sister and Rory rekindling their relationship?

"Uh, are you two okay?" I asked.

"Should I tell her? Or you?" Nuri asked.

"I should explain," Desiree said. She stood up. "Juniper, there's something you should know. Everyone should know."

"What? Are you okay?"

"Yes. More than okay, actually." As Desiree spoke, I noticed Nuri had put a hand on the back of her wrist. I had a feeling I knew where this was headed. "Thank you for never asking me about the secret that Esme had on me. When she gave me that so-called loan, I had been younger. Insecure and nervous. I didn't want people knowing..." She struggled to say the words.

Nuri stood up next to her and put an arm around her waist. "It's okay. You weren't ready to come out back then. Everyone has their own journey."

"Are you two together?" I asked.

They each nodded before leaning their heads against each other and touching foreheads. How adorable were my sweet friend?. I felt awful that the secret Desiree had felt she needed to hide was her relationships. How relieving to see they could be together now.

"Congratulations! That's wonderful news," I said.

"Thank you, Juniper," Desiree said.

"Yes, thank you. More than you could ever imagine," Nuri added. "You've helped us both remove such burdens."

"You both did it yourselves," I said. "I'm just excited for you."

I put down my tea on a side table and hugged my friends. After such a turbulent week, I was relieved to have something to be happy about for them both. Desiree saw her younger sister Keisha and went over to talk to her, leaving me alone with Nuri.

"Nuri, there's something I want to show you," I said.

"What is it?" she asked. "Is it the letters? I really don't want those back."

I crooked my finger and walked her around the library. "Right over here…" I had to pull over a step stool to reach one of the highest shelves. "We keep a lot of family treasures up here, out of the way of most guests." I climbed up and reached to the shelf, pulling down a small, leather book.

"What is that?" she asked.

"Do you recognize it?" I handed the book to her. Its leather was worn and faded, but you could still make out the dark Hebrew letters on the front cover.

"Oh, is this?" She carefully opened up the book, which was written almost entirely in Hebrew. "Is this the prayer book I bought at the auction?"

I nodded. "The same one. My grandmother treasured it. She said it felt like a piece of home had returned to us."

Nuri's eyes watered. "I'd forgotten about that day."

"You had done something special for us then," I said.

"Is that why you wanted to help me with the auction?" she asked.

"One of the many reasons."

Her face lit up. "That's why you said something about returning the favor."

I shrugged. "Anytime."

"I'm still going to pay you back," she said.

"Look, why don't you get through what happens next, and then we'll figure it out, okay?" I said.

"I'm talking with my lawyer more next week. He thinks that I'll need to face some sort of punishment, but if I can explain what happened and help with the case against Betsy, he's hopeful I won't have to face anything severe. Maybe some fines? It'll get worked out. But I want to own up to my mistakes and take responsibility. I want to make amends," she said.

# CHAPTER THIRTY-EIGHT

"Nuri, I know. You're a good person. You'll figure it out."

"Thank you for understanding, Juniper." She hugged me. "Oh, I meant to ask."

"What?"

"You mentioned your grandmother. Did you find out why her paintings were in the unit, too?"

"Well, Noah and Susannah haven't fully cracked the code in Esme's ledger, but they figured out the names at least. Guess who was not in there?"

"Nana Z?" Nuri asked.

"Nana Z," I responded. "Plus, I found some of her papers. She was a very organized person. It looks like she donated those paintings to an Artist's Guild auction event, and that Esme won them."

"That must be a relief."

"Considerably," I replied.

# Chapter Thirty-Nine

I thought I heard the tea kettle singing again. I walked into the kitchen, but to my surprise, it wasn't on the stove. Then I recognized the sound: the clarinet. My dad had begun to play.

Everyone followed him like the pied piper, crowding into the library. In the center, my dad played on our family's historic clarinet. My father had once told me that the clarinet was considered to be the closest instrument to the human voice. He explained that it used many of the same signature styles as cantors, the vocalists who lead the congregation in song and prayer.

His clarinet whined with the *krecht*—a shrill and perfectly imperfect whine, which blasted across the house like a sob. Clover must have agreed, because he began to howl in return. My father, to his credit, put down the clarinet and laughed heartily, welcoming the small dog up to their improvised stage.

"We have a new member of the band," he said, while giving my pup a pet.

"Can I join?" Violet waved her arm excitedly from where she was perched on my mother's lap.

"Everyone is welcome," my mom said, rubbing her hair. "They'll play, and we can sing and dance!"

"All of us?" Azalea asked. Her gaze around the room appeared concerned for the furniture and antiques. I agreed that it was too tight for this group to fit in the small room.

"How about outside?" my dad asked.

"Let's set up a speaker on the verandah, Ash," Mom suggested.

Within a few minutes, we were all in the front yard, as the songs from my parents' band played over a small speaker on the porch. My family lined everyone up into a circle and encouraged us to grab hands. We danced a jubilant *hora*—or circle dance—around and around. My friends and family laughed, kicked, switched directions, and ran. Clover bobbed in and out of the group, yipping and jumping, until he broke out into a few happy "zoomies" around the grounds.

Someone grabbed chairs from inside, and the men took turns heaving different people up in the middle of the circle, as the rest of us danced around. It reminded me of Azalea and Rory's wedding. While it had been largely secular, my parents had played a few songs during the reception, including the famous *Hava Nagila*, a well-known Jewish folk song. Within the opening bars, everyone instinctively joined up in the *hora* with the happy couple in the middle. They had been lifted up in two chairs, each holding onto the end of a napkin. It was joyous and beautiful, and that spirit was exactly what we needed.

"Wow! That looks amazing." It was Sneezy—I mean, Sarah, from the photographer's studio.

"Oh, is it already time?" I looked at my watch. I'd forgotten that I'd booked her to do a family photograph. When Sarah had said she wanted to build her photography portfolio, I had reached out to see if we could do something while my family was in town. She readily agreed. With Olivia's legal issues, Sarah doubted she'd have a job much longer, so she decided it was time to go out on her own.

"Don't worry about it. I'm going to take some candids. Just have fun!"

We continued dancing, singing, and running around. After such a chaotic week, it felt cathartic. I couldn't wait to see Sarah's photos.

After the music died down, we got everyone together for group photos. Sarah did an excellent job rounding us all up and patiently took every group we requested. Then, we went back inside the Wildflower Inn for dessert, inviting her to join us.

Azalea pulled me aside. She wanted to see how I was holding up.

"I should ask you the same thing, hostess with the mostess," I said, putting my arm around her shoulders.

"Exhausted but good. Really, really good," she said. When Rory walked by,

I noticed an extra twinkle in her eyes.

"Things are back to normal between you two?" I asked.

"Not quite so fast. But we're getting there. We both know it's important to take it slow. Make sure we don't make the same mistakes we did before," she said.

"That's smart," I agreed. "I'm trying to do the same thing with Leo."

"Good idea. Is that your resolution for the new year?"

I laughed. "No, but I've been thinking about that."

"Oh, really?" Azalea asked.

"I probably should do something creative like you're doing with the painting classes. But I think I have something else in mind," I said.

"Tell me."

"At first I thought about learning Yiddish or an instrument," I said.

"Those are great ideas."

"And maybe I still will. But there's something else."

"What?" Azalea asked.

"Well, you know how I talked with the realtor…"

"Noah Danvers? The guy you thought might have murdered Marcus Howard?" she asked. Then she stopped. "Wait, are you thinking about moving out of the Wildflower Inn?" Her face paled.

"Same guy, very much did not hurt anyone, and no, I'm not thinking about moving out. I'm thinking about moving in. Permanently. Talking with him really made me consider what I wanted to do. And getting some other house isn't it."

"That's great," she replied, putting her arms around me for a quick hug.

"But I'm not going to stay in one of your guest rooms. You need that room." Especially if this grant was suddenly going to fall through. Even if I continued to pay my sister rent, she could use the extra money.

"How does that work? Where will you live?" Her eyes grew big. "In the Carriage House?" She began to protest about it being too small for all of us to stay there, but I shushed her. Hopefully politely.

"No, I'm not going to move into the Carriage House either. Instead, I'm going to sell my townhouse in D.C. Then I want to have someone look at both the attic and the basement. I'm hoping we can renovate one of those spaces," I explained.

"You think that's possible?" Her voice was hopeful.

"Anything's possible," I replied with a wink. After this week, that felt true. I had my family together for the first time in ages. We had our extended family of friends, which continued to grow. While there were still issues to resolve, I firmly believed we could overcome anything coming our way—so as long as we were together.

# A Note from the Author

In the story, Nuri has created letters supposedly from Jane Austen (1775 - 1817) while living at Chawton Cottage, part of the estate of the grand Chawton House in Chawton, Hampshire, England. Both the "Great House" and the Cottage have turned into museums open to the public. With the Cottage serving as the Jane Austen's House Museum. You can take a virtual tour at https://janeaustens.house/online-exhibition/virtual-tour-of-jane-austens-house/.

Austen spent the last eight years of her life there, where she published all six of her novels, including *Pride and Prejudice*. She passed away at the age of 41, possibly of Addison's Disease, Hodkin's Lymphoma, lupus, or even some think it may have been arsenic poisoning! Austen left behind an unfinished work entitled *Sanditon* (or *The Brothers*). Can you imagine if Nuri had attempted to forge an original version of that book? But it would likely have attracted more attention than our forgery circle would have wanted.

Like Juniper's family, I've always loved klezmer music, the traditional folk music of Central and East European Jews going back centuries. Klezmer is a Yiddish word, contracting *kley* (Hebrew for instrument) and *zemer* (Hebrew for song). The word first appears documented at a Jewish council meeting in Krakow, Poland 1595. This is particularly poignant for me as I have family dating back to Krakow in the 17th century, when my multi-great-grandfather Hillel Weigert lived.

Klezmer can be mournful, but it's typically joyful. A band often has several different instruments, such as clarinet and hammered dulcimer but also violins, accordions, various brass instruments, and percussion. If you want to listen to Klezmer music, I've put together a playlist (including a raucous version of *Hava Nagila*) on YouTube at https://bit.ly/klezmerplaylist.

Like Azalea's family, mine is an interfaith one, although we belong to a local synagogue and had a rabbi at our wedding. We also had a live band that did a beautiful rendition of *Hava Nagila* during the reception. Getting hoisted up in the chairs as everyone danced in circles around my husband and I was incredible. This was the inspiration for the dancing scene during Rosh Hashanah at the end of the book.

Speaking of Jewish traditions, let's talk a little about *kashrut*, also known as keeping kosher. There are many rules, but one of the most basic was not to have a dishes that combined meat with any sort of dairy. In fact, you were supposed to wait six hours after eating meat to have any dairy products!

The rule stemmed from the *Torah*, which says, "Do not boil a kid in its mother's milk" (Exodus 23:19). This is commonly interpreted to be about kindness and not cooking a lamb in its mother's nurturing milk.

As such, for those who keep kosher, you wouldn't have meals that include meat with any sort of dairy. Many people use margarine or other non-dairy options instead of milk when making sides and desserts. But with a dairy meal, someone can use all the butter, cream, and cheese anyone would ever desire. So much delicious goodness.

As always, I have some recipes from the story on my website at https://www.daphnesilver.com/recipes, and I hope to add more soon.

**JOIN MY NEWSLETTER**

Join my newsletter list at www.daphnesilver.com to get the free short story, "A MIDSUMMER'S NIGHT SCHEME!" A rum runner's mansion, a 1623 copy of Shakespeare's "First Folio," and a performance of a *Midsummer's Night Dream* set in a speakeasy... what more could a history loving librarian want? Juniper Blume had simply planned a fun night out with her sister Azalea. She certainly didn't expect to stumble upon a rare books' puzzle in a classic locked room style mystery. Will she figure out the truth before the final curtain drops?

# Acknowledgments

Thank you to the so many people who made *The Tell-Tale Homicide* possible, including Shawn Reilly Simmons and Deb Well of Level Best Books, Anne Newman, Rosalie Spielman and Cathy Wiley, the Sisters in Crime Chesapeake Chapter (especially theZoom writing group), Kristen Harbeson, my mom, and my family, especially my husband Matt and our kid Nate.

Much appreciation to those who won character naming opportunities in auctions for various causes. It was fun including your chosen names! Thank you to Julianna Magnus, Laure Rolfe, and Emily Goehner.

Thank you to everyone reading! I'm grateful to all of you, especially those who have left reviews, asked their local library and bookstore for my books, follow me on social media, subscribe to my newsletter, and participate in the Silver Sleuths team. You all are amazing! If you haven't signed up yet, you can do so at www.daphnesilver.com. When you join the newsletter, you'll also get the free short story "A Midsummer's Night Scheme."

# About the Author

Daphne Silver is the Agatha-award winning author of the Rare Books Cozy Mystery series. She's worked more than twenty years in museums and symphonies and has the great fortune of being married to a librarian. When she's not writing, she's drawing and painting. She lives in Maryland with her family. Although she's not much of a baker, she won't ever turn down a sweet lokshen kugel.

AUTHOR WEBSITE:
  www.daphnesilver.com

SOCIAL MEDIA HANDLES:
  www.facebook.com/daphnesilverbooks
  www.instagram.com/daphnesilverbooks

# Also by Daphne Silver

As Daphne Silver:
*The Tell-Tale Homicide* (Level Best Books, 2024)
*Crime and Parchment* (Level Best Books, 2023)

Under my legal name Lauren R. Silberman:
*The Jewish Community of Baltimore* (Arcadia Publishing, 2007)
*Wicked Baltimore: Charm City Sin and Scandal* (History Press, 2011)
*Wild Women of Maryland: Grit and Gumption in the Free State* (History Press, 2015)
*Chesapeake Crimes: Storm Warning* (2016)
*Fish or Cut Bait: A Guppy Anthology* (2015) (as Lauren Moffett)